William Hussey is the award-winning author of over a dozen novels, including the Crime Fest award-nominated *Hideous Beauty* and *The Outrage*. Born the son of a travelling showman, he has spent a lifetime absorbing the history, folklore and culture of fairground people, knowledge he has now put to work in his Scott Jericho thrillers. William lives in the seaside town of Skegness with his faithful dog Bucky and a vivid imagination.

Also by William Hussey

Killing Jericho
Jericho's Dead

JERICHO'S DEAD

WILLIAM HUSSEY

ZAFFRE

First published in the UK in 2024
This edition published in 2025 by
ZAFFRE
An imprint of Zaffre Publishing Group
A Bonnier Books UK company
4th Floor, Victoria House, Bloomsbury Square, London, WC1B 4DA
Owned by Bonnier Books
Sveavägen 56, Stockholm, Sweden

Copyright © William Hussey, 2024

All rights reserved.
No part of this publication may be reproduced,
stored or transmitted in any form by any means, electronic,
mechanical, photocopying or otherwise, without the
prior written permission of the publisher.

The right of William Hussey to be identified as Author of this
work has been asserted by him in accordance with the
Copyright, Designs and Patents Act, 1988.

This is a work of fiction. Names, places, events and
incidents are either the products of the author's
imagination or used fictitiously. Any resemblance to
actual persons, living or dead, or actual
events is purely coincidental.

A CIP catalogue record for this book is
available from the British Library.

ISBN: 978-1-80418-165-2

Also available as an ebook and an audiobook

1 3 5 7 9 10 8 6 4 2

Typeset by IDSUK (Data Connection) Ltd
Printed and bound in Great Britain by Clays Ltd, Elcograf S.p.A.

Zaffre is an imprint of Zaffre Publishing Group
A Bonnier Books UK company
www.bonnierbooks.co.uk

In loving memory of Bill Hussey Sr
(1946–2023)
Beloved dad, grandad, and legendary showman

Chapter One

'IT WILL BE THE DEATH of me here, I swear to God. No, I'm not being overdramatic. You people haven't the faintest idea what's going to happen to me inside the walls of this house.'

The man who claimed he communed with ghosts strode out of the untenanted vicarage and towards the sleeping fairground. Phone clamped to his ear, celebrity psychic Darrel Everwood did not acknowledge the woman who trotted at his heels, following him down the porch steps, across a barren garden and through a squawking, lopsided gate. He didn't catch the roll of her eyes or the billow of her cheeks as she let loose an exasperated sigh. Slipping out from beneath the shadow of the house, Everwood pulled the phone from his ear and stared at it, as if doubting its very existence. Then, holding it a hair's breadth from his mouth, he bellowed:

'Yes, I am serious! You tell those pinhead producers that I know exactly how this nightmare is going to go down. I've seen it. I've been told. A spirit has communicated with me and it ... What? Hold on a fucking minute. Are you ... ? Don't you dare laugh at me! Don't you fucking dare! I'm a lamb to the bloody slaughter here.'

And with that, he thumbed the screen and threw the mobile to his assistant, who caught it with accustomed ease.

'Those greedy bastards will dance on my grave, Deepal, I swear,' he muttered, casting the impassive presence at his side a narrow glare. 'Oh for Christ's sake, let's just get the hell out of here. This whole thing was a gigantic mistake.'

They crossed the short patch of ground that separated the austere Victorian rectory from its newly arrived, rather gaudy neighbour. Enclosed within a large clearing inside Redgrave Forest, the fairground sat like a decorous bauble, its flash and colour reflected in the uncurtained windows of the old house. Reflected there too, the retreating figures of the psychic and his PA as they swept along the fair's main drag, passing between vague columns and spirals that loomed against the lifeless October sky. Shapes that, at the flick of a switch, would immediately define themselves into thrill rides and Ferris wheels.

All around the clearing, the trees groaned and shushed while inside the fair, wires and guy ropes cut a song out of the breeze. A little background melody to cover my tread as I moved through the shadows, my feet finding steady spots upon the duckboards. So this was Darrel Everwood. I'd only ever seen him on television before, play-acting at possession, exploring supposedly haunted ruins, reassuring the bereaved that their loved ones could indeed reach out from beyond the veil. Now this handsome huckster, who had earned a fortune from such parlour tricks, came off more like an overtired toddler, petty and somehow ridiculous.

And yet as I trailed him to the car park that stood beyond the main gate, I began a feel a familiar sensation prickle beneath my skin. A hunger, a restlessness, a yearning that for the past four months I had tried my best to ignore. I had been a detective before my disgrace. After being thrown out of CID, prosecuted, and imprisoned for an attack on a murder suspect – a violent, far-right thug who'd gone by the name of Lenny Kerrigan – I had been forced to return to my fairground roots. To the family and friends I'd once rejected and who, in my hour of need, had taken me back without question. What followed had been a downward spiral of self-pity, addiction and despair, a state I'd only been rescued from when a series of bizarre murders had reawakened my interest in the world. Those dark days of last summer now seemed a lifetime away, and for a little while I'd thought I was done with puzzles. That I could do without the lure of a mystery and the desire to rebalance injustice. That in finding my partner Harry again, I had discovered a saner, brighter star to guide my life by. All lies, of course. Well, if not lies then a feeble attempt at self-deception.

That was why I now followed this man and why his words plucked at the strings of my curiosity: *You people haven't the faintest idea what's going to happen to me inside the walls of this house ... I'm a lamb to the bloody slaughter here.* Intriguing words, yet surely no more than a prima donna's bluster. Perhaps the strain of Everwood's upcoming TV special – a multi-media phenomenon that seemed to have captured the attention of the entire country – was getting to him. Was that why he'd made this unannounced inspection of 'Britain's most haunted house' before the big event. There were, after all, only four days to go until he would be expected to summon his ghosts live on national television.

As Everwood's souped-up Beemer sped out of the clearing and into the tunnel of trees that led to the main road, I glanced up at the immense billboard overlooking the car park:

IN PARTNERSHIP WITH JERICHO FAIRS, EVERTHORN MEDIA
WELCOMES YOU TO
PURLEY RECTORY
THE MOST HAUNTED HOUSE IN BRITAIN
JOIN US THIS HALLOWEEN NIGHT
FOR A LIVE EDITION OF TV PHENOMENON
GHOST SEEKERS
WITH CELEBRATED MEDIUM DARREL EVERWOOD
SPOOKY FUN FOR ALL THE FAMILY!

I liked this no more than my fellow Travellers, but in recent years special events around which a fair could open for a few days were a necessary evil. For some time, the fairground had been a dying industry, its overheads enormous, its appeal to the public little more than a fading sense of nostalgia. To survive we had to piggyback on more modern spectacles. This haunted house bullshit was just the latest in a long line of stunts that, to my mind, cheapened the purity of our heritage.

The aspect of the whole thing that grated most was to see our family name associated with a two-bit chancer like Everwood. In principle, I had no problem with harmless con artists. In fact, it could be argued that showpeople themselves had their roots in thrills and spills trumpeted with dubious claims: *Roll up, roll up! Gape in wonder at the Living Mermaid! Behold the thrilling diabolism of the Two-Headed Horror!* But Darrel Everwood was no benign sideshow huckster. His claim to communicate with the dead was not only absurd but deeply damaging. For one thing, there was the case of Debbie Chambers, the little girl who had gone missing from her front garden during the Easter holidays.

In an interview with a leading tabloid newspaper, Everwood had claimed that the child had died only hours after being abducted and had been buried somewhere close to the Chambers' residence. For Debbie's parents, clinging to any scrap of hope that their daughter might still be alive, the subsequent media shit-storm had proved devastating. If I remembered rightly, Mrs Chambers' attempted suicide had been prevented only because her husband had forgotten his briefcase and returned home from work unexpectedly. Even then, cutting her wrists had led to permanent nerve damage and a vow from Mr Chambers that, if he should ever meet Darrel Everwood in person, he could not be held responsible for his actions. Perhaps this recent additional public pressure went some way to explaining the hysterical outburst from Everwood that I'd just overheard.

A stir among the trees behind me distracted my thoughts. Turning, I caught a sudden, dashing movement in the undergrowth. Soon after our arrival here, some of the Traveller chavvies had taken to playing in the forest, their boisterous chase games ringing through the otherwise deserted woodland. Predictably, there had already been complaints from the few neighbouring farms.

Away to my left, I spied a child-sized skeleton racing between the trees, and all at once, I was thrown back to a long-forgotten October afternoon. Like little Joey Urnshaw, I too had insisted on wearing my costume every day leading up to Halloween. I think our fair must have been open in Hampstead back then because I remember my mother guiding me across the heath towards the posh houses that sat in the vale. As we walked hand in hand, she'd told me all the spine-tingling tales she could remember from her favourite ghost story writers – classic creepers by the likes of Algernon Blackwood and M. R. James. I'd hung on her every word until we reached those attractive nineteenth-century villas that abutted the heath. There I'd dashed from house to house, ringing doorbells and shouting, 'Trick or treat!'

Hardly a door was opened to us, and traipsing homeward, my little plastic cauldron had rattled with only a scatter of sweets. My mother said nothing, though I can still picture the look on her face. A pinched fury that made her lips pale. Traveller chavvies never did well at Halloween, not compared to the local kids, but this was a new low. We'd stopped at a shop just outside the fairground where she'd purchased enough pick-and-mix to fill a dozen novelty cauldrons. Then, brushing back my curls, she'd said, 'Don't mention this to your dad. It'll only make him wild.'

Even then I'd wondered if it wasn't her own anger that worried her. I have very few memories of my mother losing her temper, but when she did it was always a sight to behold. Everyone avoided her during those times, even my father. Now, caught up in this memory I hadn't thought of in years, I wondered if perhaps the rage that so often coiled under my own skin – a fury born of cruelties and injustices, large and small – might have deeper roots than I'd realised.

As Joey Urnshaw disappeared again among the trees, a voice called out to me from across the car park.

'Revolting man, isn't he?'

I turned to find Angela Rowell coming towards me. When we'd arrived yesterday, the housekeeper of Purley had received us by storming out the door of the Victorian rectory and shrieking at Joey's old man, Big Sam Urnshaw, like a banshee. His lorry had trespassed over the agreed boundary of the fair; didn't he know the stipulations of the contract? No vehicle must come within fifty metres of the house. If he didn't get his load shifted right away, Miss Rowell would be on the phone to the Earl of Aumbry, absentee owner of the property. Looking suitably horrified, Big Sam had jumped back into his cab and backed up halfway across the clearing.

Standing beside me, she now jabbed an outraged finger at the unilluminated billboard.

'As I said to your father when negotiations for this absurd spectacle began, I'm not a tremendous fan of travelling circuses.' I let the mistake pass; it is, after all, a common one. Fairs are not circuses, circuses are not fairs, and although there is some degree of overlap, those groups of travelling people remain quite distinct. 'But next to this charlatan, I would welcome a hundred carnivals,' Miss Rowell continued. 'The sheer nerve of that man!' I turned to her. The housekeeper's hands were clasped so tightly together that the knuckles stood out, sharp and bloodless. 'They . . . That's to say, they . . .' She shook her head. 'They don't like it up at the house, you know.'

'You mean the earl?' I said. 'I thought he never came here?'

'Not in years. As far as Lord Denver is concerned, Purley is a mere curiosity in his property empire. I think he enjoys the bragging rights of owning the most haunted house in England, but otherwise, he's pretty much indifferent to the place.'

'So you're talking about?' I raised an eyebrow.

'The residents.' She held my gaze for a moment before letting it slip to the ground. 'The personalities who call the house their home. They cannot abide an imposter, Mr Jericho.'

'You mean the ghosts?' I said, making a heroic effort to keep a straight face.

'*Personalities*,' she corrected. 'And jealous ones at that. Mark my words, they shan't tolerate the likes of Mr Everwood within their walls, playing his dishonest games. There have been consequences in the past for those who have sought to exploit this house.'

'Really?'

'Oh yes,' she said matter-of-factly. 'Madness. Suicide. Accidents. Murder. However it manifests, the residents of Purley always take their pound of flesh.'

Chapter Two

It might have been easier to dismiss Angela Rowell had she been anything like the ludicrous figure on the billboard in front of us. I hadn't managed to get a clear look at the man as I trailed him through the fair, but I knew the public image well enough. In his guise as celebrity medium, Darrel Everwood was cradling a crystal ball while simultaneously holding out two crooked fingers to the viewer in what I supposed was either a warning or a blessing. Mascara gave a piercing quality to his stare while his trademark cocky grin completed a look that set many a bereaved heart aflutter. Still in his twenties, cynics argued that Everwood owed his success as much to a pretty face as to his dubious hotline to the dead.

Miss Rowell, meanwhile, was a very different kettle of fish. With her bouffant hair cemented into place, she looked like a Margaret Thatcher clone that had fallen upon hard times, her once-expensive Harris Tweed patched and mended so often there were probably only scraps of the original suit remaining. Her shoes too were old and scuffed, one buckle hanging on for dear life. And yet this sixty-something held herself with a kind of faded dignity, like a battle-scarred warship, docked and awaiting decommission. Everything about her appeared constrained. Even the sleeves of her blouse were pinched so tight that the fabric dug into her skin. Around her left wrist hung a rubber band which she touched self-consciously when she saw me looking at it.

'An old habit,' she said sharply. 'Picked up from the first housekeeper I ever worked under. You glance down at your watch to check the time and the sight of the band acts as a kind of aide-mémoire, reminding you of any task that might have slipped your mind.'

'Except you don't wear a wristwatch,' I observed. 'And surely if it's an old habit you'd get used to the presence of the band. It wouldn't remind you of anything.'

'That hasn't been my experience, Mr Jericho,' she said. 'Not at all.'

A pause, filled by the constant murmur of the trees. In that brief silence, I reflected not for the first time that all Travellers are born detectives. Our ability to speak the spiel and cajole a punter lends us a natural flare for conversation and, occasionally, an ear for confession; the necessity to observe minutely and to quickly assess the public in order to earn our living proves another useful attribute; our vast knowledge of human nature, accumulated by anyone who engages as we do with every strata of society, completes the package. It was these skills that my old mentor DI Pete Garris first saw in me and which tempted him to persuade me to join the force. A decision he would later come to regret.

'I beg your pardon, Miss Rowell, but you were saying something about the gho—' I corrected myself. 'Personalities of the house punishing anyone who tries to exploit Purley Rectory. But what about the tours? Don't you guide those yourself? And what about us?' I nodded towards the sprawling hulk of the fair, all set up a stone's throw from the imperious Victorian building. 'Aren't we risking bringing down the curse on ourselves?'

If she detected any playfulness in my tone, she didn't bite. 'I show utmost delicacy and respect whenever I take a tour around the house, Mr Jericho. As for yourselves?' She almost allowed herself a smile. 'Your father has assured me that he has nothing but the highest regard for the history of Purley.'

I very nearly rolled my eyes. The number of people in this world immune to my dad's charm could probably be squeezed into one of his Waltzer carriages. Figuratively at least, the head of Jericho Fairs certainly appeared to have got under Miss Rowell's tight tweed.

'What did you mean, though, about the consequences of disrespecting the residents?' I asked.

It wasn't an idle question. What with helping to build up the fair, I hadn't yet had time to look inside the rectory myself, but those Travellers Miss Rowell had taken on the tour had almost all returned with stories of an unnerving, oppressive atmosphere, of sudden cold spots and indecipherable whispers behind the walls. Admittedly, many showpeople are congenitally superstitious, but even some of the harder-headed specimens appeared to have been affected by the spell of the house.

'An early example came in the interwar years,' Miss Rowell said. She spoke almost robotically, as if reciting from a tourist brochure. 'By then, the rectory had already gained a worldwide reputation for its hauntings. So much so that the International Institute for Psychical Research sent down a small team to look into it. No one really knows what happened the night of their séance, only that in the months following, both lead investigators died in separate railway accidents and that the medium they'd employed succumbed to a sudden and aggressive brain tumour.'

'Sounds like a few unlucky coincidences,' I said.

'If you like,' Miss Rowell retorted. 'Though I mistrust coincidences.'

I gave a wry smile. 'A former friend of mine used to say the same thing. And I suppose there have been other tragic stories associated with the house since then?'

'You'll have to take the tour, Mr Jericho,' she said flatly.

'But have you always sensed them?' I asked. 'I think my dad told me you'd been housekeeper here for almost twenty years. Was it an immediate thing as soon as you walked through the door or did it take a while for you to pick up on their presence?'

I was genuinely curious. Ever since our student days back in Oxford, my partner Harry had always chided me for my 'unbending rationalism'. It was one of the points of difference between us, his romantic soul, inspired by his passion for music and composition, rubbing up against the hard edges of my scepticism. And I suppose like most sceptics, I have always been fascinated by the conviction of true believers. This believer hooked her forefinger through the elastic band around her wrist before blinking hard and letting the band slacken again.

'Are you mocking me?' she asked quietly.

I shook my head, a little stunned. 'I swear, I'm not. But you seem completely convinced of your ghosts and yet dismissive of Darrel Everwood's. I just wondered why.'

'Men like that.' She spat out the words, jabbing her finger once again at the billboard. 'Duplicity runs through their veins like poison. Their kind of deception is wilful, unforgivable, cruel. Honesty is a precious commodity in a world like this. It shouldn't be thrown away on the altar of mere entertainment. But I . . .' She appeared to catch herself, her hand moving to cradle her stomach. 'I can't stand here gossiping all night. I have a to-do list a mile long from these television people. Apparently, Purley isn't "old-timey" enough for the *Ghost Seekers* audience. How on earth they expect me to make a nineteenth-century rectory *more* old-timey, I have no idea.'

She turned on her heel, and battered shoes squelching in the mud, stalked back through the fairground towards the dark hulk of the house.

I looked after her for a moment. Something in her condemnation of Everwood had jarred with me. For all his absurdity how could she, a believer in the paranormal, be so convinced he was a fraud? And really, even if she was certain of it, what did it matter to her? There had been something like venom in her words, but of a distant, almost abstract kind. And now another thought occurred to me: if Miss Rowell's story of a house of spirits exacting revenge upon those it deemed unworthy was common knowledge, did this explain Everwood's outburst? Did he truly believe himself to be in danger here? A lamb to the psychic slaughter? Much as it might seem ridiculous to me, my reality was not theirs.

I watched until Miss Rowell entered the blank portico of the house and then headed into the fair myself.

It had been raining heavily for days before we arrived in the ancient fenland city of Aumbry and had pulled our loads into this clearing in the woods. Strips of metal grating and good old-fashioned wooden duckboards now ran in grids between the rides and side stalls. I hopped between these, making for the area where Haz and I had set up yesterday morning. A few Travellers were stirring as I passed through, torches in hand as they fired up their gennies and wiped down their cashboxes, old aunts tottering behind in fingerless gloves, clucking their tongues and handing out flasks of tea. I spotted my dad talking to Big Sam Urnshaw and chucked them both a wave.

'All right, son,' my dad grunted.

'How's the fella?' Sam called out.

'Haz is fine,' I shot back. 'Says he'll find you a hook-up on Grindr when he gets a minute.'

'Cheeky joskin!' Sam laughed.

Dad shook his head while his oldest mate slapped him on the back. I couldn't help but smile. It's amazing what familiarity could achieve. Just a few months ago, I would never have dared make a joke like that on the fair. Part of the reason I had left the life at eighteen, heading to university and the freedom I had believed awaited me in Oxford, was to escape the constraints of this place. Half convinced the community would never really accept my sexuality, I suppose I'd harboured a lot of grudging resentment. And, truth be told, I thought prejudice still existed in the hearts of some of them. It was, after all, a tough, hard-scrabble sort of existence, built largely around stereotypes of masculinity. So it was ironic that an outsider like Harry had been the one to break down many of those barriers, just by being his warm, open, generous self.

After we had found each other again in Bradbury End last summer, Harry had discovered a kind of refuge with me at the fair. The only reason he'd been in the town of Bradbury at all was because a killer had blackmailed him into playing a role. Harry had been just another unwitting actor in that blood-soaked drama that had reawakened me to the world after my imprisonment and disgrace. But when the tragedy was done, we had both wanted to put that little town and its horrors far behind us. The easiest exit route was to hand the keys to Haz's rented bungalow back to the estate agent, and in effect, run away with the fair. After all, that's the beauty of communities like mine – if you're willing to work hard, you can make yourself a new life from scratch. You can be happy. That's what we told ourselves anyway, and we were. For a time at least.

I moved away from the main strip and into the side ground where the novelty games and less showy attractions were stationed. These didn't require the same safety checks as the big rides and so their owners were not yet stirring. Passing an empty cashbox, I caught my reflection in the booth's murky glass. For weeks now, Harry had been gently pestering me about needing a haircut. He was right. A mess of blue-black curls was currently spilling over my ears. Otherwise, I looked better than I had in years. A combination of Haz's home-cooked meals and the hard labour of working on the fair had recut muscle I'd lost during my time in prison.

Still, there was something I didn't like about the winter-grey eyes of this figure. The persistent hunger, that old yearning. Back in Bradbury End, five innocent people had been slaughtered, mutilated, desecrated, all to serve up a puzzle that might save me from my self-annihilation. And all the work of a madman I had once called a friend and mentor. Now I woke screaming from nightmares, haunted by the memory of what DI Peter Garris had done to rescue me from myself.

And yet that old hunger was back. The need for a puzzle, for a shadowland of complication and of violence. I turned away from the glass, disgusted with myself. I needed to leave this man behind. I had to, for my own sake as well as Harry's. I owed him that much at least.

But it seemed that the world would not allow me this chance. I was just debating whether to check on mine and Harry's new ride or to head back to our trailer when I suddenly realised I was being followed. The creak of a duckboard behind me, the flick of a shadow out of the tail of my eye. You might think, so what? Over two hundred souls called this fairground their home. But Travellers are a chatty, boisterous breed. To see someone up ahead and not call out a greeting would be considered the height of rudeness, even if you've spoken to them only a moment before. This clearing was remote too, miles from the bustling centre of Aumbry. It was unlikely that an innocent joskin would have wandered into the fair before opening time. And then there was that low, threatening grumble emanating from behind the side ground where the trailers were set up. In my mind's eye, I could picture the juks starting out of their boxes, Webster among them, straining now at their leads, nostrils flared, black lips pulled back over vicious teeth. A stranger had entered their domain and they were eager to make his acquaintance.

I willed them not to startle him. Not yet.

I wanted words with him first.

Chapter Three

I WELCOMED IT AT ONCE. THE chance to unleash those brutal instincts that I'd denied myself for four long months. I wanted this man who pursued me to be my enemy. The implications of this, I could fret about later. For now, I focused on the opportunity to indulge my rage. If he intended harm to me or my people then he would pay, not only for his sins but my own – my inability to save the victims of Bradbury End; my complicity in the final murder that had occurred there; my guilt at not seeing my old boss Peter Garris for the monster he truly was; my now faltering relationship with Harry.

All of it.

I flexed my fingers, remade my fists. But who was he? Approaching the warped mirrors that fronted Tommy Radlett's funhouse, I chanced a sideways glance. There a figure rippled in the glass, half a dozen paces behind me. Allowing for the distortion of the mirror, I made out a broad-shouldered man, slim at the waist, long-limbed, a build not unlike my own. Black jeans, a cap of some kind shadowing his features, dark T-shirt straining to accommodate pale biceps ribboned with veins. Lightly dressed, but not a hint in those smooth, fluid movements that he was bothered by the cold. Maybe it was the adrenalin coursing through him, maybe some other less natural substance. Whatever the truth, I could see I was going to have my work cut out.

My mind blazed through possibilities as we approached the end of the side ground. My friend was patient, purposeful, a practised hand. I could tell from the noiseless way he moved that, like me, he'd once been trained in the art of the shock takedown. No tension in his body language to alert his target, nothing threatening at all apart from the sheer size of the man. But I knew even without looking that he'd also possess the innocent, open face of a gentle giant. The kind you could take home to tea with your granny. The kind that wouldn't betray itself, even when the beating started. I knew because his face was my face.

Only one real possibility then. They'd caught up with me at last. Truth be told, I was always on high alert for them and had expected a visit before now. My friend here was a professional. A foot soldier of one of the big gangland bosses I'd worked for after leaving university and then 'betrayed', simply by joining the police. Despite the fact I'd never revealed any of their dirty secrets, a few had promised they'd deal with me nonetheless. Once you're in you're never truly out, you see? In that way, organised crime isn't all that different from being a showman.

I made a sudden turn, off the duckboards, and across the sucking mire of the side ground. Nimble as he was, my shadow couldn't levitate and I could hear the slurp of his boots behind me. We passed between the hoardings of a shooting gallery and a hook-a-duck stall. Up ahead stood the corral of trailers, and off to their right, a web of washing lines with a few damp sheets fluttering dankly in the breeze. The question as I headed towards the lines was, which of them? I knew I'd been practically untouchable during my time on the force – even the most psychopathic of mobsters is wary of taking down a serving police officer – but after my disgrace and release from prison? I could think of one or two who might still nurse a grudge.

We were within a few metres of the clotheslines when the juks' persistent grumble broke into a scattershot of barking. My gaze snapped to trailer doors and windows, caught the glow of TV lights on drawn blinds. Travellers always protect their own, but I didn't want backup. Not tonight. However it came off, I wanted this confrontation all to myself. And so, ducking under the first bedsheet, I shouted a command and the juks fell silent.

I yanked at the damp sheet, sending plastic pegs popping into the air. Then I was back under the clothesline, my fists twisted so firmly around the sheet that the soggy chill of it scorched my knuckles. My pursuer's senses were keen, he'd be used to surprise attacks, and so I knew that brute force was my only option. He was already stepping away when I lunged forward and wrapped the icy material around his head. Something familiar in that face before it vanished under the suffocating white. A word, perhaps my name, deadened by the sheet. I didn't allow myself time to register any recognition. Hesitation now could be lethal.

It took the man seconds to overcome his panic. Just a few moments of scrabbling at the chokehold of the sheet before his experience kicked in. Trying to save himself that way would get him nowhere, and he knew it. He had to disable the attacker, not the weapon. By the time he jolted sideways, pulling me with him and spearing his elbow into my gut, I'd dragged him as far as the forest. Despite the sudden winding, I managed to regain my footing and throw him hard against the nearest tree. I heard the dull smack of his skull on the trunk, saw the bedsheet torn away from his head. Ignoring the pain in my ribs, I sucked down as much air as I could and launched myself at him again.

Christ, but this guy was strong. I'd been a scrapper since childhood, almost all Traveller chavvies are, and through either the charm of my personality or simply because I possessed the kind of face people liked to punch, a lot of my adulthood seemed to have been spent brawling. But I'd hardly ever come up against such a tough bastard as this. He was trying to say something while at the same time landing a left hook to my upper arm that sent me spinning into the undergrowth. I scrambled to my feet, ignored the click at my shoulder joint. He was speaking again, but this was a well-worn tactic. If a punishment beating isn't going to plan then a 'friendly' word mid-confrontation, maybe an offer to defuse the situation, is often gladly accepted by the other party. Then, once his guard is down, the hurt can really begin.

The sky was moonless, the darkness thick in the forest. I couldn't see his face properly. He held up his hands, palms out, a truce declared. I slouched towards him, panting, playing into this fiction. My heart hammered out a fast, skittish beat. I could sense the rage inside me, straining like the fairground juks at their leashes. His words were lost against the blood roaring in my head. I moved quickly into his orbit and aimed a jab at the crook of his right elbow. He anticipated it, snatching at my wrist with a grip like iron, bending my arm backwards until

I saw stars. I rolled with the counter-attack, and dropping to one knee, used my free arm to drive an elbow into the big tibial nerve in the back of his leg.

Another man would have screamed in agony. This man let out only a short grunt. Still, the spasm did its work and his legs came unhinged, felling him to the forest floor. Meanwhile, I groaned to my feet and dug the phone from my coat pocket. Its torchlight flashed across the bedsheet, billowing on a branch and smeared with dirt, before finding my pursuer. Sprawled in a bed of autumn leaves, he was laughing against his pain and holding out a hand to me.

'That was a snide move, Scott,' he said. 'But for old times' sake, I forgive you.'

In the well of his palm, I saw the cigarette burn like a white sun, its rays radiating to the edges of his hand. At the sight of it, my anger vanished. I suddenly remembered us in bed together, in the quiet confessional moments after making love, my finger circling that old scar as he told me the story of its origin. I had held him when the tears started in his eyes. Tears from a man whose job it was to inflict pain and to jest at scars. In the end, he'd broken down completely, reliving his youth on the Humber estuary. The mother who had abandoned him, the abusive father – a fisherman – embittered by the death of his industry and the shame of being unable to provide for his growing son.

I stepped forward now and pulled the flat cap from his head. Those denim-blue eyes, almost black in the dark of the wood, blinked up at me. Mussed by the removal of his hat, a shock of red hair stood out like flames while his pale skin complemented the white teeth behind that pained grimace. He flapped his fingers at me and the veins that ran like rivers down his huge arms pulsed in time with the movement. A giant indeed, gangland enforcer Benjamin Halliday was even bigger than the last time I'd seen him.

'Benny,' I murmured. 'What the hell are you doing here?'

Chapter Four

MAKING LOVE? HAD WE EVER done that? I wondered, as I helped Ben Halliday to his feet. Honestly, I think we both would have laughed at such a sentimental description of what was really nothing more than good old-fashioned casual sex. And yet, I had comforted him when he'd told me about his father and the abuse he'd suffered in that cottage on the estuary. For my part, it had been a rare act of compassion in those dark days after university when Haz and I had first parted ways.

'Nice way to greet an old mate,' Ben said, massaging the back of his thigh. 'I thought you showpeople were supposed to be hospitable.'

I shook my head at him. 'Not sure where you got that idea. Anyway, what do you expect when you creep up on someone in the dark?'

Though I could see he had lived some hard years since the last time we'd met, still the wrinkling of that snub nose made him look twenty again. His fingers curled gently around my shoulder. Just a twinge from where he'd hit me, though I expected a mighty bruise come the morning.

'Suppose I should've called out,' he said. 'But I wasn't sure it was you. And anyway, I didn't expect you to come at me like that. I mean, you were always a bit on the mardy side, Scott, but Christ Almighty!' He puffed out lightly freckled cheeks. 'I hope your shoulder's OK.'

'And your thigh,' I said.

He grinned, circling his big hands around his upper leg. 'Not bad, are they? Squats morning, noon, and night. It's agony, but the boys love 'em.' He straightened up, his gaze taking me in. 'Not looking too bad yourself. Do you ever age, Scott Jericho? I swear—'

'Enough with the charm,' I said. 'What are you doing here, Benny?'

'I got out.' He shrugged. 'Just like you. Finally, anyway.'

I turned, and limping a little, he began to follow me out of the trees.

'You mean you left Noonan's outfit?'

'I know,' he grunted. 'Took me long enough, eh? Oh, I recognised the name, by the way. Jericho Fairs? Wondered if maybe you'd gone back to the travelling life, though last I heard you'd joined the filth. Noonan still wants your head for that little stunt, in case you're wondering. You should hear the way he boasts about what he'll do if he ever gets his hands on you.' I'd forgotten the strength of Ben's Yorkshire accent, how it plumbed every vowel so that a word like 'boast' emerged as 'burst'. The London gangsters had always had trouble deciphering his dialect. 'Said he'll do for you in the end.'

I nodded. 'Let him try.'

Mark Noonan. After what had happened between me and Haz in Oxford – his breaking up with me following the death of his cancer-riddled father; a mercy killing on Haz's part for which he'd never truly forgiven himself – I had not wanted to live much inside my head. And so I'd left university and fallen into a kind of work that didn't require me to think. Work, in fact, in which thinking at all was aggressively discouraged. The only talents of mine that were required rested in my fists, and so I'd hired myself out to a few mobsters on a freelance basis. Noonan had been the least objectionable – not into prostitution and light on the drugs side – his operation had focused on counterfeit sports gear, smuggled cigarettes, and a bit of loan-sharking. From the beginning, I'd set out what I was prepared to do for him as an enforcer and what I wasn't. It mainly involved putting the frighteners on his rivals and collecting debts owed by other gangsters. I couldn't say I was proud of those years, but I was able to live with myself. Just.

'So what happened?' I asked.

We had now reached the trailers and he'd shaken off the cramp in his leg. Doors were yawning wide and a bustle of Travellers was spilling into the night.

'Mark wanted to make me one of the husbands,' he said. 'And you know how that always ends up.'

I grimaced. Noonan offered 'husband' status to a couple of his favourites every year, usually on his birthday, making a kind of sick pageant out of the whole thing. It was a protected, cosseted position for the prettiest boys in his gang, but Noonan was famously jealous. There were stories of husbands who had lied and cheated on him and who afterwards found themselves one eye short of the standard pair. In a twisted way, mobster Mark Noonan was something like the Purley Rectory house-keeper Miss Rowell – they both prized honesty.

'I only knew one man who could stand up to him,' Ben said, touching my collar. 'Only one he was afraid of. Only one who threw the husband offer back in his face. I remember how you'd look out for me when he got into one of his rages, Scott. I was always grateful for that.'

I pulled his hand away. It had been more than five years since I'd last seen Ben Halliday and time hangs heavy on such men, but there was something else here. His pupils sat like pinpricks in their denim-blue irises and there were claw marks on his upper arms where he'd scratched his skin raw. Quite a feat for fingernails bitten almost to the quick. I searched his face.

'What's going on with you?'

He tried to bluff it out until a wave of exhaustion seemed to overcome him. 'Codeine.' He sighed. 'Tramadol. All the usual prescription pain meds. It's what Mark's started dealing these past few years. Thought it was how he'd keep me, I reckon. Get me hooked on the stuff so that I'd never leave. He's lost it, Scott. Made the amateur mistake of sampling his own product. Fentanyl patches, for Christ's sake. The kind of heavy-duty stuff they give terminal cancer patients who can't bear the pain anymore.'

'And you?' I asked.

'What can I say? It's taken a while but I'm down to just a few pills a day.'

He rubbed the pad of his thumb across that faded burn mark as he spoke, and I wondered if what he'd told me was true.

'So what are you doing here, Ben?'

'Bodyguarding,' he said, suddenly bright again and patting the imposing barrel of his chest. 'We can't all be hard bastards *and* clever sods like Scott Jericho, you know. I know where my talents lie. After leaving Mark, I spent a few months working as a bouncer at a casino on the south coast.' That accent again, lyrical in its way, 'coast' spoken like 'cursed'. 'Met some media type there who liked the look of me and put me up for a job with this celebrity he represented.' He licked his lips. 'Look, Scott, I know your family's involved with this here Halloween TV stunt. You won't grass me up, will you? About what I did for Noonan? About the drugs? I need this job.'

'I won't say a word,' I promised. 'Who's your client?'

He pointed over my shoulder to the car park and to the distant, unlit shape of the billboard.

'That psychic crackpot.'

'Darrel Everwood?' I rubbed my chin. 'Funny, you're the second person I've spoken to tonight who thinks he's a fraud.'

Ben held up his hands. 'Oh, I don't say he isn't the real deal. I've been working for him for a while now, been to quite a few of his gigs, even stood in the background when he does his private readings for celebrities. Honestly, you wouldn't believe some of the names – rap stars, politicians, Premiership footballers, even the odd Saudi prince. Guy's raking it in. Or was. And I gotta say, he puts on a good show. I think you'll agree, Scott, we've seen some fucked-up things in our time. It would take a lot to scare us, right? Well, when Everwood starts chatting with these dead relatives, then tells the punters things he couldn't possibly have known? Family secrets, personal details?' He blew out those freckled cheeks again. 'It keeps me awake at night, that's for sure.'

'So why do you call him a crackpot?'

He ran the tip of his tongue across his teeth. 'Not because of the ghost stuff. Only, in a way, maybe it is connected. I mean, nattering with the dead? It has to scramble your brain a bit, right? Truth is, he's paranoid as hell. Although, I guess he's had quite a lot of crap thrown at him after the bust-up with his ex. Did you see how that all went down online?'

I shook my head. I hadn't seen much news at all since Harry and I left Bradbury End. After Peter Garris had used the mercy killing of his father to blackmail Haz into playing a part in the mystery – a part in which he was an innocent red herring, designed to intrigue and baffle me – I had been keen to protect the man I loved. Harry hadn't asked about Garris's larger plan and remained ignorant of the murders committed four months ago. I suppose my idea of us rebuilding a life together as part of the fair had included a desire to keep our world small and insular, without such daily horrors as those doled out by newsfeeds. After all, we'd both had enough horror in our lives. All I really wanted was to safeguard that almost childlike innocence that was so much of Harry's nature.

Ben laughed, snapping me out of my thoughts. 'Jesus, you must be the only person in the country who hasn't heard about it. Everwood had been dating this social media influencer – probably met her at some posh do where nobody drinks anything and the bog seats are all lined with coke. Anyway, although she's considered quite a stunner by our hetero cousins, Darrel is a greedy boy. He was knocking off her assistant on the side. Miss Instagrammer actually finds them at it and tries to shove Everwood's mystic crystal ball where the sun don't shine.

'Next thing you know, she's putting up videos and doing interviews claiming he's a scam artist. Says that all the humble bragging about his background growing up on a council estate is one hundred per cent horseshit. Says he was a kids' party magician before he read some old book that inspired him to get into the medium business. Anyway, the online trolling and hate mail has been flooding in ever since. I kid you not, he's had actual turds posted through the letter box. I mean, who does that?'

'Are you saying that's why he needed a bodyguard?' I asked. 'Because of some unwanted mail and a few bitchy comments online?'

'Part of it. But it isn't just spiteful nerds having a go, Scott. I've seen the messages. Scumbags saying he's such a liar and a cheat that his dogs deserve to be set on fire for it.'

'That is sick,' I agreed. If anyone ever threatened to do that to my faithful old hound Webster? Well, let's just say some emergency dental work would be required. 'Funny thing is, I happened to spot your boss a few minutes ago coming out of the old house,' I said. 'Looked like a spur of the moment visit.'

I glanced over to the western fringe of the fair, just now in the shadow of the old rectory. EverThorn Media had set up their production fleet there – expensive Jayco and Enterra trailers that made even the showiest Traveller homes look like sardine tins on wheels. They had arrived during the morning, but I didn't think the full production team itself had arrived with them. Ben confirmed my suspicion.

'Oh yeah, he's been tetchy for a while now. Wanted to check the place out again before the big day.'

'He must really be worried then?' I said. 'About some of the threats? Or is it something else?'

For a moment, Ben didn't say anything. He stared out across the expanse of the clearing, beyond the fair to the turreted chimneys of Purley.

'Strange thing is, I don't think he actually takes the threats all that seriously. But the pressure of the whole celebrity deal, this image he has to maintain, the fact it's suddenly crumbling, and then the sheer weirdness of the world he's created for himself? I think it's caused a kind of mental breakdown.'

Ben turned to me. 'You see, Darrel seems absolutely convinced that he's going to die here.'

I nodded. 'I overheard him say something a bit melodramatic myself. That this place would be the death of him. But surely he meant that figuratively. Like a professional disaster, the end of his career, that sort of thing.'

Ben looked at me for a while, as if considering his response. At last, he sighed, 'No, Scott. You don't understand. The man believes he really will die here in four days' time. He's absolutely convinced of it.'

Chapter Five

*I*T WILL BE THE DEATH *of me here, I swear to God. I'm a lamb to the bloody slaughter.* Had Darrel Everwood really meant those words literally? I held Benny with my gaze. 'He thinks someone's going to kill him?'

Behind us, the cacophony of the fair suddenly erupted across the clearing. Dance beats from the Waltzer, the clockwork clank and grind of the runaway train, my father's booming voice on an automated loop welcoming punters to Jericho's Fair. In the car park, chaps in hi-vis vests started waving the first cars into the bays.

I shook my head. 'If he truly believes that, then why come here at all?'

'He doesn't think *someone* will kill him,' Ben said. 'Not exactly. But he thinks if he comes here then . . .' At a loss for the right words, his brow furrowed. 'He told me that there's something bad waiting for him here. That he feels it. That maybe it's always been waiting for him, right from the very beginning, and that even if he tries to avoid it, this thing will still reach out and find him. I know it sounds barmy, but if you'd been there, if you'd heard how he said it? He even had me half-convinced.'

'Sounds like he's talking about fate,' I suggested. 'Or maybe a reckoning? I guess that would play into the trauma of what's happened to him recently. Being publicly questioned and exposed. But what does he expect you to do about it? You're a strong lad, Ben, but you can't protect him from his own paranoia.'

'He's looking for a way out, that's my guess,' Ben said. 'Something solid he can pin a reasonable fear on. If he can go to the producers and say, "Here's a tangible threat to my safety, so I'm not doing the gig," maybe they'll reorganise the whole thing.'

'You don't think he's scared of the reputation of the house itself?' I thought back to my conversation with Miss Rowell and her conviction that those who exploited Purley often came to a sticky end. When Ben denied that Everwood had ever mentioned Purley in those terms, I asked again, 'So, why's he continuing with this whole bloody farce? From what you've told me, he's successful enough to pull out of the event if he wants to.'

'He was,' Ben said. 'But all that was before little Miss Instagrammer's public meltdown. His publicity team have gone into damage limitation overdrive, but a lot of the mud has stuck. Tickets for his gigs have collapsed, theatres have pulled bookings, old celeb pals are giving him the cold shoulder. Darrel Everwood is toxic goods right now. And between us, he spends brass like there's no tomorrow. Long story short, he needs the money.'

I nodded. 'Well, it'd be devastating for the fair if he did cancel. We're only pulling in punters over these few nights because of the excitement leading up to the TV show. So I'm not sure if I should wish you well, Benny. All I can say is, it was good to see you.'

I'd started to move away when that iron hand caught my wrist again. Unbalanced, I was pulled around to face him. His breath steamed the night air, faint wisps drifting against my lips.

'I missed you, you know,' he said. 'After you left Noonan and joined the police. I know it was never anything more than just sex between us, but I wanted to say—'

'No.' I prised his fingers from my arm and repeated, 'No.'

A curse, an apology, a question – I can't say what he called after me. My mind was reeling, my blood pounding almost in time to the roar of the fair. I headed straight for it, desperate for its numbing clamour to envelop me. To hide me. What if someone had seen Ben and me together in that moment? And what if they then happened to mention it to Haz? This unexpected intrusion of my old life made me nervous. And yet it wasn't only those years I had spent doing Mark Noonan's dirty work, or the intimacy I'd shared with Ben that unsettled me. For weeks now, things hadn't been right between me and Haz, and I had no concrete idea why. Was it the fact that my old mentor had involved him in the murders at Bradbury End? The mystery Detective Inspector Pete Garris had constructed for my benefit, sacrificing innocent victims, remaking them to echo the freaks from a century-old fairground legend? Although as I say, Harry had never learned the full details of the case, had never in fact asked about the larger drama in which he'd played his role, questions from that time must still gnaw at him. His fear concerning what answers I might provide, and my own dread of revealing those details, might account for this drifting between us. And yet at the same time the reason felt deeper than that.

All I sensed was that we were hanging on by the slimmest thread and that it wouldn't take much to sever it entirely. I couldn't bear that. I had lost him once, all those years ago in Oxford, and the despair that followed that parting had driven me into the outer darkness of my nature. I needed Harry, a light to guide and steady me.

I came to a stop. Tried to let my thoughts settle. The first of the crowds were streaming in, squeaking and squabbling as they always do. In a few days, this Halloween event would be over, I told myself. The fair would move on and us with it. Benjamin Halliday and all he represented would be gone. Then there would be time for Haz and me to talk, to figure things out, to start again.

I bustled on, shouldering my way between the throng. Travellers called out greetings from their stalls and in answer I plastered on the most convincing smile I could. Turning a corner, I found the kiddies' carousel we had rented from my dad. Old Man Jericho, as he was known to all, owned a lot of the rides and stalls operating on his fair, but not all of them. Many were the property of individual Traveller families who paid Dad a rent to travel with his operation. Dad provided all the organisational logistics – licences to trade, negotiations with councils to open on public land, security details – as well as a community of which most who travelled with him would remain members throughout their lives. Our own little ride sat at the heart of the show and appeared gleaming and ready for the night's trade.

Sal Myers and her daughter Jodie straightened up from their work, my goddaughter flicking a wet sponge in my direction. Buckets of soapy water stood at their feet, suds sprinkled in their matching auburn hair. I went over and cupped Jodie's raw little hands in mine, rubbing warmth into them.

'You didn't have to do this,' I said.

'Someone had to,' Sal muttered. 'The ride looked a proper state before Jodes and I got to work. Didn't it, love?'

The mirror image of her mother, Jodie treated me to an identical scowl. Then that pixie face cracked into a wide grin and she tugged at my sleeve. 'Wanna hear the song I've been practising with Uncle Haz?'

Not waiting for an answer, she launched into a surprisingly soulful rendition of 'Hallelujah' by Leonard Cohen. Even Sal stopped glaring at me for a full ninety seconds. As Jodie hit the final note, me, her mother and a passing family all broke into spontaneous applause. Haz had worked his usual wonders and it was pretty clear that the munchkin had found her forte. She'd certainly abandoned her former ambition of following in my footsteps and becoming a detective. Smart girl.

'Where is Haz?' I asked, leaning in and tweaking her nose.

I looked up to find Sal gazing at my knuckles. Specifically at the burn marks from the wet bedsheet.

'I need you to go back to the trailer and put the buckets away, sweetheart,' she said, her eyes still fixed on my fists. When Jodie started to moan, Sal threw her the kind of look that turned pissed-up punters sober on the spot. I gave the little girl a reassuring wink and she sighed glumly and heaved away at the first bucket, dirty suds splashing her dungarees.

'So,' Sal said when her daughter was out of earshot. 'Been finding trouble again?'

'Just a tussle with the laundry.'

'You know something, Scott, I ... Yes, *what*?' A customer had approached with two small kids, asking if the carousel was open yet. That forbidding stare soon sent them scuttling.

Sal then marched straight over and prodded me in the shoulder. The very spot where Ben had landed his jab. I winced. If anyone possessed true psychic abilities, it was probably my oldest friend. Ever since our childhood days as Traveller chavvies, playing hide and seek in unlit ghost trains, teasing the ancient aunts, leaning into the innards of rides with oil-sleeved uncles, learning the clockwork mechanisms of our world, we'd always been close. Perhaps too close. I could never hide a thing from Sal Myers.

'If you're pulling your usual shit, I will end you,' she said. 'And don't even begin to claim you don't know what I'm talking about. Just because we haven't all interrogated you about Bradbury End doesn't mean we've forgotten. Not me, not your dad, and most of all not that doe-eyed puppy dog you're lucky enough to call your boyfriend.'

She was right. Haz hadn't asked about any of it. Not a single question since I'd found him waiting for me on Travellers Bridge the night Lenny Kerrigan, the far-right group leader and final victim of Peter Garris, had died. He knew Garris had blackmailed him for a purpose, he knew I'd been investigating something strange going on in the town, and that was all he wanted to know. I wasn't surprised. It had always been in Haz's nature to shy away from upsetting truths. It was the reason he had broken up with me after the mercy killing of his sick father – because he knew that I knew what he had done and, back then, he hadn't been able to face the truth of it. But Harry Moorhouse was no fool.

I remembered him visiting the hospital following Lenny Kerrigan's assault on me in that alleyway back in Bradbury and him saying, 'How is this ever going to end? He could have killed you.' More unspoken truths. More secrets, growing like weeds between us.

But Haz wasn't the only one avoiding questions. As Sal had said, no one on the fair had pried into those final days in Bradbury. Except that wasn't quite true. After Kerrigan had been reported missing, my dad had come to find me. By then we'd accepted his offer of travelling with the fair and I'd been busy setting up the children's carousel he'd rented us to make our living.

'I'll ask you once,' he'd said, leaning on a merry-go-round horse, his expression neutral. 'Did you do for him?'

I had told him, 'No,' and that was the end of the matter.

My father's question hadn't been an idle one. Kerrigan had been the murder suspect whose case had led to my downfall. This snivelling coward had petrol-bombed a Polish food store, resulting in the death of three innocent children. Losing my temper with his shit-eating smirk, I had attacked Kerrigan mid-interview; a stupid, reckless act that had been punished with prosecution and imprisonment. After my release, the monster had dogged my footsteps until, at last, DI Peter Garris had made him the final victim in the Bradbury End mystery. Despicable as he had been, the fact that I had abandoned the mutilated but still living Kerrigan to his fate continued to haunt my conscience. I still saw him in my dreams, as I had seen him in that little library back in Bradbury, his body twisted and broken, a shattered mouth pleading with me to save him. I had simply turned my back and left him to Garris's scalpel.

'Nothing's going on,' I now assured Sal. 'Not like in Bradbury anyway.'

She searched my face for a moment before nodding. 'Then tell me what's wrong between you and Harry.'

'What do you mean?' I stared at her. 'Has he said something?'

'He doesn't need to,' she sighed. 'That boy wears his pain in his eyes.'

I looked up into the smoky darkness. No stars there, no light of any kind, except the pulsing heartbeat of the fairground. Sal knuckled my chin.

'I'm worried about the pair of you. You've seemed so distant recently.' She had spoken softly but her old edge soon returned. 'Bloody hell, Scott, why do you have to be so ... *you*?' She swatted my shoulder and I grimaced again. 'I'm here if you need to talk, all right?'

'Talk about what?'

We both turned around like a pair of guilty schoolkids.

Haz stood with his long, nervous fingers twining between the drawstring of his canary-yellow cagoule. At first, I thought he might have been crying, but then he wiped his eyes and said something about the smoke from the burger truck. Those gentle jade eyes, crinkling at their edges as he looked at me. Not quite a smile. We seemed stuck for a moment until, eventually, he came over and I wrapped my arms around him, kissing that mop of mousy brown hair. It felt almost paternal, not the sort of embrace shared by lovers.

'Where've you been?' I asked.

'Choir practice,' he said, pulling away and showing me his music bag. 'I told you this morning. We ran over a bit, sorry.'

I nodded. Our circuit for the fair had been pretty limited lately and Haz had found a choir group in the nearby city of Aumbry. He'd even started composing again. In fact, his face only seemed to light up these days when he spoke about his music.

'Oh God,' he said, glancing at Sal's grimy work dungarees and then at the spotless carousel. 'I'm sorry, have you done all this? And I'm late for opening night as well. I really am the worst joskin-turned-traveller ever.'

'Don't worry about it,' I said. 'Knowing Sal, she'll have already decided how we can pay her back. Anyway, you head on over to the trailer and have a wash. I'll open up and then you can take over running the ride for the rest of the—'

'Opening can wait,' my dad's voice, the word of God itself on the fair, called out to us. We turned to find him and Big Sam Urnshaw steaming in our direction.

'I don't like the look of this,' Sal murmured.

She was right. There was something stony and relentless in my father's expression. A look that I had seen before and which never failed to remind me of his contained fury after my mother's death. Others had seen it in different situations and it always signalled one thing – someone from outside had harmed one of his people. That look. It almost made me feel sorry for whoever had been so foolish.

Chapter Six

My dad and Big Sam approached and together with Sal and Haz we formed a circle.

'What's happened?' I asked.

Dad wiped a finger across his salt-and-pepper moustache while Sam ground his teeth. Like most large, loud men Dad was a sentimental soul and I could see the emotion shimmering in his eyes. But his cheeks were dry and so it wasn't as bad as it might have been. No one was dead, at least.

'It's Aunt Tilda,' Dad said. 'Something's upset her.'

I almost laughed. Something upset Aunt Tilda on an almost daily basis. Chavvies playing too boisterously around her trailer. Joskins and their 'strange gorger smells'. The price of tea bags was enough to launch her into fits. Dad must have seen my scepticism and shot me a baleful glare.

'It ain't no moody bollocks,' he barked. 'If I find out who did this, they'll be in their box and buried ahead of time, I swear down. It's a wicked trick to play on an old girl.'

Haz reached out and laid a comforting hand on the back of my father's. It was amazing really. If I'd done such a thing, the old man might have belted me one. As it turned out, he just smiled and gave my boyfriend a grateful nod.

'I'm all right, son,' he said. 'But Tilda ain't. She's asking to see you. Both of you.'

'Me too?' Haz asked in a wondering tone. 'You're sure?'

'You come as a pair now, don't you?' Big Sam grunted. 'Sal, would you be all right looking after the juvenile until they come back?'

'Course.' Sal nodded, unconsciously patting the head of a carousel lion. 'Tell Aunt Tils I asked after her.'

Without another word, my dad turned and led us through the crowds towards the quieter end of the ground. It was a spectacle that never failed to impress me, how punters would automatically make a path for him, as if they knew on an instinctive level that he was the master of the show. As we walked, I shot a few questions at Big Sam but he said it would be better if I saw for myself. I knew this was the old man's instruction, and I suppose it made me proud. He understood how I liked to approach a puzzle, fresh-minded and without preconceptions.

I glanced again at Haz. Here was another mystery.

'How was practice?' I asked him.

'Fine.' He nodded. 'Good.'

'Still working on that Mozart piece?'

'Yes. "Lacrimosa".'

'Remind me of those lyrics again.'

'I'm not sure—'

'The ones you sang for me a few nights ago,' I persisted. 'You remember.'

He cut his gaze away. '*Lacrimosa dies illa; Qua resurget ex favilla; Judicandus homo reus.*' He spoke in a sing-song voice but without its usual melody. 'Full of tears will be that day;

When from the ashes shall arise; The guilty man to be judged.'

'The guilty man,' I echoed and thought again of how he had so ostentatiously shown us his music bag when I asked where he'd been. Another little puzzle to add to my growing collection, alongside Miss Rowell's strange revulsion of Darrel Everwood and the latter's apparent certainty that he will die here in four days' time.

I kept Harry in view for the remainder of our walk to Aunt Tilda's. A blaze of colour in those endless cheekbones, his shoulders slumped, his head bowed. I wanted to reach for him, to ask what was wrong, but fear kept my hands at my sides. If I pushed too hard, that final thread might snap and then what would become of us?

We came at last to the red-and-white striped tent, set a little apart, on Aunt Tilda's orders, from the other stalls. Apparently, it gave the impression that even her fellow Travellers (who were under strict instructions to bring her tea and sandwiches only when there were no punters about – their joskin smell putting her off her scran, so she said) were a little afraid of her, adding to Madam Tilda's allure.

A sign outside the tent did the business too: LOVE! DESTINY! FATE! MYSTICAL PROGNOSTICATIONS – FORTUNE TELLING, CRYSTAL BALL GAZING, PALM READING, TAROT CARDS. ENTER NOW AND MEET THE FUTURE.

The antiquated charm of the fortune teller's tent was a rare sight on modern fairs. My dad, who could never be accused of being a sentimentalist where money was concerned, nevertheless gave Tilda her pitch practically rent-free. She had been a friend of my mum's and I still had fond memories of them together, shelling peas on their trailer steps, trading gossip between each other like a game of pass the parcel.

Pushing aside the damp canvas flaps, Dad led us into the tent. Almost at once the chaos outside was muted. Here incense fragranced the air while lamps shaded with coloured veils cast an eerie light across the painted enlargements of tarot cards that hung around the walls. These consisted of the usual suspects: the Sun, the Moon, the Devil, the Hanged Man, the Wheel of Fortune, the Hermit, the Lovers, the Fool and the rest. An obligatory crystal ball sat at the centre of a circular table that was covered in a red damask cloth. The only incongruous detail was a small electric heater chuntering away beside Tilda's high-backed chair.

The mystic herself rose to greet us. A small, hunched figure, her stubby fingers mounted with rings up to the second knuckle, Aunt Tilda possessed a wide, generous mouth, her blonde hair only now turning grey in her seventy-third year. She walked with a stick in her right hand, and just occasionally her features would tuck up with pain. A case of crippling arthritis meant she rarely stood if she could help it.

'You wanted to see us, Aunt Tils?' I asked gently.

I bent down so that she could kiss both my cheeks. She then moved on to Haz.

'Ain't he got an handsome mooie, this mush,' she said, her voice redolent of a forty-a-day habit.

'She says you've got a nice face,' I translated for Haz. Old-timers like Tilda used the secret Traveller tongue more than most and some of her words were a mystery, even to me.

Turning a gummy gaze upon us, her expression darkened. 'Someone broke into me tent this afternoon. Didn't chor nothing but left me a little treat.' She waved me closer. 'You ain't got the sight, Scott Jericho, but you can see almost as well as any genuine dukkerer. I wanted your opinion on it.'

She swept her hand towards a small wax figurine lying beside the crystal ball on her table. It was a crude effigy, childish in its way, and yet horribly sinister. For one thing, the face was featureless and had, in fact, been spooned out so that all that remained was a shallow well carved into the head. Steel sewing needles peppered the rest of the body like the quills of a porcupine, while the arms of the figure appeared a little foreshortened. Attached to the left leg was a scrap of paper with 'Ex 22:18' shakily inscribed in pencil and below this, a sort of floral design encompassed by a circle.

While I took in these details, I sensed Haz beside me on his phone. He stiffened, and leaning in, whispered: 'It's a biblical citation. The Book of Exodus, chapter twenty-two, verse eighteen. In the King James version, it says—'

'"Thou shalt not suffer a witch to live",' Tilda croaked, hobbling back to her chair. Haz went to kneel beside the old woman, folding her arthritically twisted hands between his.

Meanwhile, I followed Haz's example and googled the six-petal flower motif drawn below the citation. It was a relatively obscure symbol, but I found it eventually.

'It's called a hexafoil,' I said, turning to Big Sam and my dad. 'Designed after the lily to represent purity. Apparently, they often used it in Gothic architecture as a sign of protection and to ward off evil.'

Tilda stirred. 'Also known as a witch mark, used by some of the old religions to guard against witchcraft and the evil eye. And then there's the poppet.' She hovered her hand just above the needles that forested the doll. 'Folk magic used to cause harm to whoever the doll is meant to represent. All makes a pretty pattern with the Bible passage, doesn't it?' She looked at Haz and winked. 'Someone doesn't like me very much.'

'When was it left here?' I asked.

Big Sam answered. 'Sam Junior and a few of the chaps set up Auntie's tent an hour ago. She came to inspect it and found that nasty old thing on the table.'

My gaze roamed around the interior. The tent had been securely anchored down on the outside, no one could have got under it. 'Were the flaps tied up when you came to do your inspection, Auntie?'

She shook her head.

'The boys forgot both the ties and the padlocks.' Big Sam grunted. 'I'll have their guts for bloody garters.'

Approaching the table, I knelt and examined the effigy from every angle before picking it up. 'Anyone touched it?'

My dad came over. 'Tilda says not.'

'No fingerprints,' I murmured, turning it over carefully in my hand. 'Must've used gloves of some kind to mould it.'

'Does that worry you?'

'I'm not sure. It shows a certain premeditation. As if it isn't intended to be a single, isolated act. As if there could be a sequel. Is there any CCTV running here?'

'Nothing much worth nicking in this corner of the fair,' Dad said. 'So no. But look, don't you think it's probably just some stupid game? Maybe the local farm kids getting their own back. They've been rucking with our chavvies ever since we got here.' He lowered his voice. 'Maybe they thought they'd give one of us a good scare as payback.'

'They'd have to do better than that,' Tilda snapped, folding her arms across her chest.

I smiled. I was pretty sure that most of Madam Tilda's gift was down to her sharp ears, listening into the hopes, dreams, and anxieties of her punters as they queued up outside her tent. But when I looked again at the effigy, my smile died.

'I don't know, Dad. This? It seems consciously ritualistic. Perhaps even overdone to a certain extent – the Bible quote mixed up with the poppet doll and the hexafoil. A jumble of ideas from different sources. But still, there's nothing rushed or playful or giddy in it, like some kids' revenge. I mean, would a bunch of children even know what a hexafoil was?'

'So what do we do?' Dad asked. 'Call in the gavvers?'

'There's nothing the police could do,' I said, flashing back to my days in uniform and the standard procedure for investigating things like poison pen letters and threatening messages. 'The tent was left open, nothing's been taken. It might sound strange, but this wouldn't even constitute harassment because it's a first event and not part of a pattern of behaviour. There are no fingerprints in the wax so I doubt there would be any DNA, even if the gavvers could justify actioning a forensic analysis. Which they couldn't. Honestly, there isn't a crime here anyone could be charged with.'

Big Sam was saying something, bellowing in his empty way, asking what we paid taxes for if not to protect our pensioners. My dad was reassuring Tilda that I'd get to the bottom of it all. Haz was still kneeling beside her, whispering comfort while the old mystic herself didn't appear to be listening to any of them. Her moist eyes were fixed on mine, a question there I couldn't read. Unable to meet her gaze, I felt myself drawn to one of the tarot cards adorning the walls.

From his perch, the Devil glowered down at us, bat wings spread wide, his brow emblazoned with a pentagram, a look of sullen mischief on that bestial face. I felt an involuntary shiver.

'Will you excuse me a moment?' I said. 'I have to make a call.'

Chapter Seven

'Has he moved from the house today?'

The phone crackled and I heard an asthmatic gasp as the private detective repositioned himself in his driver's seat. In my mind's eye, I could picture Gary Treadaway shift a family-sized bag of crisps out of his lap and brush the crumbs from his stomach.

'Not a step beyond the garden gate. Oh, he popped outside around noon to water them sorry-looking hanging baskets by the front door, but there hasn't been a peep out of him since. In fact, lemme see.' Another wheeze and shuffle. 'Yep, I can see him right now through me binoculars watching the telly in the front room. He's been there a good hour or more.'

I nodded. It was at least a fifty-minute drive from Peter Garris's house to the city of Aumbry and the forest clearing where the fair was set up. I had just needed to confirm in my own mind that my old mentor hadn't set me another of his puzzles.

Treadaway and his staff were a covert security measure I'd had running ever since I abandoned Lenny Kerrigan to his fate in Bradbury End. After confessing to the murders, Garris had assured me that the impulse to kill was no longer part of his makeup. That although he had once been a serial murderer, those savage appetites of his youth were long since sated. He had only 'come out of retirement' for my benefit, to set me the puzzle that had rescued me from self-destruction. But I knew I could no longer trust the word of my old friend. And so I continued to visit him. Unannounced spot checks and superficially clumsy attempts at surveillance on my part, all to ensure that he was behaving himself. It had lured Garris into a false sense of security. Although it was stretching my income to breaking point, the private detectives who monitored DCI Peter Garris in my absence provided the reassurance I needed that his urge to kill had not been reawakened. However, all this was a temporary solution. I couldn't go on paying the detectives forever.

'Thanks,' I muttered.

I was about to disconnect when Treadaway piped up. 'Boss says your next payment's due on Friday, by the way. Just a friendly reminder.'

I cancelled the call. Then, while the murmurs continued in the tent behind me, I stared at the phone in my hand. Directly above 'GARY, Private Detective' in my contacts list was 'GARRIS, Peter'. My thumb hovered over the name as I battled the almost irresistible urge to hit 'call'.

In the days before I had discovered who he was, *what* he was, I wouldn't have hesitated. I'd have hurried to share my every thought and theory with him, bouncing my plan for action off that logical, experienced intellect. Despite everything, I knew he could help me now, if he chose. But this was a trite business, wasn't it? A wax effigy left in an old mystic's tent? Hardly worth compromising my morals to consult a serial killer.

Shoving the phone back into the pocket of my trench coat, I re-entered the tent.

Four faces turned to look at me. I felt their expectation like a dead weight.

'Just an idea,' I muttered. 'Didn't pan out.'

My dad nodded. 'We've been talking about what you said regarding this thing seeming a bit ritualistic, what with the Bible verse and everything. Well, Tommy Radlett happened to notice this religious-type lurking around the forest road yesterday afternoon. He was handing out pamphlets to the chavvies who were playing in the woods. You know how we sometimes get nonces hanging around the fair, looking out for kiddies? Well, Tom told the little 'uns to stop rokkering with the mush and to jel out of it.'

'Stop talking to the man and run away,' I translated for a puzzled-looking Haz.

'Then Tom phoned me and I went down there to have a word myself. He was a youngish joskin, about your age. Clean-shaved, a bit bug-eyed, looked like he cut his own hair from the state of it. The usual black suit a preacher might wear, but at least a size too small for him. Charity shop number would be my guess. Still, he'd had money once, and whatever converted him to the good Lord, it must have happened in the past couple of years.'

'How do you know that?' Haz asked.

'He was wearing these glasses. Designer frames, Cartier, but one of the arms was broken and taped and the lenses had been replaced, probably because his eyesight had got worse since he'd bought them. Thick, Coke-bottle lenses that looked ugly in the frames because he couldn't afford to have the thinner kind.'

Haz frowned. 'Maybe the glasses weren't originally his? Maybe he found them and had the lenses replaced?'

Dad searched inside his pocket and brought out a torn sheet from the front of the preacher's pamphlet: 'REJECT SATAN, REJECT SIN, REJECT WORLDLINESS AND AVARICE, ENVY AND GREED. EMBRACE JESUS CHRIST AS YOUR LORD AND SAVIOUR BEFORE THE HELL-FIRE CONSUMES ...'

'A puritanical prick like this doesn't pick up expensive glasses off the street and keep 'em,' Dad said. 'He'd hand them in as lost property to the gavvers. But he might hold onto a pair from his old, sinful life, thinking that to throw them away would be wasteful. From the state of them, I'd guess this big life change happened a year or two back.'

I couldn't help but smile at Haz's quietly awed expression. It was how he had often looked at me in the old days when I performed my 'tricks'.

'I learned from the best,' I murmured to him, and turned my attention back to the torn scrap of paper. 'So you confronted this guy, tried to take one of his pamphlets, and he wrenched it back.'

'Said his message of salvation wasn't for the likes of me. That he could tell just by looking into my face that I was beyond the grace of God.' Dad chuckled – a sound so rare that we all looked at him. 'Anyway, I told the dinlo to be on his way and didn't think much more about it, until this happened. A fire-and-brimstone mush like that might well think fortune telling was the devil's work.'

I glanced at Tilda who was quietly shaking her head. As she didn't speak, I let the gesture pass.

'I gotta go see to the dodgems,' Big Sam said. 'The plates are still out of alignment. Tils, why don't you stay up at our trailer tonight? I'll get Sandra to make up the spare bed.'

Dad agreed. 'And if you want to open tomorrow, I'll have one of the chaps stand guard outside the tent. I still think this is all a prank, but to be on the safe side we'll keep a close eye on you. Unless Scott has anything to add?'

I shook my head. At that moment it was difficult to see what else could be done. In a strange way, the oblique threat of the doll reminded me of that uncertain terror harboured by Darrel Everwood. His fear that some dark fate awaited him at Purley Rectory was almost embodied in that gruesome wax poppet. And in their very different ways, weren't Tilda and Darrel cut from the same psychic cloth? A religious fanatic who saw a simple fortune teller as a witch deserving of biblical punishment would surely view Everwood in similar terms. But it was such a vague connection, and when I asked Tilda if she'd ever met or spoken with Everwood, her denial seemed to make it even more unlikely.

'I've seen him on the telly, of course,' she said. 'Done very well for himself, that one. But I doubt he has the true gift of a seer. Smoke and mirrors is his game, if I'm any judge.' *But not yours?* I let the question go unspoken. 'Never met him, though,' she continued. 'Why would I? They don't put ugly mugs like mine on the telly.'

She cackled and then hushed us as we all demurred.

'I don't have to be a mind-reader to know when I'm being flattered.' She shooed her twisted fingers at both Big Sam and my dad. 'Now, off with you. The boys here can walk me over to your trailer, Sam. I shan't open the tent tonight, but tomorrow?' Her lips tucked in with annoyance. 'No God-botherer's going to scare me away from my living.'

After they left, Haz and I helped Tilda out of her chair. Her knobbled knuckles affectionately brushed the side of our faces before she turned back to the needle-pierced poppet. She hesitated a moment and then gingerly picked it up.

'Feels mulardi, don't it?' she said, then looked at Haz. 'Haunted, I mean. But not by spirits. By a living person's spite and wickedness. It feels ... personal.' Glancing up from the doll, she met my gaze. 'Oh, I know you ain't a believer, Scott Jericho. You never was, but still I see shadows all around you. Around both of you.' Her eyes appeared to lose their focus as she suddenly grasped at Harry's sleeve. 'A man with silver hair and a hole in his body where terrible agonies wormed their way inside. Black pain like nothing he believed could ever be real. But he's smiling now because the hole is empty and the pain's gone. You took that pain from him, and he thanks you for it. His smile is your smile.'

Haz's eyes went wide and he pulled away from her.

'I don't ...' He gazed at both of us, a look of someone betrayed. 'I can't.'

And with that, he wrenched the tent flaps aside and vanished into the night. I was about to call out to him when Tilda grabbed my wrist.

'And you,' she said, her voice smoother, somehow less of a toadish croak. 'The ghosts of those little Polish kiddies. The ones that evil-hearted man Kerrigan murdered. They're gone now. They've been avenged, and so they have stepped beyond the light and out of this world. They won't haunt you anymore. But you have other spirits now, don't you? New and terrible shades. They look to you for justice, Scott Jericho. They scream like starving juks for the soul that took them before their time. They cling to you with the cold and certain grasp of the grave. They were murdered to save you and now they reach out. All of them. But him ... *Him* most of all. The child killer, broken and remade.'

It was a shadow on the wall of the tent that caught my attention. A lone punter in the passing crowd, his darkness distorted by strobing lights and the windblown canvas. That was all. And if the shape paused and turned its misshapen head towards us, as if listening in through the shivering doorway? Well, people will stop to read Madam Tilda's sign, won't they? ENTER NOW AND MEET THE FUTURE! But I didn't want him to enter. Didn't want that twisted arm to reach out and pull the flap aside. Didn't want the bloated corpse of Lenny Kerrigan to drag itself over the threshold. Didn't want that still-bleeding face, red and slick as a freshly dipped toffee apple, to turn and grin and plead, as it had back in Bradbury End:

Juh-i-co. Huh-elp. Muh-ee.

And of course it didn't. Because there are no ghosts.

When I turned to Tilda again, she was smiling her gentle smile, as if nothing had happened.

'Shall we go?' she asked. 'It's cold in here and I feel a chill in my bones.'

Chapter Eight

I WAS RELIEVED TO FIND ONE of my dad's chaps waiting outside. Together we tied and padlocked the flaps, ensuring Tilda's tent was secure for the night. Part of me had wanted to take the wax doll so that I could examine it again later, but on reflection, I didn't think I'd get much more out of it. Anyway, I was desperate to find Haz. That look he'd given us before running off? It had made my blood run cold.

'Take her to Big Sam's trailer,' I said to the chap. 'His wife Sandra should be up there. Don't leave until she's safely inside.' I then bent down to give Tilda a quick kiss on the cheek. 'It's only foolishness, I'm sure.'

She looked at me, her expression distant again. 'Whatever happens, it's nobody's fault. I want you to remember that. Now, go find that handsome boy of yours.'

The ground was heaving. Punters surging and dawdling, tumbling dizzily off rides, lovers feeding each other wisps of candyfloss. I moved between them with the born ease of a showman, making for the side ground and our carousel, where I prayed I'd find Haz. At one point I thought I saw Ben Halliday, a glint of flaming red among the bobbing heads, and then another familiar face I couldn't quite place. A small, drawn-looking man dragging at the arm of a harassed woman in an olive-green anorak. The crowd swallowed them again and I dismissed the nagging recognition.

Stretching onto my toes, I finally made out the carousel. Sal was collecting money from parents while Haz went around checking their kids were safely mounted upon winged unicorns and magic carpets. My nerves were singing by the time I reached them. Jodie was busy nattering away to a distracted Haz who, on glimpsing me, appeared to fumble with a wailing child's seat belt.

'How's Aunt Tils?' Sal asked, stepping in front of me.

'He didn't tell you?'

'Hasn't said a word since he came back.'

'She's fine,' I said. 'Just a nasty practical joke. I'll fill you in later.'

Sal levelled her eyes with mine. 'You take him back to the trailer right now. He looks like he's had a bad shock.' When I started to protest she cut me short. 'Me and Jodes can mind the ride, it's no trouble. Just sort things out, for Christ's sake.'

'I will.' I touched her elbow. 'Thanks.'

Sal then called her daughter over, receiving an almost adolescent pout from the seven-year-old. Haz was definitely Jodie's favourite person and she hated being parted from him. Looking at my boyfriend's sad, sweet face, it was a sentiment with which I could only sympathise. Haz pretended to be busy with his cash pocket until I unclipped it from his belt and handed it to Sal.

'Come on,' I said.

'No,' he answered, trying to snatch it back. 'I said I'd mind the ride tonight and I will. I have to—'

I took his hand. 'Come on.'

We didn't return to our trailer. Instead, I led us to my father's old Colchester and the kennel that stood at the bottom of the trailer steps. Hearing our approach, a weary head poked its way out of the wooden box. Haz knelt and immediately started making a fuss of the old boxer dog while I grabbed Webster's lead from the hook outside my dad's door. The juk gave a great, full-bodied yawn, and lead attached, plodded along loyally beside us.

We barely exchanged a word as we left the main gate and followed the boundary of the wood. Not a hint of movement among those trees. I guessed that whatever night creatures called this place their home had been frightened away by the glare and bellow of the fair. I glanced over at the great sprawling expanse of it now, planted in its latest setting. Our home, our community, our livelihood; a pulsing, vibrant beacon that drew the wide-eyed thrill-seeker and yet at the same time hid so much from their wondering gaze. An ancient way of life that held its people and its secrets dear, allowing only a select few newcomers, like Harry, into its midst. The fairground of my forebears, of my youth, of my present, of my future, ever moving, ever changing, ever the same.

Webster tugged on his leash and I clicked the release button, allowing him a few more metres of freedom. The old mutt snuffled in the undergrowth, his head turning this way and that, doleful eyes following things invisible to human sight. Breathing deeply, I caught the smell of bonfires on the air. Perhaps prompted by this autumnal scent, the Halloween image of a burning pyre suddenly ignited in my head – a figure lashed to a stake, screaming, writhing, caged in fire ...

'I'm sorry, what?'

I realised Haz had been speaking.

'Nothing,' he murmured, slipping his hand out of mine. 'Doesn't matter.'

I was about to say something when Webster bristled at my side. I glanced down to find his hackles raised, his teeth bared. His attention was fixed on the blank facade of the house in front of us. Purley Rectory seemed to have loomed out of the clearing without me being aware that we'd even approached it. I told Webster to hush and followed Haz to the low iron railing that ran around the front garden. A patch of grassless, flowerless scrub so desolate that even weeds appeared to shun it.

The house itself was a big, square, red-brick building in the style of the Gothic Revival. All sharp angles and overly ornate flourishes. Planted into the steep, sloping roof, a regiment of towering chimneys stood like guardians on a battlement. It was a house of contrasts. Features leaped out and caught the eye: one window larger and misaligned with the rest, an eave hanging out of balance, a small, pagan face randomly etched into a cornerstone. The overall effect was one of clutter and disorder, as if the architect had been unable to bear contemplating any single part of his design for too long.

Above the overhang of the porch, a light shone at a first-floor window. With the rest of the house in darkness, that single bright chink gave the place a watchful air. I wondered if Miss Rowell was still busy inside, trying to comply with the production team's request to make Purley more 'old-timey'. Just to the right of the rectory stood those expensive trailers, each with a *Ghost Seekers* decal slapped onto the side.

Suddenly, Haz turned to me, his eyes bright. 'Did you tell her?' Webster glanced between us and whined.

'Haz.' I sighed. 'Of course not. I would never—'

'Then how did she know? About what happened?' He crossed his arms, cupped his elbows with his hands. 'About my dad.'

'Harry.' I tried to reach for him but he pulled away. 'Think about it. You're thirty-two years old. Like most people our age, you've probably lost an older relative at some point in your life, and what are the odds that person had grey hair and a smile a bit like yours? Tilda didn't say who it was – it might have been your grandfather.'

'She said he had a hole in his body full of pain.'

'OK,' I agreed. 'But did she say what kind of pain or where it was located? It might have been cancer or heart trouble, anything at all. I mean, who doesn't have an elderly relative with aches and pains?'

'She said I took his pain away,' Haz muttered.

'She said you "took his pain from him",' I corrected gently. 'A kind word or a joke can take someone's mind off their pain. Don't you see? This is how dukkerin—' He shot me a questioning glance. 'Fortune telling, mediumship, talking with spirits, call it what you like, this is how it works. The "psychic" makes general statements that sound specific and you fill in the blanks.'

'So why did she say those things?' he asked. 'To be cruel?'

I shook my head. 'She might have thought it would bring you comfort. She's been playing this role all her life, remember. I don't even think she knows she's making it up.'

Making it up? Then how did she know about Peter Garris's victims and about Lenny Kerrigan? Because those too had been generalities, I reasoned, and in the moment I had mistakenly interpreted them as specific knowledge. Everyone on the fair knew about my history with Kerrigan, while the rest of it was all just coincidence and illusion – the human mind seeking patterns in things that weren't there.

'So none of it's real,' Haz said. 'Not Aunt Tilda's dukkerin, not even the ghosts of this ugly old house?'

While Webster returned to nose around in the undergrowth, I slipped my hand back into Harry's. It felt ice cold as I threaded our fingers together.

'People make their own ghosts,' I said. 'This world is dark enough without the spirits of the dead troubling anyone.'

'Perhaps.' I saw his jaw set tight. 'But you're not a total pragmatist, Scott. I know you're not. I mean, if you only see the world in terms of facts to be weighed and analysed, why do you love books so much? Invented characters, made-up stories? And how come I catch you sometimes, sitting up in our trailer at night, so lost in your reading you don't notice the tears on your cheeks? I see those tears. I see the person behind them.' He smiled what had now become a rare smile. 'Words, books, poetry, they move you in a way you can't explain. Not rationally. It's the same with me and music. When I hear a certain melody, when I sing, when I write something that captures some fragment of how I feel. It's more than all this.' He threw out his hands, sweeping the forest and the fair. 'I suppose you'll say that what I'm describing is just neurons firing in the brain. Dopamine hits to help make this whole sad spectacle of life seem bearable so that we can keep the human race turning on its wheel. But I know you sense it, just like I do. Some kind of essence we can't explain. Something beyond ourselves.'

'I don't deny people feel that way,' I said. 'And yes, spirituality has inspired incredible art and music and literature. You could even say our entire culture is based on it. The search for something bigger than ourselves. But do I think it has any substance in reality?' I shook my head. 'You're wrong, Haz. I *am* a pragmatist. Show me evidence and I'll believe there's something more than those little firing neurons. Until then, it's all just wishful thinking.'

He nodded. 'So anything you can't touch and observe and evaluate is a lie?'

'Not a lie. There's no deliberate deception.'

'Even love,' he said quietly, his gaze flicking across the confused tumble of the rectory.

'Look, I think we're wandering from the point,' I said. 'I promise you, I haven't said a word to anyone about what happened with your father. I would never—'

'But you did,' he countered. 'You told *him*.'

I took a deep breath. 'Is that what this is about? Harry, do you want to talk about Garris?' I felt my stomach knot. 'About what really happened in Bradbury End?'

'You don't understand,' he said. 'You just—'

He had started to turn away when, reaching out, I caught the strap of the music bag he still carried over his shoulder. The clasp snapped and the bag fell to the ground. Dropping Webster's lead, I went to pick it up and at once felt the utter weightlessness of the thing. Unable to resist, I pulled back the front flap and glanced inside the bag. Nothing. No sheet music, no notebook stuffed with his compositions, not even the old-fashioned tuning fork he always carried because he mistrusted the digital kind. Only the stub of a pencil at the very bottom. For some reason, I dug this out before he snatched the bag away from me.

'I'm sorry,' I said. 'Haz, wait!'

I grabbed at the sleeve of his cagoule but the material slipped through my fingers and in the next instant he was running, a confused Webster lolloping at his heels. I stood there, frozen, looking down at the fragment of pencil in my palm. And then I felt something else – a smooth, pliable softness at my fingertips. Some substance that had come loose from Harry's sleeve as I'd tugged at it. Lifting my hand to the light of the fair, I saw a spot of white wax adhering to my fingernail.

And suddenly, I was picturing myself back in Aunt Tilda's tent, the faceless wax doll in my hand, the scrap of paper pinned to its leg. 'EX 22:18'.

A biblical scrawl done in pencil.

Chapter Nine

Did I really believe that this gentle, empathetic man who'd relieved his father's suffering, who had comforted Aunt Tilda in her distress, who'd shown me more tenderness than anyone I had ever known, had crafted that sick effigy in order to frighten an old woman out of her wits? Of course not. And yet, in the passing horror of the moment, had I pictured him moulding its soft white flesh? All I'll say is that the mind often paints images that it would shame us to admit.

And after all, there was the fact of the empty bag. If that had merely been a prop used to sustain the alibi of choir practice, then where had Harry really been spending his time these past few weeks? Returning to the fair, I ran over those absences in my head. Always a Tuesday and Thursday evening, a couple of hours each time. He had returned flushed and exhilarated, re-energised and somehow more youthful, as if the years of guilt he'd endured since his father's death had been lifted from him. Since we'd reconnected, he'd never been that way with me.

My thoughts strayed to the inevitable conclusion, and angrily I thrust it away. The idea of Haz cheating was almost as absurd as him sitting in some secret room, carving wax poppets. Still, something was badly wrong between us, and as I returned to the carousel, I could see that Sal thought so too.

'What have you done, you bloody dinlo?' she snapped at me. A few punters cast her looks and she rolled her eyes and spat back. 'You don't even know what a dinlo is, so jog on.'

'Where is he?' I asked.

'Taken Webster back to your dad's. Then he says he's going into Aumbry to find a hotel for the night. I tried to talk him out of it, but he said he needed some space. Scott, don't.'

She grabbed my shoulder – that spot again where Ben had landed his jab. 'I know you're worried.' Her voice took on an uncharacteristically gentle tone. 'I know, believe me, but tearing after him tonight will only push him further away. He'll be up the trailer now packing an overnight bag. Stay here with me and Jodes and work the juvenile with us. It'll take your mind off things.'

Jodie had been waiting out of earshot, her fingers twining together just like Haz's when he was worried. I called her over, told her everything was fine, and the munchkin wrapped her arms around my waist.

'You don't hate Uncle Haz, do you?'

That caught me like a punch to the gut. 'Course not, sweet pea. I could never.'

Just an hour ago I wouldn't have believed that anything could drive Aunt Tilda out of my thoughts. Now, while I took their cash and gave every customer the cheery showman's spiel I'd learned at my father's knee, I went over those last moments with Haz again and again. What had I done? What had I said? What hadn't I seen?

It was almost midnight by the time we shut up shop. Chaps were wrangling the last stragglers out of the gate while Sal and I fixed the weatherproofing around the carousel. One of the aunts had come by hours ago and taken Jodie away to bed. Before she left, the munchkin made me promise that Haz would come home soon.

Ten minutes after shutdown, I was locking the trailer door behind me. Exhausted, I took off my coat and went and crashed on the locker settee, slipping my phone out of my pocket just as a text came through. My hopes that Haz had replied to one of the half-dozen I'd already sent were dashed. It was from Sal, telling me to turn on the TV to some late-night discussion programme I'd never heard of. I hunted out the remote from the sofa cushions and absently flicked the switch.

While the show droned on in the background, I let my gaze play around the trailer. Structurally, it was the same creaky tin box it had always been, but Haz had worked his magic and transformed the interior into something resembling a home. Colourful throws, scented candles, his vintage Garrard turntable and record collection, my mum's books neatly stacked on a cinderblock bookcase by the bed. It was small and cramped, but it was ours. Or it had been. Now his bag and some of his clothes were gone. The sudden emptiness felt palpable.

Finally, I drifted back to the TV. An interviewer with a plummy Etonian drawl was introducing a tall, narrow-shouldered man in a well-cut suit. He was aged about fifty and what my mum would have called 'well-preserved', no slackening at the jawline and just a trace of grey around the temples. The only marked lines in his face were those bracketing a somewhat humourless mouth. He wore stylish tortoiseshell glasses and had a habit of almost constantly adjusting his cuffs in a fussy, preening sort of gesture.

'It's my pleasure this evening to have as my guest a noted figure from the world of popular science. Dr Joe Gilles—'

'*Joseph*,' the doctor said, that dour mouth puckering. 'Only my mother and my partner call me Joe.'

'Dr *Joseph* Gillespie,' the interviewer appeased. 'Tonight, Dr Gillespie is here to discuss his new investigative documentary, *Ghost Scammers*, in which he aims to debunk all claims of the supernatural and especially those of mediums and clairvoyants. The programme will air on Halloween night, at exactly the same time as renowned—' Gillespie actually blanched at the word '—celebrity medium Darrel Everwood and his team of "Ghost Seekers" broadcast their live séance from Purley Rectory. Reputedly the most haunted house in England. Dr Gillespie, bearing in mind the long-running success of Darrel Everwood's show, is *Ghost Scammers* a deliberately provocative title on your part?'

'Yes,' Gillespie deadpanned. 'Next question.'

The interviewer's smile broadened. I imagined he could see his obscure little programme trending on social media.

'You are by training a physicist, Dr Gillespie,' he went on. 'A serious scientist. And yet in recent years, you've waged what can only be described as a crusade against believers in the supernatural. Some might ask, why do you waste your time on such nonsense?'

Gillespie raised his eyebrows. 'Because it is *dangerous* nonsense. Humanity spent its infancy terrified of sprites and demons, but if we are ever to grow into maturity as a species, we must abandon the terrors of the cradle. The supernatural not only diverts the ingenuity of the human mind away from the really important questions of existence, but it can also be immensely harmful. People throw away their hard-earned money on these psychic conmen and do damage to themselves in the process. Psychiatry has shown us that grieving is a natural process. It is healthy to let go. Mediums, with their bogus claims of an afterlife, keep the mourner stuck in the crisis of their loss. A cruel and unnecessary paralysis.'

I sat forward. For all his arrogance, I couldn't help agreeing with Gillespie.

'But you seem, if I may say, particularly fixated on Darrel Everwood,' the interviewer observed.

'He is the most obnoxious of a bad lot, yes.'

I suddenly thought of Miss Rowell and her marked antagonism towards Everwood, then of the public backlash he'd recently suffered. I wondered if there were many people like Ben Halliday who still had sympathy for him.

'And of course his ex-fiancée has recently played into your hands,' the interviewer said. 'The videos she's released in which she claims that he's a fraud.'

'Hell hath no fury like a woman scorned,' Gillespie said drily. 'But then hell doesn't exist. Mr Everwood's duplicity does.'

'But this isn't just personal to Darrel Everwood. This *is* a crusade. I want to play the viewers an audio clip from a podcast you recently took part in.' The interviewer turned to the camera. 'I should explain, Dr Gillespie was invited to challenge the skills of a once-famous spiritualist, Miss Genevieve Bell. Miss Bell and Dr Gillespie were tasked with "psychically" reading the same subject in separate sessions. Here the podcaster reveals the results.'

The camera trained itself on an impassive Gillespie as the audio started to play.

'Miss Bell, in your reading you claimed that the subject's late mother made contact with you,' the podcaster said. 'That, from the spirit world, she had provided ten facts about her son. Of those facts, four were verified by the subject and our research team as correct, two were so general as to be statistically insignificant, and four were incorrect. Dr Gillespie, you approached the subject by a method of cold reading: analysing his age, sex, dress, manner of speech, body language, and facial expressions in response to your statements. Of the ten facts you provided, nine were verified as correct, with the subject himself remarking that you were clearly the more gifted medium.'

Dr Gillespie's voice broke into the audio, cutting off the podcaster. 'And, of course, the truth is that I am *not* a medium. Nor are there any spirits whispering in poor Miss Bell's ear. Her entire life has been constructed on a lie so transparent that even she cannot now fail to see it.'

A weak, plaintive voice responded, 'But they *do* speak to me, Dr Gillespie. They always have. Ever since I was a little girl.'

'Oh yes, I've heard your silly life story,' Gillespie scoffed. 'But it is results that matter. I won, you lost. Accept it, my dear. *Learn* from it.'

The clip came to an end and the interviewer turned back to the doctor.

'Poor woman.' Gillespie sighed. 'I sat with her afterwards and explained how she does her tricks. Eliciting cooperation from her subjects, picking up physical clues from them, shotgunning them – as we sceptics call it – with a huge quantity of general information before refining her guesses and then presenting those guesses as facts. The pitiful thing is, I think Miss Bell actually believed she *was* psychic, unlike Darrel Everwood who is fully aware of his chicanery.'

The interviewer shifted in his chair. 'But isn't there an element of cruelty in what you do, Doctor?'

A photograph appeared on a large screen behind the two men. It showed a child of about eight or nine years old, sitting hunched in a wicker chair, knees drawn up to her chin, forearms clasped around her shins. She appeared to be very thin, big dark eyes bright in their hollows. Although the photo looked to be from the eighties or early nineties, the little girl had a striking Edwardian quality to her, an impression reinforced by the slightly oversized black lace gloves she wore.

'Genevieve Bell was notoriously reclusive,' the interviewer said. 'This photo from her childhood was one of the few we could source. You are aware, Dr Gillespie, that Miss Bell died quite recently? Not long after your podcast with her, in fact. Do you harbour any regrets about how you treated her?'

Gillespie tutted as if the question was beneath him. 'Of course, I'm sorry she died so tragically, but please, let's not sentimentalise the woman's legacy simply because of her unhappy end. In life, she victimised others. Preyed upon their grief and credulity, although as I have said, perhaps unwittingly.'

'Very well, then shall we return to your upcoming documentary?'

'Willingly,' Gillespie said with relish. 'In advance of transmission, I shall be going down to Purley Rectory tomorrow to protest this *Ghost Seekers* nonsense. I would encourage any rational citizen to join me there and help combat Everwood's pantomime. This kind of thing should be stopped. *Must* be stopped.'

He turned that stern and uncompromising gaze upon the camera.

'I hope you and the viewers take me seriously when I say this. There is nothing I will not do to rid humanity of the stain of superstition. Nothing.'

Chapter Ten

I WOKE SCREAMING, SHEETS TWISTED AROUND my body, every muscle tensed. Somewhere out in the dark, an unsecured piece of tarpaulin cracked in the wind, and in the riptide of my dream, I imagined it as the snap of burning wood. It took a few breathless seconds for the images to lose their power and for my heart to settle.

In the nightmare, I had stood before the same witch's pyre I'd pictured while walking with Haz. Around me, the baying of an unseen mob, eager for the flames to do their holy work. Their fury was directed at a writhing figure staked at the heart of the bonfire. No agony she endured seemed to satisfy their hatred. Close by, warming his gloved hands above the flames, stood a man in a long black cloak and a tall Puritan hat. All at once, the mob fell silent, stunned perhaps that the still-burning woman appeared to have freed herself from the stake.

She came at me fast, lurching out of the inferno on the charcoal sticks of her legs, the wind tearing at her flesh and dispersing it like black snow across the clearing. It was then that I saw the great jumbled mass of Purley Rectory grow up behind her, red fire reflected in its windows. I tried to step back, to turn and run, but the dream held me in place.

Inside the raging cowl that flickered about her head, I saw the witch's skin, white and melting, like a wax doll thrown into a furnace. It was Aunt Tilda's face. It was Harry's. The two bubbling and mingling together as they slipped away from the skull.

'Thou shalt not suffer, Scotty!' they shrieked at me in their weird hybrid voice. 'Thou shalt not!'

I tried to look away but again the dream wouldn't let me. I was forced to watch them fall, to explode into dust at my feet, and for that dust to re-form into the shattered body of Lenny Kerrigan. Flowers immediately began to grow around him, marigolds the colour of consuming fire.

'You wanted a puzzle, my boy. The world has given you one. Take it.'

I looked up into the face of the man in the Puritan hat.

The unremarkable face of dormant serial killer, Peter Garris. He laughed that oh-so-rare laugh of his, dry as the corpse-dust at my feet.

Now, the nightmare over, I tugged the damp sheets from my body and went to the sink. I poured a bowl of cold water and washed myself down with a flannel, scrubbing the dark bristle of my jaw, my chest, the hair under my arms, feverishly cleansing myself of the dream. Afterwards, I simply stood there, wet and shivering, looking out through the little window above the sink.

I had fallen asleep breathing in the scent of Harry's pillow, my phone in my hand. The last text I'd received had been from Sal following the interview with Dr Gillespie:

Could cause us trouble?

I'd replied, saying that the doctor's planned demonstration against the *Ghost Seekers* event probably wouldn't amount to much. Anyway, despite his arrogance, I had found myself agreeing with virtually everything the man had said. Darrel Everwood was a fraud and our association with him cheapened the reputation of Jericho Fairs.

Beyond the window, a grey dawn was silvering the mist that blanketed the wood. In the distance, I could make out faint wisps stealing in and then retreating from the door of Purley Rectory. I don't know why, but I half expected to see Haz there, draped in the shadow of that somewhat sinister old house. I stayed at the window, watching and shivering until the cold forced me back to bed.

After another hour of staring at my phone, I dug out the remote control and switched on the TV. More time passed, mindlessly flicking between breakfast shows until the face from the billboard snapped me out of my daydreaming.

Darrel Everwood was sprawled in a flamboyantly relaxed attitude across a studio sofa while, perched opposite, the breakfast hosts grinned as if this was the most outrageous thing they had ever seen. That trademark cocky smile was firmly in place, although perhaps a little strained, like a high-tension wire about to snap. Still, Everwood played to the camera brilliantly, mascara-rimmed eyes twinkling with mischief.

'So, Darrel, you're here to tell us about the *Ghost Seekers Halloween Special*,' the female host began.

Everwood sat up, suddenly alert. 'Miles, Rosanna, this is gonna be the biggest séance we've done yet,' he said, in a Cockney accent about as convincing as Dick Van Dyke's in *Mary Poppins*. 'I kid you not, this Purley Rectory gaff is wall-to-wall spirits. Even sitting here, I'm getting vibes from the place. Like, the old girl is reaching out to me across the miles.'

The male host seemed to be lapping it up. 'So you're expecting fireworks on the night?'

'Fireworks, Miles, my man? Forget Guy bloody Fawkes, this is gonna be a psychic nuclear detonation! And it won't just be broadcast in this country. We've got deals with major networks across the globe, as well as all the major streaming giants, doing a live simulcast. But look, I have to be serious and level with you for a minute. Which camera am I on?' Miles pointed and Everwood stood and approached the screen, his hands pressed together as if in prayer. 'Viewers at home, this All Hallows' Eve, we are going to be opening channels of paranormal energy never experienced before. I cannot guarantee there won't be pushback from the spirit world. As some of you know, Purley Rectory has a long and bloody history. So I'm begging you, for your own sake, if you've got young kiddies or you have a heart condition, anything like that, *please* don't watch this once-in-a-lifetime TV event.'

I had to hand it to Everwood, he might be peddling some premium bullshit, but he peddled it with all the showmanship of a modern P. T. Barnum.

Rosanna visibly shuddered as the psychic took his seat. 'Sounds thrilling! Now let's have a little look at you in action from an old episode of *Ghost Seekers*.'

The screen switched to a grainy, night-vision shot of Everwood stumbling around the corridors of some ancient building. Dust motes spiralled in his wake while his eyes stood out, stark and luminous in the pitch darkness. A caption read: 'Morstan Keep,

3.13 a.m.'. Suddenly there came a hollow groan, the kind of structural fart a medieval castle probably gives off every five minutes. Still, Everwood staggered back against the nearest wall, as if the afterlife had reached out and personally insulted his fake tan. In the next instant, his mouth dropped open and a high-pitched keening sound came from the back of his throat. Then his entire body started to shake, shoulders jigging up and down, arms thrashing, making me wonder if someone had accidentally plugged him into the mains. The whining stopped abruptly, and turning his head from side to side, he shrieked at the camera, now with a vaguely Glaswegian twang:

'Get out! Get out of my hooose!'

The clip ended and the transmission switched back to the studio. Miles and Rosanna stared at their guest with frank admiration.

'And that was back in series twelve when you were—'

'Possessed by the spirit of Matthew McDowell, sixteenth-century laird of Morstan Keep.' Everwood nodded. 'Quite a ride, but it'll be nothing compared to Purley.'

'All right, Darrel, now there's one thing we should address before we let you go,' Rosanna said, her Botoxed brow actually finding a crease, so the audience knew she was serious. 'As you may be aware, celebrated sceptic Dr Joseph Gillespie—'

'Celebrated by who?' Everwood laughed. 'His mum?'

'Dr Gillespie will be showing his documentary, *Ghost Scammers*, on the same night on a rival channel. He claims that he will expose the "tricks" you use to fool people into—'

'Fool people, Rosanna?' Everwood leaned forward and touched his middle finger to his temple. 'OK, so can I just ask, was it annoying when your car – your BMW convertible with the custom paint job – didn't start this morning? And was it any compensation when the bloke from the RAC turned out to be such a babe? Nice brown eyes and a very cute bum, am I right?'

'But how on earth did you . . . ?' Rosanna gawped.

'Anyway.' Everwood grinned, waving aside her amazement. 'You were saying something about that old dinosaur, Gillespie? You know his problem? Jealousy. Well, he was never going to pull the girls by talking about quadratic equations and pulsars, was he? So he decides to come after me to increase his street cred. It's sad, really.'

'But can we ask about the recent bad press you've experienced?' Miles put in. 'Your fiancée—?'

'That's . . . It's . . . What I mean to say is, that's the subject of ongoing legal proceedings that I can't . . .' For the first time, Everwood's voice faltered. He looked down at his hands, his shoulders slumping. His supreme bravado suddenly appeared to abandon him. No longer the bratty toddler I'd seen storming out of Purley Rectory, he seemed like a different kind of a child altogether, lost and uncertain. Head still bowed, he went on, 'I'd just like to remind everyone of something. I grew up on a council estate in Peckham. Had to drag myself up, in fact. I didn't get everything handed to me from birth like the Joseph Gillespies of this world. I've had to make a living from the talents God decided to bless me with. And you know something, despite all my success, I'm still like any ordinary, working-class geezer out there. As Charles Dickens said, "If you prick me, don't I bleed?"'

'Shakespeare,' I groaned at the trailer ceiling.

'And you know what else? Every bit of my success, I owe to you.' Reanimated again, Everwood lifted his head and thrust out his arms towards the viewers. 'The great British public, and I love you for it.'

I switched off the TV and turned my face into Haz's pillow. Then, rolling onto my back, I stared up at the weak autumn daylight shivering against the ceiling. Something Darrel Everwood had just said chimed strangely with the nightmare that had woken me. A half-remembered fragment of my childhood, some Halloween story of my mother's linking the two. Not from a book she'd read to me but a tale passed between her and Aunt Tilda as they sat on their trailer steps. Some gruesome history recalled to entertain a morbidly inclined child ...

It was no good. The memory wouldn't come. Anyway, I was still exhausted from a troubled night and there were hours yet until I was needed on the fair. Turning onto my side, away from Haz's half of the bed, I tried to go back to sleep.

Chapter Eleven

I MOVED AMONG THE GHOSTS AND goblins, the monsters and blood-spattered corpses, an ordinary man in a sea of carnival freaks. The word had gone out first thing via social media and virtually every punter seemed to have heard the call. Halloween had come early to Jericho Fair, and it was half-priced tickets for anyone who showed up in costume. This I knew was the brainchild of George Jericho, a man who knew more about pulling in the trade than any marketing guru alive. My guess was that it was an early counter-attack against Dr Gillespie and his demonstration.

There was no sign of the doc just yet, however, and it was already after seven. No sign of Darrel Everwood either. After spending most of the day in bed, I'd finally hauled my carcass into a pair of faded blue jeans and a black polo neck only an hour before opening time. It was then that I realised I hadn't eaten since yesterday. Usually, Haz could be relied on to ply me with a wholesome meal at regular intervals, and it felt pathetically ridiculous that I was already slipping back into old neglectful routines. Anyway, a hot dog from Layla Jafford's truck took the edge off my hunger.

I glanced again at my phone. Nothing. On Sal's advice, I'd resisted sending any more texts.

'He'll come round in his own time,' Sal had said as we set up the carousel. 'But if you push him now, then he might just stay away for good.'

I looked up. 'Sounds like you know more than you're telling. Come on, Sal, do you know what's going on with him?'

'I swear, I don't,' she promised. 'But I've got to know that boy a little these past few months. Whatever you've done or not done, he's hurting right now, and he doesn't need you and your questions poking away at him. When he comes back, just be patient and *listen*. You're a good listener, most of the time.'

All showpeople are detectives at heart – observation combined with a deep knowledge of human nature is how they ply their trade – and so it didn't surprise me that, without Sal uttering a word, the news had got around. I guess it was kind, how many of them came over and asked how I was doing. Big Sam even looked like he was going to burst into tears. Most surprising of all was my dad's reaction when I ran into him five minutes before opening.

'You heard from the joskin?' That word for a non-Traveller spoken more gently than I'd ever heard it. When I shook my head, he sighed. 'Your mother and I used to have a lot of rows, if you remember. She'd disappear for a few days and then come back, right as rain. Or right as she ever was. We're a hard breed to rub along with, us Jerichos, but that boy's a good 'un. Don't lose him if you can help it.'

'Thanks, Dad,' I murmured.

'Anyhow,' he went on. 'I've got a chap minding your ride tonight—' When I tried to protest, he cut me short. 'I'll pay his wages. I want you out patrolling.'

'Is this to do with Aunt Tilda?' I asked.

'No. I have a man watching out for her. But you saw that uppity gorger Gillespie on the box last night? Well, I don't want him bringing *his* circus onto my ground. I know you're leery about us working with these telly people, but we need this event to be a success. Winter's coming on, and if we don't take some posh over the next few days, we'll feel it soon enough.'

Despite Dad's reassurances, I kept a special lookout on Tilda's tent during my patrol. The chap was always at his post, sizing up each punter as they passed through. Once I caught sight of the old mystic herself, poking her head out of the flap.

'Heard about the pretty joskin,' she croaked at me. 'Never you mind. I read your cards special this afternoon: after dealing the Tower – upheaval, broken pride, disaster – came the Star and the Lovers combined – faith, hope, and rejuvenation. All will be well, my darlin'.'

I thanked her and moved on.

Halloween really had shown up ahead of schedule. A kind of giddy ghoulishness seemed to have caught hold of the crowd as the most popular attraction of the night appeared to be old Tommy Radlett's ghost train. Queues of excitable vampires, overstimulated zombies, and hot-dog-chomping werewolves impatiently awaited their turn. Meanwhile the place heaved with miniature figures dressed up as superheroes and Disney princesses, all clutching hard-won hook-a-duck prizes and those ubiquitous plastic cauldrons.

About half an hour into my patrol, I ran across the preacher. I found him by the funhouse, handing out his pamphlets to a group of bewildered-looking teenagers. He was just as my dad had described him – a gangly figure with a bad haircut, dressed in a raggedy charity shop suit. His face was almost emaciated and those broken Cartier glasses kept sliding down his long nose, making me wonder if they'd once fitted a larger, more well-nourished head.

'That'll do,' I said to him, taking the pamphlets from the teens and handing them back. 'On your way now.'

The kids appeared to think I meant them and scuttled off gratefully. Meanwhile, the preacher nodded over his pages before looking up at me with a sort of ingratiating intensity.

'"Everyone who hears these words of Mine and does not act on them, will be like a foolish man who built his house on the sand."' He closed his bulging eyes, his smile becoming almost orgasmic. 'So said the Lord, our God.'

'And what are *your* words, Mr . . . ?'

'Pastor.' He inclined his head. 'Christopher Cloade. And may I have your name, brother?'

'Scott Jericho. Are you willing to shake hands with a filthy sinner, Christopher?'

He juggled his pamphlets and gripped my hand with surprising force, especially for a man who looked like the breeze might take him at any moment.

'Jericho, like the biblical city, whose great walls fell at the trumpet blast.' He glanced around himself, at the hoopla and the shooting galleries, at the welcoming faces of the Travellers. 'If you stand with the heathens of your race, Scott Jericho, you too shall fall.'

'Right.' I sighed, taking one of his tracts and flicking through the pages. 'So you've got a hard-on for that Old Testament bully boy, have you? That blood-soaked maniac who insisted that, once the walls fell, every Canaanite in Jericho must be slaughtered – man, woman, and child. I know my Bible too, you see? And before you say it, yes, the devil *can* quote scripture. I've seen it done, more than once. In a former life, I was a detective and you'd be surprised how many holy monsters I put behind bars. Or ...' I glanced down at the title page – 'The Church of Christ the Redeemer: REPENT BEFORE ME AND SEEK SALVATION'. 'Perhaps you wouldn't.'

'We are all monsters,' he replied evenly. 'And the worst of us can be saved.'

'Even the ones I've seen?' I asked. 'The killers, the torturers, the child molesters.'

He lifted rapturous eyes to the heavens. 'Should *they* ask His mercy, they will be the *most* exalted.'

'I can see that idea is a great comfort to you,' I said, leaning in. 'Two years ago, was it? About then anyway. Yes, the wear on those glasses and the studied way you've starved yourself, all in search of penance. Well, maybe it was that at first. Now you enjoy the suffering, don't you? The daily denials and the howl of your stomach. I bet you've forgotten all about the child.' I gripped him by his frayed collar and shook the smile from his lips. 'I know a convicted pervert when I see him. So get your scrawny arse off my ground, or I'll take those pamphlets and force each and every one down your scraggly throat. Understand?'

I released him and he staggered back, clutching his works to his chest.

'I am needed here,' he practically shrieked at me. 'This is an evil place. Not only the celebration of this pagan festival, not only the gambling and debauchery of your carnival, but in the very earth.' He turned towards the silently watchful house. 'A rectory, a haven for men of the Word, now corrupted. A house fit only for demons and those who seek their counsel. Like the witch of Endor, whom Solomon sought out and—'

'Exodus chapter twenty-two, verse eighteen,' I said. 'You know it?'

'Of course.' His Adam's apple bobbed in that turkey throat.

'Tell me then, are you into scaring old ladies as well as little kids, Pastor?' I asked. 'Because if you are—'

I stopped mid-threat. The mix of fear and defiance had drained away from Christopher Cloade. Now a new and starker terror appeared to take hold of him. A bright blue vein sketched itself along his temple while those bulbous eyes grew even larger in their sunken sockets. Most of the pamphlets fell from his grasp and were taken up by the wind, promises of hellfire set to dance. I turned and glanced over my shoulder to where I believed his gaze was focused. Just the usual grinning vampires and white-sheet ghosts, and a little distance off, Ben Halliday escorting a dowdy-looking couple from the site. The same couple I'd seen last night – the small, weary man and the harassed woman in her green anorak.

'So it's true,' Cloade said, his voice almost a whisper. 'What they say about Purley . . .'

He didn't spare me another glance but twisted clumsily on his heel and moved quickly in the direction of the gate.

Dismissing his ramblings, I headed the same way, towards Ben and the couple I now recognised from the news reports of the time as Mr and Mrs Chambers, parents of the missing child, Debbie. As I followed them, Ben talking firmly but gently to the pair, I wondered if Darrel Everwood had at last found his excuse not to return to Purley. After his baseless assertion that Debbie had been murdered and buried close to the family home, and then Mrs Chambers' attempted suicide, Everwood had received that mild threat from the father – that if they should ever meet, the medium would be sorry. On TV this morning, a publicity-primed Darrel had been forced to show enthusiasm for the event, but here was his opportunity to call the whole thing off.

At the gate, Mr Chambers pulled his arm roughly away from Ben. The latter held up his hands while some angry words were thrown at him. Then Chambers looped his arm around his wife's waist and they both trudged off towards the car park. Still unnoticed, I stepped a little nearer as Ben took out his phone.

'Deepal? Yeah, it's them again,' he said. 'They're practically stalking him now, aren't they? Although I can't say I blame them. If I had a kid that had gone missing and some silly twat said something like that ... Yes, Deepal, I know he's jittery as fuck, but still ... No, no sign of Gillespie yet. And you say you're gonna be here with Darrel in, what, five minutes? Cool, I'll meet you up at the house. Oh, one last thing, the interview Gillespie did last night on the telly. Remember when the presenter mentioned that medium – the one Gillespie humiliated on the podcast ... ? That's right. Well, the funny thing is, I reckon Darrel knew her too. He mentioned her name to me anyway ...'

I'd lost sight of the Chambers but Cloade was still there, lingering by the gate, looking back at the fair with an expression I could only describe as haunted.

'She didn't just die, though, did she?' Ben was saying. 'I looked it up before I went to bed. The poor cow was murdered.'

He ran strong, freckled fingers through his hair.

'And not just murdered, neither. Butchered, so they say.'

Chapter Twelve

GENEVIEVE BELL. I REMEMBERED THAT tiny, broken voice from the podcast, insisting that her talent was genuine and that the dead had spoken to her since childhood. Something else from the interview then flashed into my mind. Gillespie saying that Genevieve's death shouldn't be sentimentalised because in life she had *victimised* others, and then his boast that he would stop at nothing in his crusade to wipe out superstition.

Returning to the fair, I followed Ben's example and used my phone to look up some of the online reports concerning the tragedy. As ever with a murder case properly managed, the Major Investigations Team in charge had fed the media only the barest crumbs. Perhaps twenty years ago, when Genevieve Bell had been at the height of her fame, this would have been different. Then, journalists might have dug deeper for any juicy titbits concerning the killing of a celebrated teenage psychic. But as I read about her life and death, it became clear that Miss Bell had long since retreated into obscurity, and so the scant facts offered up by the police were all that had been reported.

These amounted to: the badly battered corpse of a thirty-nine-year-old woman had been discovered by the victim's frail mother in the early hours of last Thursday morning. Due to Mrs Bell's advancing dementia, there had been a significant delay in contacting the authorities. Evangeline Bell, the victim's elder sister, was eventually reached by her mother, and following a hysterical and garbled conversation, called a neighbour to check at the house – Cedar Gables, Marchwood. Genevieve had been dead some hours. Burglary was not suspected to be the motive.

Evangeline, who lived in Edinburgh and had since travelled down to be with her mother, said the family was in a state of complete shock. Her sister hadn't an enemy in the world. Police would only say that the body was so brutally mutilated, DNA analysis was required for identification. The press had then speculated that the motive may have been deeply personal or else the work of a random psychopath.

I summarised these facts in my head from the various reports. They were so thin that, from my experience of working such cases, I guessed something highly unusual had taken place at Cedar Gables. Unique details would be kept back as an investigative tool and to weed out false confessions. DNA analysis for identification was suggestive, however. Not a cheap nor a quick tool when easier methods were at hand. The fact it had been resorted to in order to establish beyond doubt the identity of the victim must mean that the killer had—

'Scott, I need you down by the forest road.' My dad swarmed towards me. It was the only appropriate verb. At moments of crisis, he seemed to grow in stature, dominating the situation. 'Gillespie's arrived and is kicking up trouble with the press. Everwood's on his way too and— Ah, balls. There he is.'

A bulky black Bentley that looked something like a presidential protection vehicle came hurtling along the forest road, scattering punters in its wake. Some hurled insults, others dug out their phones to take video. I could see the hashtags already: #RoadRageDaz #DarrelEverwanker. A smaller, dark blue Volvo swept in behind the Bentley, containing, so I assumed, the assistant, Deepal, who'd just been speaking to Ben. Without slowing, both cars blazed through the car park and made for the production trailers set up beside the rectory.

'What do you want me to do?' I asked Dad. 'The main road's public land, I can't make Gillespie leave.'

'But the forest road isn't,' the old man grunted. 'Just make sure he stays where he is.'

As I valued human life a little more than Darrel Everwood, I decided not to take my ancient Mercedes on a slalom chase down the avenue of trees that led to the main road. Instead, I jogged towards the junction. Halfway there, I could already make out the lights of a camera crew and a small but noisy crowd gathered around a man standing on a platform. Even from the back, I recognised that preening posture.

I came up alongside the mob – mostly Gillespie fanboys and girls with superior expressions and badges in their lapels with slogans like *Thank God He Doesn't Exist* and *Born Again Atheist*. Which was ironic, for they were looking up at the doctor with all the rapt attention of true disciples. Basking in their adoration, as well as the news cameras' glare, Gillespie was in full flow.

'... the pathetic sideshow that is going to take place here on Halloween is just another example of gullibility being exploited. Darrel Everwood and his kind are like a brain cancer growing on the collective intellect. They must be burned away, cut out, destroyed utterly. Only then can we—'

'What about Genevieve Bell?' someone shrieked from outside the cordon of admirers. 'Don't you feel any sympathy for her?'

Gillespie adjusted his cuffs in that self-conscious way of his. 'I've already said that what happened to Miss Bell was a tragedy. As a humanist, I mourn the loss of any life, even one that had been wasted on the trite nonsense of spiritualism. But Everwood is a different matter.' I'd come around to the front of the platform and so could see the contemptuous curl of his lip. 'He deserves to be pilloried for the falsehoods he spreads. For playing the fool and allowing—'

'Oh, give it a rest, Joe.'

Another interruption, this time from a woman in a bright red puffer jacket. Her arms were folded across her chest and she was giving Gillespie the kind of look a parent might bestow upon a child that refuses to stop picking at a scab. She had a no-nonsense beauty about her, high cheekbones and full lips, dark eyes full of disdain. I recognised her at once from the previous evening. So Everwood's PA hadn't gone up to the house with him but had been dropped off here in order to deal with this unfolding shitshow. Despite the protests of his supporters, she barged through the mob and joined him on the platform. For once, Gillespie's facade cracked. He seemed at a loss as the enemy took command and addressed the news crews.

'On behalf of Darrel Everwood, I'd like to assure everyone at home that Dr Gillespie's *bizarre* accusations are entirely false. Darrel not only possesses a rare and powerful gift, it remains his greatest joy to share that gift with the world. Instead of frightening people with talk of a godless, uncaring universe,

Darrel has comforted thousands with the truth.' Her tone altered to just the right side of saccharine. 'You *will* see your loved ones again. They *are* still with you. And if you tune into *Ghost Seekers* this Halloween night, Darrel Everwood will prove it.'

Shouts from the Gillespie mob, a scattering of applause elsewhere. The doctor himself tried to wrest back control by addressing the cameras again, but one by one, the bright lights began to blink off.

'Quite a performance,' I said as the woman descended the platform. Shouldering the Gillespieites aside, I made a path for her. She glanced at me suspiciously as I walked with her along the forest road. 'Scott Jericho,' I said. 'Son of George. Also an old friend of Ben Halliday.'

'Ah.' Her brow cleared. 'Yes. I'm Deepal Chandra, Darrel's PA. Ben's mentioned you. He's a good man.'

'He is. So I was wondering—'

Her phone chirruped and Deepal held up a finger. 'Sorry. The boss.'

A voice, certainly Everwood's but without the mockney accent, came through the loudspeaker. 'Deepal, for Christ's sake! Has anyone seen them? Those sad-eyed bastards are turning up everywhere I go – the house, TV studios, even my bloody local. Now Ben tells me they're here, lurking around the gaff like a pair of gloomy-faced fucks, and all because I said their daughter was dead. Well, it's been six months, hasn't it, so where the fuck is she? I'll tell you this, you can bet your sweet arse it was them two weirdos that killed her, and now they're stalking me to divert suspicion. In fact, I bet they're all in it together – them and Gillespie, conspiring to make me look mad. Please, Deepal, just sort out this fucking mess!'

Deepal rolled her eyes and tucked the phone into her pocket.

'Slightly paranoid?' I suggested.

'Perhaps,' she said diplomatically.

'He's talking about the Chambers, isn't he? They were here earlier. Ben had to show them off the ground.'

She looked at me. 'So maybe *not* all that paranoid, after all? The truth is, they have been making a nuisance of themselves for a while now. I know, I know.' She held up her hand to an objection I hadn't voiced. 'They've lost their daughter. Allowances should be made. But Darrel has actually been pretty patient with them.'

'And it wouldn't look good if he took out a restraining order?' I said.

'That too,' she conceded.

Coming towards us down the road, I spotted Miss Rowell. The housekeeper of Purley gave me a sharp nod of acknowledgement before hurrying on her way with a clipped, 'Late for my bus.' She looked more than usually dishevelled tonight, tweed jacket buttoned awry, muddy splashes at the knee of her skirt. Glancing back, I caught sight of her running a finger inside that elastic band she wore around her wrist. She seemed more focused on it than where she was going and ended up almost colliding with a group coming the other way.

I wanted to question Deepal more about Everwood, but arriving at the car park, her phone rang again and she hustled off in the direction of the house. In any case, I had to report to my dad. I eventually found him fixing a loose caster on one of the Waltzer carriages. When I said I didn't think we'd have any more trouble from Gillespie tonight, he nodded and told me to go grab some food.

Queuing up at Lyla Jafford's catering truck, it struck me that I hadn't checked for any messages from Haz. Not since my run-in with Christopher Cloade. It shamed me to admit it, but the human drama of the night – all those seemingly random connections – had fed the puzzle addict within me, so that even Haz had been driven from my thoughts. Instead, I'd wondered about the paedophile preacher, with his religious antipathy to superstition that so strangely mirrored Dr Gillespie's rational convictions. And then Miss Rowell's uncharacteristically hurried flight down the road, as keen to be away from Purley and the fairground as the Chambers were to remain. The housekeeper and the grieving parents unknowingly united in their contempt for Darrel Everwood. Everwood, who may have known Genevieve Bell, a woman murdered so brutally as to be unrecognisable ...

My head snapped around, towards the side ground and the distant shape of the fortune teller's tent. In the next instant, I was running, no longer the graceful showman sidestepping punters, now shoving them out of my path. I ignored their startled cries. All I could hear was the drum of my heart and the slap of my boots in the wet earth. Closer, closer, the red-and-white canvas of the tent. The doorway flaps, sealed but unguarded. No sign of the chap my dad had sent to keep watch. It would be all right, I told myself. There was no reason to be afraid. And yet, in my mind's eye, I pictured again that little wax poppet with its caved-in skull.

The doll, like Genevieve Bell, without a face.

Chapter Thirteen

THE SIGN HOOKED ONTO ONE of the door ties, I knew from my earliest childhood. The wood, chipped and weathered, the letters repainted a hundred times: MADAM TILDA'S ON HER TEA BREAK. BE BACK SOON! Next to that faded inscription, a scatter of bright red flecks. I pulled my hand into my sleeve, unhooked the sign and laid it as carefully as I could on the ground. I was then forced to use my bare hands to pull apart each of the tightly knotted ties until the canvas doorway fell open. Already knowing what I'd find – wanting more than anything to be wrong – I stepped inside the tent.

It was an abattoir.

That was how it struck me right away. The copper tang of freshly spilled blood. Pints and pints of it, pooled in the divots of the groundsheet that covered the uneven floor. Little rivers still finding channels down which to run. A glimpse of hell, fragranced with incense and illuminated by the soft light of veiled lamps. And there, collapsed face up to the right of the circular table, the source of it all – a small, round-shouldered woman whose hair had only just been turning grey in her seventy-third year.

I say face up.

There was no face.

I had attended hundreds of murders, suicides, road traffic collisions in my career on the force. I'd seen death in all its tortuous spectrum. Still, I had to turn away for a moment, to hold down my stomach and hold back my tears. Later, I could let this nightmare haunt me. Later, I could give way to grief and fury. Now, I owed it to Tilda to take in the scene as completely as I could. To pick out whatever clues might lead me to her killer.

I slipped my hands into my pockets, that bit of crime scene preservation training coming back to me. Free hands are apt to wander and leave traces. Tucked safely away, they curled naturally into fists. Then I closed my eyes for a moment, took a breath through my mouth, and let my gaze fall first on the table. Like a mockery of Tilda's corpse, the wax doll was there, lying beside the crystal ball. It too was featureless. It too had been punctured over a dozen times. My eyes slipped back to the body for a second and to the long masonry nails that had been driven through Tilda's clothes and into her torso. A small comfort here – there appeared to be very little blood around those wounds, indicating they'd been inflicted after death.

'If you prick us, do we not bleed?' I murmured to myself.

A quotation I had heard just that morning, mangled by Darrel Everwood during his appearance on breakfast TV. Did that signify anything? I shook my head. There was something else about the phrase that niggled at me – something Tilda herself had once said. Not recently, but years ago. Again, I pictured her with my mother, sitting on their trailer steps, entertaining me with some gruesome tale.

I could worry at the memory later. Now, I had to make the most of what time I had alone here. Returning my attention to the doll, I confirmed that all the wounds inflicted on Tilda had been foretold by the effigy. All except one, perhaps. The crystal ball was lying off-centre, the damask cloth pulled askew. No reason for the killer to do such a thing. And so Tilda must have grasped at the cloth as she fell, not onto her back as she was now positioned, but forwards. The stick she always carried in her right hand lay beside her. She would have been clutching it when attacked and so, if struck face on, wouldn't have been able to snatch at the cloth at all. That meant she had used her left hand and so must have been hit from behind.

Trying to move my feet as little as possible, I dropped to my haunches and craned my neck until I could make out the wound. The edge of it was just visible – a catastrophic shattering at the back of her skull. I let out a sigh and straightened up. In this hell, I would take that small comfort – she'd been struck hard, had in all likelihood felt little pain, and had died not long after hitting the floor. I could tell that from the relative lack of smearing in the blood around her. No last death rattle, no thrashing.

My guess was a hammer. Some blunt implement that had afterwards been used on her face before it was put to work driving the nails home. But this was not the only tool the killer had brought with them. After death, Tilda's left hand had been almost severed at the wrist. Short, biting cuts by the look of the flesh, probably a hacksaw. Despite the precaution of hanging the sign outside, and most likely securing the ties as well, I wondered if the killer had grown anxious about being discovered and given up on this final piece of desecration. One thing they had made sure of, however, was to remove every tooth in Tilda's head.

This was what I had guessed must also have happened to Genevieve Bell. The quickest and simplest method of identification of a badly mutilated corpse was to check dental records. The fact the police had been forced to resort to DNA analysis, probably from comparison with the follicle roots of stray hairs found on brushes and pillows at the victim's property, meant that the murderer must have taken her teeth. In terms of trophies collected by serial killers, teeth were a classic. But was there more to it than that? Something tied into the ritualistic nature of these murders? My eyes strayed back to the doll and the biblical quotation affixed to its leg.

'Thou shalt not suffer a witch to live,' I said slowly. 'If thy hand offends thee, cut it off. An eye for an eye, a tooth for a tooth.'

But these weren't the only biblical references that might be in play.

Tilda had died instantly. The gore around her was run-off from the terrible wounds inflicted post-mortem. So why was there blood splatter across one of the tarot card enlargements hanging on the other side of the tent? Even the hammer blow that had felled her was unlikely to have caused a spray that reached the far wall. And so that red arc must have been made deliberately, the killer perhaps flicking the slick hammerhead against the card. Which meant the choice of card – The Fool – was significant because there were almost half a dozen hanging closer by.

The card depicted a leaping court jester in harlequin colours, a wand or sceptre in hand, bells dangling from his cockscomb hat.

'The foolish man built his house upon the sand,' I said, quoting the verse spoken to me not two hours ago by Christopher Cloade.

But the preacher hadn't been the only one with a fool on his lips tonight. Dr Gillespie had accused Darrel Everwood of playing the fool. Gillespie, who viewed all believers as hapless buffoons.

Except wasn't there something here that made a stranger like the preacher or the doctor seem unlikely? My attention returned to the stick lying beside the corpse. In life, Tilda had suffered almost crippling arthritis. She very rarely rose from her chair, always calling her customers inside with a croaky rasp. Yet she had been attacked from behind, which meant she must have struggled to the door and then turned to hobble back to her chair. She would only have endured this pain if she had wanted to greet her visitor personally, which ruled out someone like Gillespie or Cloade. Unless, of course, they *had* met before.

As my mum had once said about her old friend, Tilda Urnshaw was a close woman. Not even her nearest and dearest knew all her secrets. A vital attribute for a mystic.

But going back to the idea that Tilda had known her killer, there was one psychopath who, until a few months ago, had become a familiar face on the fair. A man who had often visited his disgraced protégé, and in so doing, had got to know many of the old-timers here. I pulled out my phone and video-called Peter Garris, angling the screen so that only my face would be in the shot. Suddenly my hands were shaking and I had to use both to hold the phone steady.

The bland, haggard features of my former mentor appeared on-screen. 'Scott. What a pleasant surprise. To what do I owe the—?'

'Move your camera around, let me see the room.'

The dead eyes narrowed. 'Certainly.'

I was given a sweeping panorama of his clinical kitchen with its gleaming pans and glistening knives. The picture then returned to Garris. He didn't beat around the bush.

'What's happened . . . ? Scott, you clearly wish to know my whereabouts and so obviously someone you care about has been hurt. I promise you, I haven't moved from the house all day. I trust it isn't your father? Or Harry?' When I didn't answer, the murderer sighed and began to move through the hallway and into his soulless lounge. 'This is preposterous. You must take a breath, think clearly and dispassionately. You know that I can help you, if you only ask—'

I ended the call.

Garris wasn't involved. That certainty was all I needed. Only, if that was true, then why hadn't I called Garry Treadaway, the private detective, to verify his location?

I pushed the thought away and returned my attention to the scene. A killer with his rituals, seemingly obsessed with the most extreme biblical commandments. Or perhaps hiding his true loathing for religion and the supernatural by making it appear that he embraced them. A murderer who foretold the fate of his victims by sending them wax dolls. I wondered if Genevieve Bell had also received one? That these two deaths were linked seemed more than probable – a fortune teller and a psychic, both brutally murdered within days of each other, both mutilated, both with their teeth taken as trophies.

I looked down at my phone. It was almost time. Just one more thing to check. Glancing back through the doorway at the ground immediately outside the tent, I saw two sets of lateral marks in the damp earth, evenly spaced. The impression of kneecaps and toes as the killer had knelt to secure the bottom ties. At first, it made me think what a risk he had taken, for at least some of his clothing must have been heavily stained. And then I saw the costumes passing by – those ghouls and monsters, all chattering and laughing together. Among them, a figure drenched in blood would hardly be noticed.

Except perhaps that whatever costume they had been wearing might not have covered them completely. A patched and mended Harris Tweed jacket unmarked, except for the hem of the skirt? I thought again of Miss Rowell hurrying down the forest road, late for her bus, those muddy splashes at her knees.

I shook my head. Cloade, Gillespie, Rowell. Was there anyone I hadn't pictured standing here, the hammer in their fist? Yes, one person came to mind, though the thought made me sick to my stomach. Because it was hateful and ridiculous and impossible. But again I returned to that mysterious spill of white wax on his sleeve and the pencil stub in his bag.

Harry in the veiled lamplight, fulfilling the promise of the wax doll.

I dialled and pressed the phone to my ear. 'Yes, police. I need to report a murder.'

Chapter Fourteen

THE FAIR WAS STILL BUZZING with light and activity, though now the rides had been silenced and the costumes were different. There is something odd and jarring about a fairground abruptly stilled. Excitement suddenly terminated leaves an eerie, brittle atmosphere behind it. These places are built for crowds that teeter on the uncontrollable, for whoops of joy, for breathless chatter, the push and pull and surge of bodies. Not for this dour, regulated procession of officialdom.

It had been two and a half hours since my discovery of Aunt Tilda and I was sitting in one of the tents the police had erected around the crime scene. I had to admit, the whole operation had swung into action with polished efficiency. Minutes after the first constables arrived, a perimeter had been established, and within the hour, the punters who were still onsite had all been processed and released, their names and addresses taken for follow-up interviews. I had remained, guarding Tilda until a sergeant and the divisional surgeon poked their heads into the tent and asked me, very gently, to step outside. Then it was the usual forensic rigmarole of swabs and fingernail scrapings before the sergeant returned to take my statement.

'Just hang on for a minute or two, will you, sir?' he had said as we finished up. 'The chief inspector will want a word.'

'Looks like you've got a pretty decent guvnor.' I nodded. 'Everything actioned very swiftly for an out-of-the-blue murder. Unless, of course, you'd expected something like this to happen.'

'Now why would you think that?' the sergeant asked, rising to his feet and looming over me. He was a big man and a free-perspirer, the armpits of his shirt damp and sagging. I considered asking him to take a step back but thought better of it.

'No operation gets out the gate this fast, no matter how violent the killing,' I said. 'But, of course, I'm happy to hang on for your DCI.'

He looked as if he was about to bite back but instead tapped his pencil thoughtfully against his chin and left the tent. And so I stayed put, waiting for the officer in charge. Before it was confiscated by a random constable passing through, I still had use of my phone. The one oversight in an otherwise immaculate investigation: in a case like this, all witness phones ought to be immediately seized to create a digital copy before being returned. Following the gavvers' arrival, there had been a flurry of texts from Sal, Big Sam, and my dad, asking if I knew what was going on. Of these, I didn't think it was wise to respond to any except the old man's.

In a few words, I explained what had happened, and after a short delay, he replied, calmly and cautiously, knowing that the police might soon have access to my phone. Outrage and promises of vengeance would not do us any favours right now. He told me that the chap that had been guarding Tilda had left his post to use the toilet at about eight fifteen. On returning, he'd seen Tilda's sign and assumed she'd gone off for her tea break. Fancying a bit of refreshment himself, he'd retired to his own trailer and fallen asleep while watching a match on the box. I for one prayed he'd have the wisdom to pack up his things and leave the fair that night. His safety among the Travellers could not now be guaranteed.

But this also made me think about how the killer must have watched and waited for their moment. Perhaps they'd even visited Jericho Fairs before and learned of Tilda's routine with her sign. That showed foresight and planning, or else they knew the fortune teller and her habits of old. In any case, it had been a brutally efficient execution. The timing meant a window of approximately forty-five minutes between the chap's departure and me finding the body at around nine.

Just before my phone was taken, I had thought of calling Haz. Despite their last encounter when she had upset him by seeming to speak about his dead father, he'd always had a soft spot for Aunt Tils. Hell, Harry had a soft spot for just about everyone. My thumb had hovered over his contact but something held me back. Perhaps the shame of my imagining his involvement, perhaps the fear that he would hear that doubt in my voice.

The minutes crawled by, and I was about to go and ask what was keeping him when the DCI stepped into the tent. He was probably only a year or two older than me, which meant he was smarter than he looked. No one reached the rank of chief inspector by their mid-thirties without having both brains and a knack for office politics. He came forward with a broad, apologetic smile and grasped my hand in both of his. It seemed at once an act of submission and assertion, his handshake overly firm but his expression contrite.

'Inspector Tallis. I'm *so* sorry I've kept you waiting.' Falling into the folding seat opposite, he took out his notebook and flicked through the pages before looking up. 'Mr Jericho.'

He hadn't needed to consult his notes. He knew my name. I wondered if it was all part of the same performance that extended to that bit of bumfluff on his upper lip. An almost adolescent attempt to grow a moustache. He was youthful looking anyway, tousle-headed, wide-eyed, all teeth, a man who'd look more at home in a school blazer than that almost creaseless suit. A man easy to underestimate, which was surely his intent.

'I'd like to start by saying how sorry I am for your loss. Miss Urnshaw was your aunt, I understand?'

'Aunt in the Traveller sense,' I answered. 'Not a blood relative, but all the old-timers here are known as aunts and uncles.'

He made a note. 'Good to know. Well, Mr Jericho, I see from my sergeant's notes that you've made some interesting observations about the crime scene. Didn't touch anything, didn't try to see if your aunt was still alive. Just stood there and took it all in, didn't you?'

There wasn't anything accusatory in his tone. There wasn't much of a tone at all.

'She'd been hit on the back of the head,' I said evenly. 'Her face had been smashed in, all her teeth removed, and her left hand almost severed. I thought it was safe to assume she was dead.'

He smoothed down the open page and didn't take his eyes from me. Despite the questioning, I think I made up my mind right then that I liked DCI Tallis.

'Still, not the usual reaction of a civilian,' he said. 'I mean you didn't disturb the body but nor did you run for help. You stayed at the scene until we arrived and then provided a catalogue of insights – victim attacked from behind, perhaps indicating he was known to her; some kind of point being made by the splattering of blood on the tarot card; indentations on the ground outside where he knelt to fasten the ties.'

'I never said "him",' I corrected. 'A reasonably fit woman would've been capable of any of this.'

'Another good point. And I understand you didn't report the doll to the police when it first appeared. May I ask why not?'

I shrugged. 'I knew you wouldn't do anything about it.'

'Did you? But still, you were troubled?'

I looked down at my hands. Willed them not to tremble as I remembered discouraging my dad from reporting the doll.

'It seemed ... malicious in a studied way, if you know what I mean?' I said. 'No fingerprints, and then the pins, the Bible quotation, the hexafoil. All of it thought out. Maybe even overdone.'

'What do you mean by that?'

'I'm not entirely sure. Yet.'

'But you were worried that there might be something more to come?'

I shuffled in my seat. 'The doll is like the murder itself. Overkill, if you like. Almost too many little touches. The teeth, presumably taken as trophies as there's no doubt about the identity of the victim. But still, it's unusual for a killer even with a dental fetish to take *all* the teeth. And then there's the fact that, although it was very elaborate – the planning of it, sending the doll, waiting for the right time to strike, performing each mutilation – there's also a sense of half-heartedness. A rush to complete everything. The fact the hands weren't taken.'

Tallis scratched his eyebrow. 'It was a public place. Maybe he was fearful of discovery.'

'Maybe. But these kinds of ritualistic killers are usually obsessive about their signatures. They take their time, take risks, even if it endangers them.'

'So what does that tell you?'

'It tells me I don't know the full story.'

The inspector cleared his throat. 'You see, Mr Jericho, all this – your sense of calm, your knowledge, observations, it's suggestive.'

'Is it?'

'Unusual name, Jericho,' he mused. 'Reminds me of a case I heard about a couple of years ago. Smart young detective. Brilliant, in fact. Rising star in CID, incredible record for closing cases successfully. Just my sort of officer. But he throws away his career after losing his temper with the prime suspect in a murder case. A hate crime in which three young kids were killed. The case collapses and our golden boy is sent straight to jail. Do not pass go, do not collect your pension. You used to be a copper, Mr Jericho.'

I nodded. There was no point denying it.

'Do you miss the job?' Tallis asked.

'Some of it,' I admitted with a shrug. 'I was never the most popular face in the department, but I enjoyed the work.' *Oh yes*, I thought to myself. *Enjoyed it too much perhaps.*

'Not a team player.' Tallis nodded. 'I'd heard that too. We don't get many from your community joining up. It's a shame, what happened. I was raised in a small seaside town myself.

My father owned an amusement arcade where I'd work for a few quid after school and at the weekends. Perhaps not a totally dissimilar upbringing?'

Much as I liked Tallis, this felt like a waste of time. 'You don't have to establish a rapport with me, Inspector. Shall we get on with it?'

He paid me the respect of closing his notebook. 'What else would you like to tell me?'

'You were on alert for another of these, weren't you?' I said. 'So *you* tell me, did Genevieve Bell also receive a wax doll before she was killed? Were her hands taken? Was her body punctured with nails?'

He scratched his eyebrow again. 'The details of that case haven't been made public.'

'I know. You run a tight ship.'

'Then how did you connect the two?'

'It was hinted at in the press. The way you had to ID her – from stray hair follicles found on personal items at the house would be my guess. So her teeth and hands must have been taken, just like with Tilda. The crucial question is, were there others before Genevieve Bell?' Again the scratched brow – Tallis's unconscious tell. 'Then Tilda was his second. Less than a week separating the two deaths. You have a serial killer targeting fortune tellers and psychics, Inspector, and unless we stop him, he will kill again.'

'Unless *I* stop him.'

Tallis rose to his feet. He was almost a head shorter than me and yet he held his ground with assurance.

'You're out of jail, Mr Jericho, but you're still not part of the game. I appreciate that the murder of your aunt will feel very personal and you'll want to see whoever's responsible punished. Believe me when I say, I won't rest until that happens. But I also want you to know this ...'

I'd followed him to the exit when he turned and laid a hand on my shoulder. Once more, I felt the tenderness from where Ben had struck me.

'If I discover that you've tried to rejoin the game, I'll sweep you right off the board,' he promised. 'And back behind bars.'

Chapter Fifteen

I MANAGED TO CONTROL MYSELF. DESPITE the vision of what I'd suffered behind the walls of HMP Hazelhurst rising up before me – the shower block with its bloodied tiles, the memory of that fire deep inside my gut as I lay shaking and weeping on the floor – I remained calm. Tallis couldn't know of the assault I'd suffered while serving my sentence. Though he'd asked, I hadn't even discussed it with Haz. Still, it was a lousy threat and I wondered if the inspector immediately regretted it. Stepping into the night together, his attitude appeared to soften.

'We'll try to get all this cleared away by the morning,' he said, gesturing towards a huddle of Tyvek-suited SOCOs. 'As long as your security remains tight, I'm happy if you want to open again tomorrow. I could spare you a few constables as well, just to keep up a presence.'

We spent a moment contemplating Tilda's tent before I noticed his gaze stray beyond the fair to the bleak silhouette of the rectory.

'Do you know the reputation of this place?' I asked. 'Those who seek to exploit it are often punished, apparently. Accidents, suicide, murder.'

He cast me a sceptical look. 'I don't believe in curses. I'm sure you don't either.'

'What *we* believe is irrelevant, Inspector Tallis. It's what the killer believes that's important. Speaking of which, have you considered *him* as a potential victim?'

I pointed over to the darkened billboard where Darrel Everwood's neon-white smile could still just about be made out. Tallis gave a non-committal shrug.

'You don't need a licence to practise spiritualism, and so there's no register of numbers,' he said. 'But there must be thousands of clairvoyants and palmists and whatever else they call themselves operating in the UK. I assume you don't know of any direct link between your aunt and Genevieve Bell?' I shook my head. 'Or of anything to connect Darrel Everwood to the case?'

I thought back to that phone conversation I'd overheard between Ben and Deepal Chandra. *The funny thing is, I reckon Darrel knew her too. He mentioned her name to me anyway.* And then Ben's assertion that Everwood was afraid to come to Purley: *He told me that there's something bad waiting for him here.* Had it been just a feeling or had Everwood also received a little wax doll? And if so, might he have spoken to Genevieve Bell about it? I told myself that it was a tenuous link at best. In any case, informing Tallis would lead to Ben being questioned, and almost inevitably, his past being exposed. He had, no doubt, faked his references to get the job with EverThorn Media. He was trying to go straight, to build a new life, and escape the clutches of mobsters like Mark Noonan. There may even be outstanding cases in which he was a suspect.

This was the noble side of my reason for keeping Ben's secret. In truth, I also wanted a go at questioning Everwood before Tallis got to him. Despite the inspector's threat, I was determined to play this game, and on my own terms.

'No connection I'm aware of,' I said.

Tallis fixed me with that steady gaze before digging into his pocket and pulling out my phone. 'Glad to have met you, Mr Jericho,' he said, handing it over. 'And for what it's worth, I'm sorry things worked out the way they did. The force really can't afford to lose good detectives.'

'I'm glad they still have a few.' I nodded, before turning away and heading into the shadows between the stalls.

Coming out into the corral of trailers, I checked my watch. It was long past eleven but there were lights in every window. Behind those glowing shades, toasts were being raised to a woman that even her elders had called 'auntie'. There would be tears and laughter as the tragedies and comedies of her life were shared, dates picked over and debated, her wisdom dispensed to red-eyed children so that fragments of her might live on. And in whispered asides between the men, the plotting of the killer's fate would have begun. If little else, this instinct for private justice was something I shared with my people.

A chained Webster greeted me at the foot of my father's trailer. Reaching down, I scratched behind a tattered ear. Juks are empathetic creatures and this one more than most. Something was happening that he couldn't solve with a growl or a snap, so instead, he licked the bowl of my palm and whimpered as I mounted the steps.

I opened the door. A welcome waft of warm air, tea and whisky on the kitchen counter, some joyous old photograph of my mother and Tilda at a wedding, freshly dug out and placed in a black frame over the fire. I barely had time to register the three people in the room before Big Sam came rushing towards me. I'd prepared myself for their accusations – why hadn't I seen this coming? Why hadn't I protected her? Why didn't I take that fucking doll more seriously? Wasn't I supposed to be some kind of clever bastard? I didn't try to defend myself. I just stood there, ready for his denunciation, welcoming his blows.

Instead, he wrapped those enormous arms around me and tucked my head into his shoulder, as if I were a child.

'Jesus, Scotty,' he croaked. 'What you've seen tonight, I can't even imagine. Come and have a drink, sit yourself down. It's gonna be all right.'

I allowed myself to be led to the big locker settee where Sal took my face in her hands and kissed my forehead. 'You OK?' she asked.

I shrugged and she kissed me again. Meanwhile, Sam took the armchair next to my dad. Grey-faced with grief and exhaustion, the old man leaned forward and shook my knee.

'So what was done to her, then?' Sam demanded half-heartedly.

'Sam, please.' I sighed. 'You don't want to know.'

'I do,' he insisted, staring up at the ceiling and wiping his eyes. 'I need to.'

Sal went over to him and took the great callused slab of his hand in hers. 'Now you listen to him, Sam Urnshaw, and just you remember Tilda as she was. A mad old woman loved by everyone. Am I right, Uncle George?'

My dad nodded, his voice unusually tight. 'The very best of old girls. She'll be remembered in our stories, always.'

As one, we seemed to turn to the photograph hanging over the fire. Two dead women, both the victims of violence, perhaps reunited now, in the minds of some at least.

'You've talked to the gavvers?' Dad said. 'What are they thinking?'

I explained that, in all likelihood, Tilda had been the second victim of a killer obsessed with ridding the world of what he considered to be 'witches'. I also told them she had probably been selected at random. Even then, I didn't believe that, but it gave the others the comfort that we couldn't have foreseen what would happen.

'You think that preacher had anything to do with it?' Dad asked. 'The one I mentioned hanging around with his pamphlets?'

'It's possible,' I said. 'He was at the fair tonight.'

Big Sam started to pull himself upright. 'If he knows anything, I'll go beat it out of him.'

'You'll stay put,' Dad said, and after a short battle of wills, his old friend sank dutifully back into the chair. 'That fucking chap. If only he'd stayed put too.'

I pinched the bridge of my nose. 'The murderer would have found their opportunity at some point. The chap isn't to blame. Look, there are people I need to see, questions I need to ask. I'm sorry, but—'

'Go,' Sam muttered. 'You find the bastard who did this. You find him, Scott, and then we'll do what needs doing.'

My dad didn't say anything but watched carefully as Sal followed me to the door. At the bottom of the steps, we found Webster fast asleep, his body draped protectively across his master's threshold. I moved to step over the juk and Sal caught my hand.

'You gonna be all right?'

'I am,' I assured her. 'This is what I'm best at. What have you told Jodie, by the way?'

She squeezed her eyes tight shut. 'Nothing yet. Thought I'd let her get a proper night's sleep and tell her in the morning. Say Aunt Tils had an accident or something, I don't know. I just hope the older chavvies don't let on ... That dear old woman, Scott. Remember how she'd peel us apples and sing us songs when we was little kids?'

'I do,' I said, rubbing her arm.

She gave me one of her searching looks, the kind that had wheedled out my secrets ever since childhood. 'Once you've got hold of this bastard, you hand him over to the gavvers. Do you understand? Whatever Sam and the others might say, I don't want you to find him if it means losing yourself along the way.'

I left her without the reassurance she needed, and buttoning my trench coat against the night air, set off towards the rectory. I'd barely walked a few steps when my phone pinged with a message:

Sal phoned me an hour ago. Scott, I've been trying to call. I'm so, so sorry. How has this happened? I wanted to come back onto the fair to see you, but the police at the gate won't let me through. If you don't feel like calling, please just message me. I love you, Haz.

I couldn't help being struck by the irony. Ever since he'd left last night, I'd been praying that he'd reach out and make contact.

Now I turned off my phone and started again towards the house. For his own sake, I needed Haz to stay far, far away from me. Until this killer was caught, I wouldn't be the man he knew.

Chapter Sixteen

'WHAT THE FUCK IS GOING on here, Deepal? I've barely been in the place five minutes and it's like all hell's broken loose. First, the bloody Bentley hits a nail or something on the road, then that Chambers bastard and his sad-sack wife show up, next we've got Gillespie badmouthing me to the local news, and now it's like *CS-fucking-I* out there. The only bright side is they've shut down that fucking fair for the night. But do either of you have a clue what's happening? No! So what am I paying you for?'

I could hear every word of Everwood's rant from outside his trailer. However, I had to step virtually up to the window to hear Deepal's response.

'I'm sorry it's taken me a while to get any intel on this, Darrel—'

'A while? It's been *hours*. What have you been doing, eh? Looking up cheap nose jobs on the internet again?'

'Boss, take it easy.' Ben's voice, smooth, placating.

'Eeeezayyy, Benjamin? Is that 'ow ah should take et?' Darrel said, mocking those broad Yorkshire inflections. 'Why don't thee fook off down't pit and let Deepal speak for her'sen?'

'It's all right, Ben,' Deepal said. 'I do have an answer, though it cost me a bit to get it. I had to bribe one of the officers for the full story.'

'Cost *you* a bit?' Everwood practically cackled. 'I doubt it'll be coming out your wages, sweetheart. Well, as I've paid for it, I better hear it.'

I wondered then if even the most loyal fan of this so-called medium might not have asked, *But, Darrel, surely you know already. Haven't the spirits told you yet?*

'There appears to have been a murder,' Deepal said. 'An elderly woman was attacked on the fairground. The constable I bribed hadn't seen the body himself, but he told me there were rumours that the corpse had been very badly mutilated. Some kind of maniac, they're thinking.'

'Who was it?' Darrel asked. 'The victim?'

All the snark and bile had gone out of his voice. He suddenly sounded very frightened.

'They didn't give me a name. I believe she was a fortune teller.'

A long pause. I thought I could hear the creak of footsteps, the chink of glass, running water. Then Everwood again, screaming, 'Out! Get out! Leave me alone!'

The door burst open and Deepal and Ben came hurrying down the steps. Before it swung back on its hinges, I caught a glimpse of the celebrity psychic. Gone was the brash swagger of the breakfast studio sofa. Darrel looked again like a little boy lost, hunched over in his chair, a glass tumbler cradled in his shaking hands. A sheen of sweat glistened across his brow and his mascara had run, painting uneven bars along his face.

Seeing me, both Ben and Deepal came to a halt. Despite the midnight chill, Ben was again dressed in a thin white T-shirt that strained to accommodate his bulk. Though just a sliver of moon illuminated the clearing, his pupils remained fixed and tiny. I wondered when he'd last taken a dose of those prescription pain meds. Meanwhile, Deepal appeared to be taking her frustration out on her hair, yanking it back and twisting it into a severe bun.

'Scott.' 'Mr Jericho.' They said almost in unison.

'What are you doing here?' Ben asked.

I didn't answer but motioned them away from the trailer and towards the iron railing that ran around the desolate rectory garden. I thought the best tactic was to be direct. I had no official capacity to ask them questions, but perhaps I might shock an answer or two out of them.

'I heard you talking about the old woman murdered tonight,' I said to Deepal. 'That was my aunt. I found her body myself and had to wait with it until the police arrived. The constable you mentioned was right, by the way. By the time he was finished, the killer had made her pretty much unrecognisable.'

Deepal covered her mouth with her hand while Ben came forward. 'Scott.' He touched the side of my face. 'Oh my God, I'm so sorry. Do you know what happened?'

'That's why I'm here,' I said. 'Your boss seemed quite upset when you told him the news.'

Deepal blinked. For a few seconds there, she had looked very far away. 'Oh, that? I wouldn't take much notice. Epic emotional swings are an hourly event. Half-hourly on a bad day.' I noticed her attention stray to the bulge of the phone in her trouser pocket. 'I suppose he might be worried about how this could affect the show.'

'Nothing to do with his reluctance to come here in the first place, then?' I said. Ben retreated a step and shot a glance at the PA. 'You told me he thought there was something bad waiting for him in Purley. That he might die here. What was that fear based on?'

'It was just one of his feelings,' Deepal said. 'You've seen what he's like. A total drama queen. He has these meltdowns before every major event, like a kind of extreme stage fright. You have to understand, Darrel built his entire career from nothing. He's come a long way since that council estate in Peckham, achieved incredible things, but that's also engendered a deep anxiety that it could all be taken away from him. And now, what with the bad press he's been getting from his ex and the added pressure from the Chambers and Dr Gillespie, that anxiety has kicked into overdrive. He knows this event has to work to get him back on track. At the same time, the burden of that knowledge means he'd do almost anything to get out of it ...' She stopped herself mid-flow.

'Anything?'

'I didn't mean that.' She flushed. 'Don't be ridiculous. He's a complete egomaniac but not even we think he'd go that far.'

'That's right,' Ben put in. 'Anyway, after we got here tonight, I stayed with Darrel in the trailer, going through security plans for the broadcast. Then I read my book while he played a game on his phone. That was until the police showed up and everything started kicking off outside.'

'You didn't leave him at all?' I asked.

'Well.' He scratched the nape of his neck. 'Only for about half an hour or so. He started getting antsy again around eight o'clock and asked me to do a scout of the forest and the fair. Said he'd lock himself inside while I was gone. I told him I'd seen Mr and Mrs Chambers off the site earlier and that Deepal had dealt with Dr Gillespie, but he insisted.'

Deepal jumped in. 'I got a call from a journalist saying they wanted to get Darrel's response to Gillespie's stunt. I went back down to the main road to keep a lookout because the reporter said he couldn't find the forest entrance. I saw Gillespie there, getting into his car and driving off just as I arrived.'

'What time was that?'

'I can tell you exactly. Eight twenty.'

'How can you be so sure?'

'I have an alert on my phone every twenty minutes to remind me to check Darrel's social media platforms. His trolls need a lot of policing. Anyway, the alarm went off right at the time I saw Gillespie leave.'

'What about the journalist?' I asked.

'No sign of him.' She caught my look. 'Nothing suspicious there. He's an old contact, but still, journos are a faithless lot. My guess is that he got a lead on a better story and couldn't be bothered to drop me a text.'

'So you returned to Darrel at about half past eight?' I said to Ben. 'And he was still playing on his phone?'

'No,' he answered carefully. 'Sorry, I forgot. When we first arrived here tonight, I found the trailer's septic toilet had backed up and couldn't be used. Darrel was fuming, of course. Anyway, when I came back from scouting out the site, Darrel wasn't there. He'd nipped into the woods for a pee and came in a couple of minutes after me.'

'How'd he seem?'

Ben shrugged. 'A bit jumpy, maybe. He hadn't wanted to go out by himself, but I suppose he couldn't hold it any longer.'

'And you didn't see anything suspicious while patrolling the site?'

'I didn't ... Wait.' Ben clicked his fingers. 'I *did* see the Chambers again. Or thought I did. I was a bit of a way off, so I can't be sure, but it was a couple – the man was small and wiry and the woman was wearing a green coat. And, Jesus, yes! They were actually coming out of the fortune teller's tent. Your aunt's tent?' I nodded. 'OK, but this was early on. Just a few minutes after eight. Do you know when she was killed?'

'Between eight fifteen and nine.'

'Then even if it was them—'

'They might have come back,' I said.

'But why on earth would a grieving couple kill your aunt?' Deepal asked.

'When it's more likely they might want to kill your employer? Speaking of which, I overheard you and Ben on the phone tonight. You spoke about another recent murder – Genevieve Bell. Ben, you said you thought Darrel might have known her.'

'He'd mentioned her name, I think,' Ben said.

'And what about my aunt's name? Tilda Urnshaw?'

'Doesn't ring a bell.'

'Are you suggesting that Darrel could also be a target of this maniac?' Deepal asked. I could almost hear the excitement in her voice as she pulled out her phone. 'If you'll excuse me, I need to touch base with Darrel's manager. I hate to say it, but if we get in front of this story then it might not be a total disaster. Brave medium forges ahead with show despite death threat. Yes, that could actually work ...' She caught my eye. 'I'm sorry, Mr Jericho. This job isn't the best environment for maintaining one's humanity.'

Nonetheless, she turned on her heel and marched away, the phone clamped to her ear.

Ben approached again, and brushing a tangled curl from my brow, he asked, 'How are you doing, Scott?'

'How are *you* doing, Ben?' I shot back. 'On the meds again? Look, I've been where you are now, very recently in fact. It's taken me almost three months to get my shit together and even now, if someone offered me a handful of sleeping pills and benzos, I'm not sure I could resist. They screwed with my mind for a while, made me see things that weren't there. Sometimes I'd even zone out for a couple of hours and have no idea how much time I'd lost.'

'What are you saying?'

'I'm saying, are you sure you saw what you thought you saw tonight? The Chambers coming out of my aunt's tent? And are you certain about your timings with Darrel? You see, fifteen minutes or so would be a pretty tight window to make him a viable suspect, but forty minutes or even fifty? I'm asking how sure you can be.'

'Scott,' he said. 'You made me a promise.'

'And I won't say a word – not about the meds, not about Mark Noonan. But I must speak to Everwood. This was my aunt, Ben. My family. You understand?'

He nodded. 'I'll see what I can do. But not tonight. He's just swallowed half a pharmacy, so whatever he says won't make much sense anyway.'

'Thank you.'

I started to move away when he spoke again. 'I heard from one of the guys on the fair that you have a boyfriend. I didn't know that when I made a move on you the other night. I'm sorry, Scott. I hope you didn't take it the wrong way.'

I didn't answer. Just buried the face of Harry Moorhouse deep at the back of my mind and moved on alone, into the darkness.

Chapter Seventeen

It was still dark when I drove away from the forest and the fair. Hitting the main road out of town, I glimpsed the spire of Aumbry's great fenland cathedral poking above those remnants of ancient woodland that had once blanketed much of this country. This was the church Harry visited twice a week for choir practice, though I'd never been invited to accompany him. I wondered again who he might have met there in my absence. Then, gripping the steering wheel tight, I refocused my attention on the road.

It was a fifty-minute drive to the killer's house. All the way, I told myself that this was simply a spot check, nothing more. A flimsy lie that could not hold. The private detectives I employed would be on guard, parked up in the shadows of that dull suburban street, keeping watch from one of their inconspicuous vehicles. There was no need for me to be here; I had other more important business to attend to. The truth was, I could not quite face the real reason I was paying my former mentor an early morning house call. The desire to speak with him, to consult that cold, logical mind, to seek his guidance about the murderer I now hunted was simply too strong.

*

In the end, the only corpse I found in Peter Garris's house was a skeletal rat decomposing in the attic, its papery bones buried under piles of old clothes. Looking down at the tiny body, I allowed myself a wry smile. I was pretty sure this rodent had died of natural causes. Turning off my phone light, I started back through the open hatchway. The foldaway steps creaked under my weight as I descended to the landing below. Having grown up in a Traveller's trailer, I'd never developed that traditional childhood dread of attics. Instead, my nightmares had concentrated on the shadowy space beneath our home – a cramped, oily gap into which hideous monsters might crawl and lie, breathlessly listening to my heartbeat above.

I hadn't known then that all monsters possess a human face. One of the blandest now stared up at me from the back garden. I remained at the landing window for a moment, returning his gaze. Impassive as ever, Peter Garris, retired detective chief inspector and dormant serial killer, raised his hand and waved. He was dressed in gardening gear, cut-off wellington boots, mud-stained corduroys, a checked shirt, and a ridiculous straw hat to keep the morning sun out of his eyes. No sign of the paisley tie his late wife had insisted he wear every day to work.

That fashion atrocity, as well as the fiction of Harriet Garris herself, had all been part of his act. A carefully calibrated performance to divert attention from the empty shell that, like those monsters under our trailer, lay patiently concealed. The house in which I stood was yet another layer of that performance. From the outside, it appeared to be the residence of any other middle-class, middle-aged widower. A neat two-up, two-down in an unremarkable suburban street, its patch of front lawn dutifully mowed, its curtains drawn at 8.30 every morning, just the hanging baskets outside the door in need of a little watering. But such oversights were to be expected. Poor Mr Garris was, after all, still in the first stages of grief.

Except he wasn't. Like love and regret and compassion, grief was unknown to him. And anyway, his late wife had never existed. I wondered if Garris's neighbours, delivering their sympathy cards and hearty casseroles, might have recoiled a little had they ever stepped over this threshold. Not because there was anything obviously disturbing here. Garris didn't display trophies from his victims on the mantelpiece or make lampshades out of their hides. No, it was the emptiness that would have unnerved them. Not a single family photograph adorned these walls, not one cherished keepsake to relieve the clinical tidiness. It was a home as vacant as the killer who occupied it.

I turned away from the window.

Heading downstairs, I wondered not for the first time, could there be a storage unit somewhere? A garage lock-up perhaps, anonymous and paid for by the year? And does he visit this place, like an old man recalling the glory days of his youth, running hands nostalgically over humming freezers and specimen jars cloudy with formaldehyde? That last night in Bradbury End, he'd confessed to taking tokens from the victims of his early kills, all the while promising that those dark appetites had left him for good.

If such a place existed, and I could find it, then all this futile watching might be over. I could lay proof before the police that even DCI Garris's reputation could not withstand. Because without corroborative evidence it was impossible to move against him. The twisted murders he'd committed four months ago, all in an effort to save me from my own self-destruction, could not be traced back to him. He'd slaughtered five people without leaving behind a scrap of DNA. But those early kills, before he'd joined the force and had no knowledge of forensic procedure, if there were traces of those and I could get at them?

I stepped off the last stair. There was, of course, a more immediate solution to all this. I could make an anonymous call, suggesting the police take a look in the eastern corner of Garris's back garden. Moving through his immaculate kitchen, with its sparkling pans and glinting knives hanging from their hooks, I stopped at the patio door. He was standing there, right beside the burial plot. If the police dug beneath those fast-growing marigolds, they would find the shattered corpse of his final Bradbury End victim. But in discovering Lenny Kerrigan they would also unearth other secrets. Ones that could endanger the person I loved most in this world.

I gripped the handle of the sliding door and stepped outside.

Garris straightened up from where he'd been pruning the marigolds. His gaze, lifeless as it seemed to me now, flicked across my face.

'So, are you satisfied that I've been behaving myself, Detective?' When I didn't answer, he bent again, and plucking a faded petal, popped it into his mouth. '*Calendula officinalis*. Give 'em a patch of blue sky and a drop of sunlight, these beauties will flower whatever the month. Perfectly edible too.' He nudged his boot against a clump of dirt. 'Of course, the right kind of nourishment in the soil helps tremendously.'

I looked down at the marmalade hue of the flowers. The fascist murderer Lenny Kerrigan had died horribly at Garris's hands, limbs snapped and twisted into strange new formations, yet some remorseless part of me still resented the beauty of his grave.

'Come now, Scott,' Garris said. 'Petulance doesn't suit you. If I'm going to continue to permit these unannounced spot checks, the least you can do is to be civil.'

Clasped in the pockets of my trench coat, my fists twitched. 'You'll permit them,' I said. 'Whether I'm civil or not.'

He chuckled. In the old days, before I'd discovered his true nature, Garris had rarely laughed. 'Very well. But do tell me, how is everyone at the fair? I must admit, I miss my visits, nattering away to your father and all the old showpeople. Perhaps one day I might—'

'If you ever set foot on any of our grounds, I'll bury you neck-deep in that flowerbed,' I said. 'And let the fiercest of our juks have at your face.'

'But not my pal Webster, eh?' he replied evenly. 'How is that good boy?' He smiled a self-satisfied smile. 'Oh, shall we just cut to the chase, Scott? That call last night, checking on my whereabouts? Something has happened, hasn't it? Something bad. So tell me, how can I help?' He spread his hands, then sighed. 'Come on now, you're here for a reason. Remember those chats of ours in The Three Crowns when we'd share all our insights into a case? You can trust me, Scott.'

I almost laughed. 'Trust you? When you used what I told you about Harry and his father's death against me?'

He blinked. 'Not against you. To help you. I can't understand why you still refuse to see that.'

'Of course you can't. Because you're a monster. You killed five people because you thought it would save me. And do you want to know the worst part? It *did* save me.' I turned my face to the sky, to the pale wash of dawn. 'And now I have to live with those deaths on my conscience. I know you'll never wrap your head around what that means, but you should know that barely a night goes by when I don't wake up screaming. That's the life you've given me.'

He nodded, wiping his palms down the front of his shirt. 'That sounds unpleasant. But even the worst nightmares fade in time. And really, what was the alternative? I remember one of those boozy midnight chats, after all of our cases had been put to bed and we'd moved on to more philosophical subjects. We agreed, did we not, that this is it?' Creaking to his haunches he picked up a morsel of dirt and crumbled it between his fingers. 'Earth to earth, dust to dust, and not a hope of heaven. Like me, you've witnessed people die. Watched as the light goes out of their eyes. Have you ever detected even a hint of something beyond?' He chuckled again and dusted off his palms. 'If I hadn't set you that puzzle back in Bradbury then all you'd be right now is a name on a gravestone.'

At his words, I felt a bright stab of fury. It would be so easy to end this man and the threat he posed. My forearm around his throat, hard as granite as I dragged him into the house. Garris's was a sheltered back garden, the neighbours' windows discreetly angled so that no one could possibly have seen him burying Lenny Kerrigan's broken body. No one to see now if I hauled the killer back through the patio door. No one to hear his muffled cry before I cut off his airway. I had never killed before, but during my thug-for-hire years, between leaving uni and joining the force, I had come close. More than once, if truth be told. I knew I had it in me. Garris knew it too.

'But you won't,' he said as if reading my mind. 'Because that really would be the end of you. And anyway, I still have that recording I took of you in The Three Crowns, as well as a few other bits and pieces that would inevitably lead to Harry Moorhouse's arrest on the charge of murdering his father. I know, I know,' he said, waving aside an objection I hadn't raised. 'The poor man was desperately ill, in agony, it was a mercy killing. But you know as well as I, that if it went to trial, there'd be no guarantee of clemency. Well then, if anything untoward should happen to me, I've arranged for the proof of his guilt to be released.'

Fury scratched behind my eyes. I did my best to tamp it down.

'Honestly though, Scott, all this conflict is unnecessary,' Garris went on. 'If you won't take my word that I have no desire to kill again, then I'm perfectly happy for you to continue monitoring my activities. In fact, I welcome these little catch-ups. I was never much of a people person, as you know, but that mind of yours? It still fascinates me. So do tell, what happened last night? I promise I can help.'

Leaning in, he rested his hand on my shoulder. An encouraging, fatherly gesture. And in that instant, as I cut my gaze towards him, I saw something in the dead marble of his eyes. Just a flicker of emotion, the stunned realisation that he'd gone too far.

'Don't,' I said.

And he recoiled as if I'd struck him.

I left Peter Garris standing beside Lenny Kerrigan's grave, the stamp of some new-found fear on his haggard features. I did not need his help. I didn't need anyone. I could solve this thing alone.

Chapter Eighteen

LOCATED IN A WOODED VALLEY just outside the pretty village of Marchwood, Cedar Gables was a stunning – if misleadingly named – house. A modernist construction of steel and glass, the home of the late Genevieve Bell was flat-roofed and so possessed no gables, cedar or otherwise. I parked at the end of a long drive pebbled with bright red stones, and getting out, took a breath of crisp morning air.

I was still a little shaky from my encounter with Garris. Why the hell had I gone there? All I'd achieved was to allow him to slither back under my skin. I was tired too; I had barely got any sleep last night. Returning to the trailer after my talk with Ben and Deepal, I had sat on the edge of the bed for some time, staring into space. Memories came and went, mostly happy fragments from my childhood in which Tilda had featured. Birthdays, Christmases, end of season parties, Tilda and my mother dancing on tables, dragging me up beside them as we roared along to old-time songs. Shy and bookish, even as a kid I'd felt like an outsider, but Aunt Tilda had tried her best to make me part of the community. She had apparently been the first to know about my sexuality too, observant old mystic that she was, and last night I had recalled a snatch of conversation we'd had just before I left for university: *Fly away then, Scott Jericho, and be happy with who you are,* she'd said, clasping my hand, her eyes damp. *I know your mum would have been very proud of the man you've become. Even them parts of yourself that you might think folk round here won't ever accept, she would have loved. I can promise you that.*

It had truly hit me then. Another good soul gone. Another link to my mother severed.

After punching a hole in the wardrobe door, then picking the bloody splinters out of my knuckles, I'd finally settled down to some online research. First, Christopher Cloade. He'd grown up the wealthy and spoiled son of a hedge fund manager, indulged in every way, until four years ago when the twelve-year-old daughter of the Cloades' live-in maid had been found in their pool house, weeping and terrified. There was no doubt as to the identity of her attacker. Clear evidence linked twenty-five-year-old Christopher to an assault on the child that only just fell short of rape. But strings appeared to have been pulled on his behalf and he'd ended up serving a mere two years. While inside, he had come under the influence of his cellmate, an evangelical who took the Bible so literally even the apostles might have told him to relax. Assured that a piece of human garbage such as he might still be saved, Christopher had become fanatical for Christ and the rest was history. He now operated a kind of roaming ministry that currently had its base in Aumbry.

Next up, Darrel Everwood. Most of his life was public knowledge, or at least appeared to be. The rough-and-tumble childhood on the estate in Peckham, the discarnate voices he'd heard since the age of five, the alcoholic mother who'd died before his eighteenth birthday. Some details had recently been disputed by his former fiancée. Her allegation that his early years weren't as grim as he portrayed. That he'd actually started out as a kids' party magician before meeting his manager, Sebastian Thorn, and forming EverThorn Media. That the whole psychic sideshow they'd created together was a scam. Old friends concurred, telling the press they'd never heard Darrel so much as mention the supernatural when they had known him.

Dr Joseph Gillespie's academic background checked out. A serious scientist until he'd become obsessed with his crusade against the paranormal – and the accompanying publicity and adoration of his followers, so some of the doctor's former colleagues drily quipped. There seemed to have been a scandal a year or two back concerning an inappropriate relationship with a PhD student under his tutelage – a situation explicitly banned by his university's professional code of ethics – but details were scant. Anyway, he was now the darling of the sceptics' lecture circuit, demanding huge fees for his after-dinner speeches.

Of the Chambers family, there were only the bare facts that I already knew from the news reports of the time. An accountant and a midwife, devastated by the abduction of their daughter from the front garden of their house just six months ago. Then, Mrs Chambers' attempted suicide following the public announcement by Darrel Everwood that her child was most certainly dead.

Unusually, for a human being living in the twenty-first century, Angela Rowell appeared to have no online footprint at all. The only thing I could find was a photograph on Lord Denver's property website under the 'Meet Our Staff' banner.

Although it had probably been taken a decade ago, I wasn't surprised to see the housekeeper wearing the same tweed jacket.

Could I really believe that any of these people had killed Genevieve Bell and Tilda Urnshaw? I knew it was a foolish question. If my recent experience in Bradbury End had taught me anything, it was that the unlikeliest of suspects sometimes turn out to be the most depraved killers.

As if on cue my phone rang. I'd received another half-dozen texts from Haz overnight, his tone increasingly concerned. In the end, I'd relented and messaged back, saying that I was fine but that I needed some time to myself. This prompted another stream of worried texts. Although he'd never asked about the details, he had seen me at work during my last investigation, and what he'd seen clearly concerned him.

> Scott, I don't know what's happening. Sal's told me a little, but I know she's holding things back. I need to see that you're OK. And we need to talk. About everything. Take care and call me when you can.

But the call right now wasn't from Haz. It was Garris. By now, he must have seen the morning news reports of a murder taking place at a travelling fair. After rejecting the call, I turned off my phone and headed down the scarlet-pebbled drive towards Cedar Gables.

I'd pulled together a rough history of Genevieve Bell from a few online newspaper and magazine archives. Following the early death of their father from a heart attack, Genevieve and her sister Evangeline, two years her senior, had been left almost destitute. Together with their mother, Patricia, they had been forced to seek the help of a distant cousin – a widow with a strong interest in the supernatural. This relative had invited the Bells to come live with her. It seemed that soon after the move, Genevieve had started hearing the voice of her deceased father. Other odd occurrences followed – objects moving of their own accord, ectoplasmic emanations glimpsed by the residents of the house, sourceless shadows scurrying along empty hallways – all seemingly focused on the eight-year-old Genevieve.

By the early nineties, word of the child's gift had spread beyond her aunt's small circle of clairvoyant enthusiasts and into the forums of a burgeoning online paranormal community. This led to reporters picking up the story and a growing public interest in the little girl who spoke to the dead. Genevieve had spent a little under five years in the spotlight before the glare became too harsh. For the past two decades, this timid, retiring woman had become a virtual recluse, living alone with her mother and providing private séances to a few trusted clients.

A photograph from the height of her fame showed the Bell sisters standing together in front of their cousin's modernist mansion. Genevieve, the smaller child, dark-haired, large-eyed, shied away from the camera, her hands raised in an almost defensive gesture. She was wearing the slightly oversized, black lace gloves I'd seen in the photo from Dr Gillespie's interview. Beside her stood the more assertive figure of Evangeline, not dissimilar in looks, but with copper-coloured hair and a defiant tilt of the chin. Her right hand was draped protectively around her sibling's narrow shoulder, and despite her being little more than a child herself, I pitied whoever was on the receiving end of that fearsome glare.

I had almost reached the house when a dazed figure came stumbling out of the conifers that bordered the drive. A woman in her mid-sixties, her snowy hair snagged with foliage, her nightdress muddied and torn. This must be Patricia Bell, the dementia-afflicted mother who had found her daughter murdered. I stepped forward and caught her as she stumbled onto the path.

'Have you seen my hat, young man?' she twittered at me. 'And my scarf? And my underthings? And my bedsheet's gone missing too. And my daughter. No. No. Silly me, I keep forgetting. So many things. Do you forgive me? Please tell me that you do.' I started to say something when she bounced onto her tiptoes and cried, 'Here's my daughter now. Eve ... E*vah!* Woo! Over here! See, I remember things sometimes. I'm just having a nice chat with Mr ... ?'

'Scott,' I smiled. 'Jericho.'

'Mr Scott, I'll remember that.'

The copper of her hair a little faded by the years, Evangeline Bell came storming out of the house. On reaching us, she pulled her mother roughly away before fixing me with a look reminiscent of that old photograph.

'Who are you? What are you doing here? Speak up then.' Turning to the grinning woman beside her, she started picking the bits of leaf and twig from her hair. 'Good God, Mother, I turn my back for five minutes and you're wandering again. How ever Gennie coped with you all these years I'll never know.'

'Gennie?' She looked puzzled. 'You mean Genevieve? She's gone now. Dead and murdered, they say. But we know, don't we?' Patricia gave me a knowing wink. 'She's still here, she speaks to me, she'll never leave. Never. She was always my favourite, you know.'

I saw Evangeline's lips tighten, perhaps biting back bitter words.

'Do you also possess your daughter's gift then, Mrs Bell?' I asked gently. 'You feel that Genevieve is still with you?'

She shook her head, an expression of utter bafflement lengthening her features. 'Eva, I want to go inside,' she said. 'It's so cold out here.'

'And I want *you* gone, Mr Jericho, or whoever you are.' Evangeline looped her arm around her mother's waist and started back towards the open door. 'We've had enough of reporters lurking about the place, asking their insolent questions. Have the decency to let us grieve in peace.'

'But I'm not a reporter,' I called after them. 'I'm here because another woman has died. Please, I only want a few minutes of your time. It was my aunt, you see?'

Ushering her mother over the threshold, Evangeline paused. 'I'm very sorry for your loss, of course, but this is surely a matter for the police. You ought to be in communication with them. I can't see how us speaking about my sister could help you.'

'I only wondered if you might have known her?' I said.

I could feel the delicacy of the moment. If I so much as took a step forward it might feel like an intrusion too far and redouble her resistance. So I stayed where I was, even as she started to close the door on me.

'Her name was Tilda Urnshaw,' I called out. 'She was a fortune teller and medium. Perhaps you or your sister—?'

She spun around, a look of horror on her face. 'Tilda? Dear God. *Tilda?* But why would anyone . . . ?'

It took a few seconds for Evangeline Bell to recover herself.

'Let me settle my mother down and then we can talk. I did know your aunt, Mr Jericho. Both Gennie and I met her when we were children. In fact, if it hadn't been for Tilda Urnshaw, none of this might ever have happened.'

Chapter Nineteen

WE SAT TOGETHER ON A bench in the grounds of the house, the stripped white branches of an aspen quivering above us, the bright chuckle of an unseen stream reaching up from the valley. I held the mug of tea Evangeline had made for me in both hands, taking what warmth I could from it. Before us, the glazed rump of the house showed a mirror image of the frosted wood. Somewhere upstairs, Patricia Bell lay sleeping.

Evangeline took a drag on her cigarette, unconsciously rubbing the small port-wine stain that marked the back of her hand. 'Filthy habit, I know,' she said. 'Gennie absolutely hated it. Our father had been a heavy smoker, you see, and it may have contributed to the heart condition that killed him. And if he hadn't died and left us penniless? Well, then perhaps we'd never have come to Cedar Gables, never have made our silly plan to ingratiate ourselves with our cousin. Never met your aunt.

'By the way, what I said just now about Tilda? I didn't mean to imply that any of this is directly her fault. It's just if, as the police suggest, this madman is killing people because he has some kind of grudge against psychics? Acht—' she shook her head '—it's a pointless game. Trying to track the path that led us here. In the end, who can say where any blame might rest?'

'Miss Bell,' I sighed. 'I think that, like me with my aunt, you're only trying to make sense of what happened to your sister.'

She snorted and picked a speck of tobacco from her lip. 'What sense can ever be made of it?'

'To the killer, there will be a logical pattern,' I said. 'However crazy it might appear to us.'

She gave me a long, appraising look. 'What exactly are you, Mr Jericho? A psychiatrist?'

'I used to be a detective,' I said. 'And if you can help me, I'd like to use whatever skills I have to find the person who did this.'

'My sister was always a victim,' she murmured, perhaps more to herself than to me. 'A victim of my mother, of our cousin, of the media, of those who wished to exploit her. Of her own inability to stand up for herself. I tried to protect her as much as I could when we were kids, but Gennie was a difficult person to help, especially when she started to believe that the game we'd invented was real. But the way in which she was made a victim in death? That was an insult. The degradation of an innocent soul.'

She threw the cigarette butt into the trees and turned to face me. 'What can I tell you that might help?'

'First, I'd like to know how you met my aunt. The police seem to believe the killer is choosing his victims at random, but now that we're aware of a connection, it might help to trace him.'

'Do you know anything of our story?' Evangeline asked. When I told her the few facts I'd discovered online, she nodded.

'As far as starting points go, it's not a bad summary. Unbeknown to my mother, our father had made a number of bad investments in the months before his death. When those investments failed, we found ourselves destitute. A cousin came to the rescue. A busybody who enjoyed playing the role of benefactor to her poor relatives. She moved us in here, and it was soon made clear that we were expected to earn our keep, our mother as an unpaid cook and housekeeper and us children as skivvies, to be seen and not heard. Bear in mind, I was about ten at the time, Gennie eight. We scrubbed and polished, vacuumed and dusted like proper little Cinderellas.

'I think my mother was suffering from some kind of acute depression. In any case, she never raised any objection to how we were treated and Miss Grice, as our cousin insisted we call her, was a very forceful personality. But for such a strong-minded, practical woman she had one surprising weakness. A complete gullibility when it came to the supernatural. Clairvoyants were always in and out of the house, taking money off her by the fistful.

'Gennie and I used to laugh ourselves sick about it. We'd sneak downstairs sometimes and watch their séances through a crack in the living room door. Even to us children, it was obvious how these fakers pulled their tricks – artificial voice boxes and tape recorders wedged between their knees, fishing wire hooked around their little fingers to make the tablecloth jump, strands of luminous gauze tucked away in their cheeks and then dribbled out to look like ectoplasm. Child's play, and yet our cousin ate it up with all the relish of a true zealot.

'Well, I thought, if it's child's play, why don't *we* give it a go? I was the leader, you see. The big sister always ready with any new game or prank. And little Gennie would simply follow along in my wake, doing everything I told her ...' She paused and pressed the side of that livid birthmark to her mouth. 'That's what doomed her, if anything. My stupid games.'

'You told her to pretend she could hear your father's voice?' I said.

'Gennie had always been a consummate little actress,' Evangeline confirmed. 'With a bit of practice, we figured out how the clairvoyants threw their voices so that it seemed as if someone was speaking from the other side of the room. We were nervous as hell the first night we tried it out. I remember running into Miss Grice's bedroom and shaking her awake, hysterical and trembling, saying that a spirit had taken control of my sister. Straightaway, I could see that we'd be all right. The excitement in her eyes! The hunger to believe.'

'And Gennie's performance convinced her?'

'Convinced her and my mother. I think on some level, Mother knew we were inventing the whole thing, but the rewards that soon started landing in our lap made her a willing accomplice. She'd had it easy with my dad, you see? Fur coats, fine dining, cruises around the Med. I honestly believe she'd have grasped at anything to get a fragment of that old life back.

'About a week after we started our game, my cousin invited one of her favourite mediums over to the house. Tilda Urnshaw. I'm not sure how Miss Grice first met your aunt, but I know she held her in high regard. My sister and I were scared out of our wits. We could fool our half-witted cousin, but a true psychic? Miss Grice set us up in the living room and Gennie went through some routine we'd rehearsed, speaking in tongues, throwing her voice, the usual nonsense. Afterwards, Tilda didn't say anything for a long time. Then she asked if she might have an hour alone with Gennie and me so that she could gauge our psychic frequencies. Miss Grice agreed and left the room.

'As soon as the door closed, Tilda came out with it. She knew what we were up to. She'd visited the house before, and although she felt that my sister did indeed possess some latent psychic ability, it was not pronounced. That said, she'd seen how our cousin had treated us in the past and how much our situation had now changed. She wanted to help us if she could. And so, for the next hour, she instructed us in what she termed "fake dukkerin" – what I believe Dr Gillespie might call "cold reading" techniques – as well as a few other tricks of the trade.

'She didn't use these herself, she'd said, but they would help maintain the illusion we'd already created. It was all about effects, smoke and mirrors, set dressing. As part of this, she reached inside her bag and brought out a pair of long, black lace gloves. She then taught my sister to mimic the paranormal ability of psychometry. That is the skill of obtaining information about a person or object by touch alone. Genevieve was to say that the talent induced headaches and hence the need for the gloves so that she wouldn't be continually bombarded with psychic images. Set dressing, you see? All to bolster our absurd story.

'When the hour was up, we knew as much about fraudulent psychic techniques as anyone. Thereafter, our lives changed completely. We were no longer charity cases but honoured guests, showered with every luxury. Our mother too. For a few years, it was heaven. We were the Bell sisters, devoted and inseparable.

'Gennie was lauded by every clairvoyant Miss Grice ushered into her parlour. But as her fame began to spread outside Cedar Gables, so my sister started to change. You have to understand, Mr Jericho, all this happened gradually, over months and years, tiny incremental alterations in our relationship and Gennie's idea of herself. I'm not sure when I finally realised that she now believed, utterly and completely, that her talents were real.'

Listening to Evangeline, I suddenly flashed back to what I'd said to Harry about Aunt Tilda. *She's been playing this role all her life, remember. I don't even think she knows she's making it up.* I wondered how many mediums began and ended this way.

'Miss Grice died from a stroke when I was nineteen,' Evangeline continued. 'By that time, my little sister had become our cousin's favourite pet. Cedar Gables and all the Grice wealth was left in trust to Gennie. But by then, things were already falling apart. The press had got wind of the child who spoke to the dead, and after a couple of years of unrelenting publicity, my sister suffered a kind of breakdown.

'I tried to talk to her. Tried to make her remember how the whole thing had started – just a silly game helped along by a well-meaning fortune teller. But Gennie had lost herself in a world of shadows and half-truths. Her entire self-worth was tied up in the identity I had helped her forge. Even though she'd begun to shun the spotlight, she couldn't let go of this crucial truth about herself, and for the next twenty years, she maintained an absolute belief of her psychic gifts.'

The wind stirred in the valley below, whistling among the rocks, crackling the frosted trees.

'Until she was shown that it *wasn't* real?' I suggested. 'The podcast with Dr Gillespie, when he demonstrated to her how she did her tricks?'

Evangeline's eyes narrowed. 'Why couldn't he have left her alone?' She spat out the words. 'You're right, Mr Jericho. I believe it was that moment that shattered my sister completely. All those years of self-deception crashing down upon her in a single, devastating moment. And then she saw the news about that man, Darrel Everwood, and the claims that he was a fraud and that he'd been inspired by her own story. She told me how responsible she felt for that. How guilty, that we'd perpetuated another generation of liars. You know, I think in the end, she was so miserable, so desperate, she probably welcomed death.'

Chapter Twenty

'But why would Gennie feel responsible for Darrel Everwood's lies?' I asked.

'Because of the book,' Miss Bell said. 'At the height of her fame, we were contacted by a publicist called Rose, I think – it's so long ago, I can't be sure of the name. Anyway, he wanted to represent Gennie. He'd already lined up a lucrative book deal with a major publisher. By this time, Miss Grice was dead and my mother was all too eager to sign the contract on our behalf. *Hearing the Dead: The Story of Genevieve Bell*. It's pretty much forgotten now, but in its day, it was a bestseller.'

'Some old book inspired him to get into the medium business,' I murmured, remembering something Ben Halliday had told me. 'So after your sister was humiliated by Dr Gillespie on the podcast, she then learned that Darrel Everwood had taken inspiration for his career from her book?'

Evangeline nodded. 'That's what she told me. Although I'd moved away in my early twenties, we'd always tried to stay in touch at least once a week. But in that last month, she was on the phone with me multiple times a day. Everything I'd been trying to tell her for the past two decades – the memories she'd buried, the truth of how it had all started – all of it was suddenly crashing down on her. She realised she'd spent her entire life unconsciously deceiving people. And now, as she read about a children's magician who'd picked up her book in a charity shop and coveted her celebrity, she began to feel a suffocating sense of responsibility.'

Evangeline plucked out another cigarette and lit up. 'I think that's how the preacher got his claws into her.'

I stared at her. 'What preacher?'

'Oh.' She waved the smouldering tip. 'Some ranting nutcase who came delivering pamphlets about a week after the podcast aired. Gennie happened to answer the door to him and they fell into conversation. He was a young man, apparently, and so had no idea who she was. But what with Gillespie and Everwood fresh in her mind, she was more than ready to hear how wicked and depraved she had been. But there was hope, of course! That's the one carrot these godly men always hold out. Just make a small donation to my church and I'll pray for your blighted soul. Salvation for sale.'

'And did she give him any money?' I asked.

'I believe so. A few thousand, anyway. To the Church of Christ the Redeemer, care of a Mr Christopher Cloade. I'm currently trying to get it back, but everything's snarled up in probate.'

'Did your sister become actively involved with this church?' I asked.

'I don't believe so. She was killed not long after that first donation.'

Links were forging everywhere – with Tilda, with Everwood, with Christopher Cloade, and with Joseph Gillespie.

'Going back a little,' I said. 'If she'd become so reclusive, why did Gennie agree to take part in the podcast at all?'

Evangeline shrugged. 'Gillespie had been shouting about his views for a while. I think she wanted to stand up for her life's work. In hindsight, of course, it was a fatal mistake. She'd been out of the spotlight for too long and so had lost whatever showmanship she'd learned. Have you listened to the thing?'

'Some of it.'

'That little broken voice.' Evangeline exhaled a dragon's tail of smoke. 'Imagine your whole world shattering in an instant. What does that do to a person?'

'I can't imagine,' I said. 'But tell me, what do you personally think of Dr Gillespie?'

She took a moment to consider her response. 'That's not an easy question to answer. In some respects, I support everything he does – opening people's eyes to science, trying to build a more rational world – but his methods and his contempt for the likes of Darrel Everwood and my sister? I don't know. I think in some respects he's just as deluded as Gennie and just as fanatical as that preacher, Cloade. It can be a dangerous thing, you know, to systematically strip away a person's certainties. It can leave them with nothing to hold onto.'

I nodded. Something about those words seemed to strike a chord with me.

'We've spoken a lot about how your childhood affected your sister. What about yourself?'

Again, Evangeline considered before responding. 'Guilt is what I feel whenever I think about what happened with Gennie,' she said. 'It was my idea, wasn't it? To play the original prank that started it all. But my sister was the one who ended up paying the price. I got to have a life. At school, I had friends, boyfriends, while she was always set apart as the strange child who spoke to ghosts. Other kids were frightened of her and so kept their distance. At first, I tried to stand up for her, to help her fit in, but eventually, it simply became easier to leave her be.

'You see, I couldn't make her understand that the fantasy we'd built together was just that. And so, in the end, I left. Took off and abandoned her and my mother to their make-believe life. We stayed in touch, of course, but when I look back?' A final draw on her cigarette, another stub flicked to the ground and stamped out. 'I should have stayed. Protected her. Somehow forced her to see the truth. But I wanted my own life. Does that make me a terrible person, Mr Jericho?'

I shook my head. 'I left the life I was born into as well. I think it makes us human.'

'Not that escaping did me much good,' Evangeline said with a dry laugh. 'One failed marriage and a kid who'd rather stay at boarding school during the holidays than come home to me. We're a rare family, us Bells.'

'I'm sure the Jerichos could give you a run for your money.' I smiled. 'But the book about your sister's life. *Hearing the Dead*. Do you happen to have a copy?'

'I'm sorry, I don't. It went out of print years ago. I believe there might still be copies floating around in the kind of charity shops where Darrel Everwood picked it up. Or online maybe. I know Gennie burned hers following the podcast. She called me, in fact, saying she was out here in the garden, making a bonfire of her past.'

'Do you remember if Tilda was mentioned in it?'

'I believe she was, as the fortune teller who first confirmed my sister's abilities. Though, of course, nothing was written about what she'd really taught us.' Evangeline gave me a hard look. 'Do you think that's why the killer went after her?'

'It's the surest link,' I said. 'Someone with a pathological hatred for psychics looking to form a specific target group. Perhaps they hear the podcast, listen to your sister being exposed by Gillespie, and then lay their hands on the book. Genevieve Bell must pay for her sins but so must the "witch" who enabled her.' We'd reached the part of my questioning that was going to prove the most upsetting. I could tell Evangeline was a strong woman but still, I hesitated before asking, 'Can you tell me what happened to your sister?'

She didn't flinch. 'I wasn't here, so I can only describe what I've pieced together from my mother's confused ramblings and the questions of the police.'

'Did Genevieve receive anything unusual in the days leading up to her death?'

'You mean the doll? I told her to ignore it. Just a Halloween trick played by the local children, I said.'

'She called you about it? Did she describe it to you?'

'It was left on the doorstep.' Evangeline frowned. 'A wax effigy with the face gouged out and the hands removed. A piece of paper attached to the leg, I think. Some kind of numbers or letters, I don't remember.'

'Had it been pierced with needles?' I asked.

She shook her head. 'Not that Gennie said. It was wet, though. Dripping with water when she picked it up, yet it hadn't been raining.'

'Water...' I murmured to myself. 'If you prick us, do we not bleed?'

'I'm sorry?'

'Miss Bell, I hate to ask, but how exactly did Gennie die?'

I think we both caught sight of the figure at the same moment. Patricia Bell standing at a wide first-floor window, her vacant gaze fixed on some unfathomable horizon.

'From what I can gather she was struck from behind,' Evangeline said. 'Which was odd, because it happened so early in the morning and my sister was very security conscious. It made me think she must have known her murderer. Let him in and taken him to the sitting room where it happened.' Just like Tilda had greeted her killer in the tent, I thought. 'They say the blow probably killed her outright, which was a mercy. Then he...' Evangeline took out yet another cigarette and lit up. 'Mutilated her somehow. The face and hands, like the doll.'

'Were her hands missing when the police arrived?' I asked as gently as I could.

She gave a brisk nod. 'I believe so. I thought it might have been a deliberate insult to her affectation. The black gloves? To deny her power of touch-sensitivity, you see? To mock it in some way.'

I nodded. Hadn't the blood smeared across The Fool card in Tilda's tent also had a touch of mockery about it? I pressed on. 'But no nails were used on the body?'

'Nails?'

'Masonry nails?'

'No. My mother said Gennie was all wet, though. Her nightdress soaked through, her hair dripping. That was all...' Evangeline shivered. 'Dear Lord, *all*? That was enough, wasn't it?'

Nails. Water. Rope. Fire. The images riffled inside my head, like the cards in a tarot deck. And suddenly I was back, cross-legged on the ground, planted between two women as they spun a true horror story to the saucer-eyed child at their feet. We'd been touring around Essex at the time and were a stone's throw from a village named Mistley. Always a morbid child, I'd been nagging my mum and Aunt Tilda for ghost stories when Tilda piped up.

'Well, you do know you're sitting on the very earth where the old Witchfinder General once plied his trade?'

'Don't you dare, Tilda Urnshaw!' my mother had said with a mischievous smile. 'The poor chavvy won't sleep for weeks if you tell him *that* tale.'

This, of course, had prompted me to beg for every gory detail.

'Matthew Hopkins was his name,' Tilda had said, leaning back on her trailer step and pointing a dramatic finger at me. 'And hunting witches was his game. Over four hundred years ago, he stalked this area, for it was the county of his birth and Mistley was his hometown. This was the time of the great Civil War, Roundheads against Cavaliers, brother slaughtering brother for Parliament or the Crown. And into this lawless mayhem, the Witchfinder came, claiming sorcery in every village and hamlet. And do you know why?' I shook my head. 'For brass, of course. It was a profitable business in them days, digging out witches and setting them to the test.'

'What test?' I had asked.

She counted them off on beringed fingers. 'The swimming test, where if they floated in the pure waters of the millstream their guilt was proven. The pricking test, where a sharp needle was pierced into any wart or blemish and should no blood flow forth, it was called a devil's mark.'

'Then what was done to them?'

'They were strung up high from the gibbet,' Tilda said, clasping her neck with both hands. 'Or else staked to a bonfire and set to burn. And watching over it all with his purse fat and his greedy eyes aglow, the Witchfinder General.'

A hand touched my arm, Evangeline's birthmark burnished by the autumn sun. I wondered absently whether that alone might have led to her torture, once upon a time.

'Mr Jericho, are you all right? You suddenly look very pale.'

Chapter Twenty-One

THE ROPE AND THE FIRE. Unless I was missing some other method of historical torture and execution reserved for witches, that meant there were at least two more murders to go.

'I'm sorry, Miss Bell,' I said, looking over at the concerned face next to me. 'I think I'm just overtired. Perhaps I could use your bathroom before I head back?'

'Of course.'

She took the mug from my hand and led me up the gentle incline of the garden. Halfway to the house, I noticed a scorch mark like a dark brand upon the grass. I guessed that this was where Genevieve had burned the copies of her book.

A big sliding glass door gave onto the kitchen. As impressive as the house was from the outside, it soon became obvious that this had been the home of a recluse. All the fixtures and fittings were at least twenty years past their best, the carpets old and frayed, tongues of wallpaper coming loose at the corners. Despite a faint stale smell and the general air of neglect, however, every surface appeared spotlessly clean. Finishing up in the downstairs bathroom, I came back into the hall just as Patricia started screeching from the landing.

'Eve! Eve, where are you? They've taken my pills and my pillows and my bedsheets and my underthings. Eve!'

An exasperated Evangeline exited the kitchen and shot me an apologetic glance before barking up at her mother. 'Please! We have company.'

'Yes, I'm sorry. I remember now.' The white-haired woman raised clenched fists to the sides of her hollow cheeks and beamed at me. 'Mr Scott, isn't it? How nice of you to visit us again.'

Evangeline showed me to the door where I thanked her for sharing so many painful memories. She waved my words aside. 'Just keep me updated on the case, will you? The man in charge, Inspector Tallis, he seems like a very competent officer. I'm sure he'll arrive at the truth eventually, but if you find out anything in the meantime?'

I agreed and took her number.

Heading back up the red-pebbled drive, I searched on my phone for any available copies of *Hearing the Dead*. Evangeline hadn't been exaggerating when she said that it was now a rarity – there were no e-book files available and the only physical copy I could source that would arrive within forty-eight hours ended up costing me almost a hundred quid. Still, I thought it was worth the investment. If my supposition was correct that the murderer had fixed his obsession for killing 'witches' on the person of Gennie Bell, then any psychic who'd encouraged or influenced her, or that she, in turn, had influenced, might be a potential victim. It appeared as if the killer was intent on eradicating the entire thread of supernatural cause and effect that centred around this individual. As if Genevieve stood as a symbol for all that he despised. If that were true, then the clues as to who else might be at risk could lie within the pages of that elusive book.

It was a fifty-mile drive back to Purley Rectory. Ample time to turn the case over in my mind. One thing I kept returning to was that primary motivation. I'd said to both my dad and Inspector Tallis that the ritualism with the doll had seemed overdone. In the case of Gennie Bell, that elaborateness had been carefully duplicated in the mutilation of her corpse, the hands entirely removed and missing, as per the effigy. In Tilda's case, however, only one hand had been mutilated, and even then, not fully severed. Did this mean that the killer's belief in the morality of his mission was already faltering? Or did it indicate something else entirely?

I suddenly pictured Dr Gillespie in the role of self-righteous butcher. As a trained academic he would have done his utmost to research Gennie before their encounter on the podcast. In fact, it was almost unimaginable that he hadn't at least looked up her book. Tracing that path of influence from Tilda, through Gennie, to his ultimate nemesis, Darrel Everwood, might he have decided to make these murders look like the work of an Old Testament fanatic, thereby diverting suspicion from himself and smearing religion in the process? It could explain why a killer who didn't believe passionately in his ritual had already grown sick of it.

Or was it a genuine zealot at work? Had Christopher Cloade really just happened upon Cedar Gables while delivering his pamphlets? He currently ministered in the nearby city of Aumbry and so it wasn't inconceivable for him to target a local fair, but to travel fifty miles outside his patch? My bet was that, after catching the podcast, he'd purposely sought out Genevieve. Just as Evangeline described it, he must have heard her self-belief shatter in that moment and had seen his opportunity. From my research last night, I'd learned that he had renounced his family's wealth, but still, his church would have running costs and a celebrity convert might be an attractive prospect. Except, why then kill her? Unless she'd had a change of heart and demanded her donation back. Then he might have justified what came next as the slaughter of a lapsed sinner.

Perhaps Evangeline Bell herself had some hidden motive for wanting her sister and Tilda dead. She might have blamed my aunt for that act of kindness that had ended up so warping her sister's life. And yet, such a motivation didn't quite work. After all, Tilda hadn't originated the psychic game, that had been Evangeline's doing. And why would she wish to kill her sister when she, Evangeline, had been the one to escape Cedar Gables? Of course, I was taking Evangeline's word for all this, but what she'd told me of their lives neatly dovetailed with everything else I'd learned during my research. Now, if sceptics like Dr Gillespie were being targeted, then I could certainly see the dominant Evangeline taking revenge for how her vulnerable sister had been destroyed, but otherwise, the image didn't seem to fit.

And what of Haz in all this? asked that treacherous voice inside my head. There is *no* Haz in this, I insisted. Then where has he been going when he told you he had choir practice? What has he been doing? Who has he been seeing? What about the pencil stub in his bag? What about the wax on his sleeve?

These questions vanished as I pulled onto the main road that abutted the forest. Immediately, I had to slam on my brakes.

The way ahead was snarled with people and vehicles, which at first made no sense. Even if Inspector Tallis had given the all-clear, it was still only midday and the fair wouldn't be open for another seven hours. I parked up on a grass verge and made my way on foot to the junction with the forest road. There, I found Dr Joseph Gillespie, back on his soapbox with his disciples cheering him on.

It was a noticeably bigger crowd than last night, and not only in terms of the Gillespieites. Nothing brings in the media like the scent of a serial killer. Even though Tallis ran a tight operation, I wasn't surprised that details had begun to leak out. If Deepal Chandra could induce a constable to take a bribe, then so could any of the reporters currently waving their microphones under the doctor's nose.

Back to his old, pompous, preening best, Gillespie appeared to be making the most of it. Although, I noticed as he spoke that he kept casting glances at the forest road, perhaps wary that Deepal might emerge at any moment and steal the limelight from him again.

'This is always the end result of superstition,' he was saying. 'It might begin innocently enough – an entertaining ghost story about some quaint old house, a love potion begged from the local wise woman, stories of devils under the bed to make an unruly child behave. But when the haunted house is burned to the ground by frightened neighbours? When the would-be lover feels cheated and persecutes the wise woman as a "witch"? When the grown child in his adult psychosis imagines there really are such things as demons? Then we see the true face of the supernatural: violence, destruction, barbarism, insanity and murder. Just such a lethal madness took hold in this place last night and a poor woman lies dead because of it.'

As every showman knows, the art of a good spiel is to leave 'em wanting more. Gillespie seemed to know this too. He refused the media's questions and, aided by his acolytes, stepped down from the platform. These same brown-nosers then tried to stop me from getting to their beloved leader. Honestly, it was pitiful – like a set of nine-stone pins meeting a fourteen-stone bowling ball.

'I'd like to talk to you, Dr Gillespie,' I said, holding one dandruff-speckled fan at arm's length as he tried to claw out my eyes.

'I'm sorry,' Gillespie replied, clearly startled. 'But I'm rather busy. If you're a reporter perhaps you could contact my press team and arrange an—'

'It was my aunt that was murdered,' I said. 'I only want a minute.'

He turned that oddly creaseless face towards me. 'My dear boy. I'm so sorry for your loss. Giles, desist!'

The acolyte Giles obeyed at once and put his talons away.

'Let's step to one side and we can talk,' Gillespie said as if he was the soul of generosity. 'I have a few minutes before my next interview. In fact, if you happen to share my views, you may wish to appear alongside me. Perhaps inform the public how much a madman's irrational belief has cost your family? The personal toll, you understand, Mr—?'

'Jericho.'

'Of course.' He patted my shoulder. 'You're one of the travelling people, aren't you?'

'I am,' I confirmed. 'And in fact, I support a lot of your opinions, Doctor. Especially what you say about vulnerable people being exploited by psychic con artists. But do you consider what *you've* just done – making a publicity stunt out of my aunt's death – just as cynical an act of exploitation?'

That dour little mouth puckered. 'I'm sorry you feel that way, Mr Jericho. I assure you, such a motive was not at the forefront of my mind. However, if you think me cruel then I'll gladly accept that criticism. Kindness is a luxury the rational world can no longer afford. If we continue to indulge the superstitious, then all too soon the human race will find itself in the shadow of a new Dark Age.

'People don't seem to understand,' Gillespie continued, warming to his subject. 'That belief in the paranormal is *not* on the wane. Indeed, ghosts and Ouija boards and telekinesis and astral projection and whatever else you care to name are now more popular than ever. You might think, so what? Let the fools indulge their inane fantasies. They aren't hurting anyone, are they? But I assure you, such nonsense has real-life consequences. Today it's a "harmless" visit to a clairvoyant, tomorrow it's belief in invisible voices telling us what to do, and demonic possession, and blood sacrifice, and religious wars. You say I'm unkind, but no one has ever read *my* books and then gone out and butchered people in the name of reason.'

'No,' I agreed. 'But they may have lost some hope that was dear to them.'

'Then they should find new hope in science,' he scoffed. 'In the perfect patterns of mathematics, in the structural beauty of the double helix, in the awesome but predictable clockwork of the universe. There is nothing there, I assure you, to inspire the slaughter of witches.'

Chapter Twenty-Two

'THE SLAUGHTER OF WITCHES,' I echoed. 'I wonder why you'd use an expression like that?'

The doctor shrugged. 'It's just a turn of phrase.'

'Is it? You also referenced witches in your press conference just now, didn't you?'

'Well, considering the circumstances of your aunt's murder – the ritualistic nature of it – I suppose a natural association of ideas came to mind.'

'Then tell me, Dr Gillespie, where did you get your information about Tilda Urnshaw's death?'

He stared at me through those tortoise-shell glasses, his suddenly wary eyes magnified. 'I believe ... uh ... I mean, it's the gossip of the area, isn't it? Perhaps I overheard one of the reporters talking about it.' He waved an airy hand. 'I really can't recall.'

'You can't recall where you learned the explicit details of a ritual murder, even though you probably only heard about it in the past few hours?' I let the question hang. 'All right. Let's see if your memory is any better concerning the events of yesterday. You were standing right on this spot when you likened people such as Darrel Everwood to a brain tumour that had to be cut away. *Burned out*. You're also on record as saying that you'd stop at nothing to eradicate belief in the supernatural. Just how far would you go to achieve that aim, Doctor?'

'You seriously think I'd murder each and every psychic in existence?' He laughed. 'My boy, I really wouldn't have the time.'

'But maybe one or two would do, as a warning to the others? Could you fit that into your schedule of after-dinner speeches, Joe?' I knew I had only moments left before the doctor's bluster gave way to questions of his own. 'What time did you leave the fair last night?'

'It's Joseph,' he corrected tartly. 'And I left at eight twenty. Before the murder, certainly.'

'You're very precise in your timekeeping.'

'I happened to glance at my watch. I was running late for another engagement.'

'*Another* engagement? But you'd finished delivering your speech to the crowds at least half an hour before you left. Why would you hang around if you were needed elsewhere?' When he didn't answer, I tried a different tack. 'What did it feel like when you lost control of your audience last night? I bet that was a unique experience for such an accomplished performer. Did it make you angry?'

'It was ... unfortunate,' he admitted.

'You should never let your disciples see you weakened, Doctor,' I advised. 'If they realise that their god is just flesh and blood – perhaps even as fallible as the believers he laughs at – what might they do then? There are always other gods, aren't there? Just waiting in the wings, ready to steal your halo.'

'I must get on,' Gillespie snapped and began to move away.

'I've just been speaking with Genevieve Bell's sister,' I called after him. He stopped and, after a brief pause, turned back to face me. 'Not your biggest fan, I'm afraid. Though, like me, she has some time for your arguments. Can I ask one last question before you disappear? What did you really think of Genevieve? I'm not talking about as a psychic, I mean as a person. A human being.'

He fiddled with his cuffs before answering. Not that preening gesture this time, but something like a nervous tic.

'She was . . . badly damaged,' he said slowly. 'Even before the podcast recording began, she looked grey, worn down. Mr Jericho, you might think that my work is designed purely to feed my ego, and maybe there is some truth in that. The spotlight can be addictive. But when I met Genevieve Bell, it brought home to me, very powerfully, the corrupting nature of the supernatural. Her life had been twisted by her convictions. Beliefs founded upon shifting sands that could no longer bear the weight of her self-deception. That was why I said we should not sentimentalise her *legacy*. After the podcast, after I'd shown her how she'd fooled herself for so many years, I'm sure she would have agreed with that statement.

'But as for the woman herself? I felt sorry for her. She was a child when this lie was sewn into the soil of her mind. In my opinion, that was a form of abuse. To deny an innocent little girl the solid reality of her world, and then to misshape her thinking so that she believed herself capable of speaking to phantoms? It was wicked, and if there really is a God of the Old Testament, then surely that act is deserving of all his fury and vengeance. It certainly reinforced my own conviction that belief in the paranormal is an evil that must be expunged. That said ...' He hesitated, picked again at his shirt cuff. 'In hindsight, might I have treated her more gently?'

'Well?' I asked.

He sighed. 'It wasn't my proudest moment.'

And with that, he walked back to join his followers.

I had just spotted a red Ford Mondeo idling not far from my own disintegrating Mercedes when Deepal appeared out of the forest road. She waved when she saw me and I walked over. It was difficult to make out from this distance, especially with the sun in my eyes, but I thought the couple sitting in the car was probably Mr and Mrs Chambers. While Dr Gillespie was no doubt right concerning the existence of ghosts, the grounds of Purley Rectory were certainly being haunted by these grieving parents. I wondered again if Ben had really seen them coming out of Tilda's tent last night or if his addiction had conjured that image from thin air?

'Damn it,' Deepal muttered when I reached her. 'Looks like I missed all the fun.'

'He put on quite a show,' I admitted.

She looked over to where the doctor was speaking to a vigorously nodding reporter. 'Sick, isn't it? Like a vulture picking over the bones of the dead.'

'Maybe,' I said. 'Although you didn't seem particularly squeamish yourself last night.'

'Touché.' She held up her hands. 'Would you think better of me if I said I'd had second thoughts about the whole "Darrel defies death threats" angle? I'm not sure his manager would have gone for it anyway. Sebastian Thorn is a cautious old dog.'

'And it would be stretching the truth a bit too, wouldn't it?' I said. 'Because Darrel hasn't actually received any direct threats.

No strange notes, no nasty phone calls, no weird wax dolls left on the doorstep?'

'Wax dolls?' Deepal frowned. 'No, nothing like that. Calls, notes, emails, yes, but that's pretty standard for a celeb.'

'Understood.' I nodded. 'By the way, I still need to speak to him. Has Ben sorted an interview for me yet?'

'He hasn't,' she said. 'And I won't let him. I'm sorry, Mr Jericho, but there's no way Darrel would ever consent to talk to you about any of this. He's paranoid as hell, remember. If you go in all guns blazing, firing off theories about your murdered aunt and how Darrel might be next, that could prompt a complete meltdown just days ahead of broadcast. Do you realise how much that would cost him, not just financially?'

'Strange attitude,' I observed. 'Especially for someone who twelve hours ago was thinking of using the danger of his position as a publicity stunt.'

'I've told you—'

'I know.' I began walking away down the forest road. 'You had second thoughts. But one way or another, Deepal, I *will* speak to Darrel Everwood.'

Coming onto the side ground, I found a large group of showpeople outside Tilda's tent. Old and young, broad-backed and stooped, they stood proudly in their finest clothes, holding onto each other as a little girl stepped forward. Stretched around the tent, a length of blue-and-white crime scene tape snapped in the breeze and made Jodie jump. My goddaughter recovered herself quickly before adding her own small bouquet to the mountain of flowers stacked outside the door. The fair would reopen today – had to, if these people were to survive the winter – but for now, they would pay their respects.

I took a sharp breath. Haz had emerged from the heart of the group. Dressed in his black suit with a pink carnation in the buttonhole – Tilda's favourite flower – he knelt and wiped away Jodie's tears. He seemed to ask a question before giving her an encouraging smile. Then, turning round to face the others, they linked hands and began to sing.

'*Abide with me; fast falls the eventide . . .*'

I listened for a while, giving way to my own tears, overwhelmed by the beauty of their harmony. I realised that my phone had been off for most of the morning, ever since I'd received the call from Garris. They'd probably tried calling to tell me about this tribute. But here wasn't where I was needed. Sal and Haz could comfort Jodie better than I ever could. My role in Tilda's death wasn't to grieve but to seek out and to punish, and so I moved away before any of them could see me.

One other person was absent from the memorial. I found my dad in his trailer, on speakerphone to a man who sounded like he'd not only been born with a silver spoon in his mouth but had swallowed the entire canteen of cutlery.

'As I say, George, I'm terribly sorry about what's happened. Awful. Just *awful*. But you're sure the police have given you the green light to reopen tonight?' My dad said yes, and catching sight of me, waved me into a chair. 'Jolly good. I'm old school chums with the chief constable, and if there had been any trouble, I could have intervened on your behalf. But there. This man Tallis sounds like a good egg, and I've been in touch with Mrs Manders, of course.'

'Mrs who?' my dad asked.

'I'm sorry, *Miss Rowell*. The housekeeper. An absolute gem. Couldn't do without her. Loyal as a dog, that one, and twice as trustworthy. Married to our old gamekeeper, many moons ago. Manders. Terrible villain. Led her a merry dance – booze, drugs, other women. He buggered off one night with one of our lesser-known Gainsboroughs and Great-grandmama's diamond tiara. That was when he and Mrs Manders were with us up at the big house in Lincolnshire. The old girl had no idea, of course. Police never caught the blackguard and she reverted to her maiden name. Hasn't accepted a raise in years. Feels she owes us, I suppose. A loyal dog, like I said, and she does a fantastic job for us at dear old Purley.'

The conversation went on for another minute or two until Dad finally managed to hang up.

'Lord Denver?' I asked.

'Bloody hell,' he said drily. 'How did you work that one out, Sherlock? His lordship called to offer me his condolences. Really, though, it was to check we were still opening up tonight. There's a clause in our contract that we only owe Denver rent for days we're open. Anyway, how've you been getting on?'

I was about to make my report when a sharp tap sounded at the door. A second later, it was open and Inspector Tallis's boyish face poked into the room.

'Sorry to interrupt, Mr Jericho, but I'd like to speak to your son.' He held out two fingers, stained bright red, as if with blood. 'Now.'

Chapter Twenty-Three

I FOLLOWED THE INSPECTOR DOWN THE steps and past a slumbering Webster. Lucky for Tallis that fierce old juk was presently dreaming or I wouldn't have fancied his chances. There wasn't much meat on the detective, true, but Webster was always ready for a snack.

En route to what I was certain would be an official bollocking, I thought about what I'd just heard concerning Miss Rowell, or Mrs Manders as she had been. Given her personal history, I wondered if her strange antipathy towards Darrel Everwood suddenly made sense. I remembered her words as she pointed up at the billboard that night. *Men like that. Duplicity runs through their veins like poison. Their kind of deception is wilful, unforgivable, cruel.* A cheating husband who had lied and stolen and then left her to face the music. Consumed with misplaced guilt following his crime, she'd left what was probably the relative comfort of Lord Denver's ancestral home to bury herself away in this draughty Victorian rectory, refusing any raise in her wages, making do in her tattered tweed. On his behalf, she had served her husband's penance. And then into her martyrdom had intruded a brash, cocky echo of the man she had sacrificed so much for.

It fitted. And yet the theory didn't feel entirely complete. Her dislike of Everwood had an abstract quality to it – a sense that it went beyond the simple comparison of two flawed men. That it wasn't just personal with Miss Rowell but philosophical. A loathing of dishonesty itself. I wondered why I kept coming back to the image of that elastic band around her wrist and to her hurried flight from Purley on the night of the murder. I recalled the hem of her skirt splashed with mud and the impressions left in the ground outside Tilda's tent – the marks of someone kneeling to fasten the doorway.

A short distance from Dad's trailer, Tallis turned to face me. 'You've been to Cedar Gables.' He held up his red-stained fingers again. 'It was raining heavily in that vicinity last night and the slush from the pebbles on the drive is all over your wheel arches. I caught sight of it as I passed your car just now in the lane. That and a conifer leaf under your windscreen wiper.'

I smiled and shook my head. 'You are good, Inspector Tallis.'

He didn't match my smile but nor did he look particularly pissed off. 'As are you, Mr Jericho. I won't threaten you again about interfering with an active police investigation, but if I find you've jeopardised my case with your own inquiries, then your balls are mine. I won't tolerate any personal vendettas, understand?'

'I'll play fair,' I promised.

'Not quite the answer to my question,' he observed. 'But I've said my piece. Now, if you're interested in helping me solve this case, I'm happy to exchange certain information. You first. What did you discover after speaking to Evangeline Bell?'

I told him about the potential victim connection with Darrel Everwood. Genevieve had mentioned his name to her sister, saying she felt guilty for having inspired 'another generation of liars', and so I could now reveal that link without shining a spotlight on Ben Halliday. I explained my theory of a killer focusing his obsession for destroying witches on Gennie Bell and her legacy. Catching Tallis's expression, I stopped mid-sentence.

'But you'd already made that link,' I said. 'That's why you offered to have constables stationed at the fair last night. You're already trying to protect Everwood.'

He nodded. 'Evangeline mentioned in her first interview with me that Gennie had spoken about Everwood. I'd been meaning to contact her again this morning and ask if the sisters had known a Tilda Urnshaw. Then I saw your car, realised where you'd been, and touching base with her, I got the full story.'

'Then maybe I can suggest an idea you haven't considered.' I explained to him my theory about the dolls, the mutilations, and the historical methods of torture and execution employed by the seventeenth-century witchfinders. 'If I'm right, there are at least two more victims to go. One to represent the hanged witch, one to represent the burned. He's going back and forth along Gennie Bell's timeline, eradicating those who influenced her and those she herself influenced.'

Tallis nodded. 'It explains the different post-mortem injuries, the different dolls. So apart from Everwood, do you have any idea of a fourth victim?'

'Not yet. But a clue may lie in a book Gennie wrote.'

'*Hearing the Dead*. Yes, I've got my team trying to track down a copy.'

'Of course you do.'

I caught his eye and we both laughed. For the first time since my imprisonment and disgrace, I felt a yearning to be back on the force, working a case again as part of a proper Major Investigations Team. True, I'd never been overly popular with my colleagues – far too temperamental and abrasive to be an effective team player – but this man, Tallis. The thought of collaborating with him made me almost nostalgic for those post-shift pints in The Three Crowns when Garris and I would happily pick apart personalities and motivations and alibis by the hour.

'So who are your suspects, Inspector?' I asked. 'You show me yours and I'll show you mine.'

Tallis shook his head. 'You show me yours and we'll leave it at that, shall we?'

'Now who isn't playing fair?' I sighed. 'In that case, can I ask if you've interviewed Darrel Everwood yet? It's possible he might know who's behind all this and is too scared to say. Either that or ...'

'Yes?'

I shook my head. 'Well, as far as suspects go, I'll give you this: according to his PA, Darrel is terrified that this Halloween event will be a complete disaster. He's desperate to get out of it if he can.'

'You're saying he'd kill two people, simply to give himself an excuse not to put on a show?'

'I'm saying he's an egomaniac with substance issues who maybe thinks he can genuinely talk to the dead. Don't forget, Genevieve Bell didn't start out believing she was a real medium. As Evangeline says, that fantasy only gradually became her sister's reality. Darrel is currently the subject of vicious online and media persecution. What if his defence mechanism is to fully embrace the identity he's created? Then he isn't a liar anymore. He's a maligned hero. Anything that would threaten that idea of himself would be intolerable to him. Exposure on national television, for instance. He might go to extreme lengths to avoid that.'

'We've tried arranging an interview,' Tallis said. 'But Sebastian Thorn, his manager, has put a block on it and called in the lawyers. Doesn't want the press getting a whiff of Everwood being involved in an active murder case.'

I nodded. 'I got the same reaction from his PA.'

'Thorn is a powerful player,' Tallis said in a contemplative tone. 'Experienced and ruthless, with friends in high places. I've been warned to handle him with kid gloves.'

'Have you spoken to Thorn directly?' I asked.

'Not yet. Just getting the man on the phone seems difficult enough. I've had to have a word with the chief constable, see if he can pull some strings so that we might be granted an audience with the elusive Mr Thorn.'

I whistled. 'A powerful man indeed, if he can dictate the timetable of a police investigation.'

Tallis held out his hand. 'Give me your phone, Mr Jericho.' Frowning, I handed it over and watched as he tapped away at the screen. 'My number, in case you get any more bright ideas.'

He handed back the mobile and I saw his full name for the first time. Thomas Tallis. Hadn't there been an Elizabethan composer with that name? Haz would know.

'Just one more thing,' I called out as DCI Tallis moved away.

'Who are you?' He grinned back at me. 'Lieutenant fucking Columbo?'

'Were there many fingerprints at the Bell crime scene?'

'Of the killer's?'

'No.' I shook my head. 'Of Gennie's?'

'Hardly any, now you mention it. Why do you ask?'

'I suppose there wouldn't have been,' I said slowly. 'Not if she'd become accustomed to wearing those black lace gloves. Doesn't matter.'

He headed off and I shoved the phone back into my trench coat pocket.

The memorial for Tilda appeared to have broken up and most of the showpeople had either gone back to completing odd jobs on their rides or were taking an afternoon nap before the gates opened at seven. I hadn't eaten since breakfast and so decided to grab a bite at the trailer. I could report my findings to Dad later.

I was already inside the tin box and closing the door behind me when I noticed Haz sitting on the bed. He was running his fingertips across the built-in wardrobe – the spot I had splintered and bloodied with my knuckles last night. Hearing the click of the door, he turned, stood up, and came to me, taking both my hands in his.

'Where have you been?' he asked.

'Where have *you* been?'

I regretted the coldness in my tone at once. I hadn't intended it. Didn't think I'd intended it, anyway. Haz flinched but didn't pull away.

'I just needed some time,' he said, his voice unsteady.

'Same here. I told you that in my text this morning. The difference between us, Harry, is that I respected your wishes.'

Why are you doing this? a voice inside my head all but screamed at me. I had no answer.

'I'm sorry,' Haz murmured. 'You're right. Of course, you're right. It's just, Sal called me saying that Jodie wanted to do something special for Tilda, and would I come back? We tried getting hold of you but your phone was switched off. She did really well. Jodie, I mean. And I thought, since I was here, maybe we could talk.' He turned his head towards the blood-flecked wardrobe before lifting my bruised knuckles to the light. 'Scott, what's happening?'

In the end, it was me that pulled away. 'You know what's happening. You've seen it before.' I went and stood at the sink, my back to him. 'But you never want to talk about what happened in Bradbury End, do you? With Garris and Lenny Kerrigan and Gerald Roebuck and the others. How can you be so incurious, Harry? Don't you want to know why Garris blackmailed you into playing that role? Don't you care about what I've sacrificed to keep you safe from him? Don't you wonder why I wake up screaming every night? No, of course you don't. Because you're a selfish coward who can never face the reality of what I really am. So don't pretend you want to know what's happening right now.'

'Scott, please,' he said softly. 'If you ask, I'll tell you—'

'Tell me what?' I snapped. 'That you haven't been going to choir practice? That there *is* no choir? That you can't stand being around me? That I frighten you and so you've found someone else? What's the truth, eh, Harry?' I watched his reflection in the little window, and in his guilt and misery saw my suspicions confirmed. He hadn't been shaping poppet dolls out of wax and murdering psychics. Of course he hadn't. That was laughable, ridiculous. He was Harry Moorhouse. All he'd done was to find a bit of comfort and safety in the arms of someone who didn't terrify him. I felt my heart sink through the floor. You stupid bastard, Jericho. You stupid, stupid ...

'Harry. I'm sorry. I shouldn't have said that.' I gripped the countertop. 'When this is all over, maybe then we can ... ?'

I turned to find the trailer door wide open and Harry gone.

Chapter Twenty-Four

I DECIDED TO PUT HAZ OUT of my mind for good. There was no coming back from what I'd said to him. I even wondered if, subconsciously, I'd done it on purpose – pushing him away as brutally as I could so that he'd never see the real me. Not in its raging, mindless totality anyway. He had someone and I was glad. Well, if not glad, in some sense relieved that at least I knew and now I could concentrate on what I did best.

So I ignored my hollow heart and sat watching the chapel door. It was dark and bitterly cold in the winding medieval streets of Aumbry. The little cathedral city on its hill dominated the flat, rolling fenland for miles around, including that distant stretch of forest which currently enclosed the fair and the rectory. The spire of the great church stood above all, like a ship mast amid a sea of glinting dykes and waterways. Most pilgrims to the city would head straight for that soaring beacon but my focus this evening was a meaner, less traditional house of God. Attached to the door of the derelict schoolhouse was a sign proclaiming: THE CHURCH CHRIST THE REDEEMER: *Enter, sinner, and beg forgiveness.*

I'd already poked my head inside an hour ago, and I had to hand it to Christopher Cloade, you couldn't accuse his poster of false advertising. The building in which his ministry was almost certainly squatting had been about a quarter full, twenty or more lost souls grovelling before his makeshift altar. The spectacle reminded me a little of Dr Gillespie and his disciples, except most of Cloade's congregation had the excuse that they were either tanked up on lager or sky-high on meth. Possibly both. I listened to a vivid description of the agonies of hell and then headed back to my bench on the other side of the street.

Before leaving the fair this afternoon, I'd strolled over to the *Ghost Seekers* production trailers in the hope I might bump into Darrel Everwood. Still reeling from what had happened with Haz, I knew I had to control my emotions. The rawness inside me could easily switch to anger if I tried to force an encounter that was rebuffed. If I was then reported to the police, that might be the end of my cosy relationship with Inspector Tallis.

On the driveway near the house, I'd caught sight of Ben replacing a tyre on that presidential Bentley. He'd glanced up when my shadow fell across him. He looked brighter today, his pale skin smoother, his pupils no longer those worrying fixed points. A grease smudge had marked that freckled snub of a nose while the old cigarette burn in his palm was almost obliterated under a film of dirt.

'All right there, Scott,' he said. 'How're things?'

I almost told him then, everything that had just happened between me and Haz. I've no idea why. Although a word of comfort from a man who'd known me in my darkest moments might have been welcome. Perhaps I had wanted that from him. Perhaps more.

'I'm fine,' I said. 'What's happened here?'

Balanced on his haunches, Ben held up a long iron nail. 'Must have hit it on the journey over last night. Just another thing to put the boss in a bad mood.'

I'd nodded, remembering that Everwood had mentioned the puncture in his self-pitying rant. 'Can I see?'

I took the nail from Ben and rolled it in my palm. It was a masonry nail, exactly the same kind as the dozen or so that had been hammered into Tilda's corpse.

'When exactly do you think this happened?' I asked.

Ben shrugged. 'Could've hit it at any time.'

'But the head is relatively clean.' I showed it to him. 'And the forest road is filthy after days of rain and from our trucks and the punters' cars. So you must have run over it pretty close to where you eventually stopped.' Which either meant that the killer had dropped it as he passed over the drive heading towards the fair or else ... I shook my head. It was a common masonry nail, the kind used by Travellers every day to repair their rides and stalls. It might mean nothing at all. 'Sorry,' I said. 'I'm daydreaming. Have you had any luck getting me a face-to-face with Darrel?'

Ben straightened up and, taking a rag from his back pocket, started cleaning his hands. 'I'm really sorry, Scott. Especially as I know it might be important in finding the scumbag who did this to your aunt, but even the police can't get access to Darrel right now. His manager, old Seb Thorn, has got involved and that guy's like a bulldog protecting his pup. If I even mention you wanting an interview, that'll be my arse kicked to the kerb, and I really need this job.'

'Have you ever met Thorn in person?' I asked.

Ben nodded. 'Just the once, when I first got the gig bodyguarding for Darrel. Bloke reminded me a bit of Mark Noonan, actually; only with a lot more style. He's one of those scary media motherfuckers you don't mess with. Sort of fella where you can feel the power of his personality just rolling off him, know what I mean? One wrong look from Sebastian Thorn and you're going to be sorry about it for the rest of your life.'

'Do you think Darrel's scared of him too?' I wondered.

'I imagine everyone's scared of him. Not that Darrel sees him all that much. The old man hardly ever leaves his mansion. He conducts all his work over the phone and through memos where "fuck" seems to be his favourite word.'

'All right.' I nodded. 'Well, I don't want to put you under any pressure, Ben. I'll see if I can find another way to speak with Darrel.'

I'd started towards the forest road when he called out: 'Are you sure everything's all right, Scott? If you need to talk, you know where I am.'

'I do. Thanks.'

Now, as I watched the doors of the old schoolhouse swing open and Cloade's bedraggled congregation swarm out into the dark, I thought back to those nights Ben and I had shared together. Apart from that one time when he'd revealed the secret of his scar and the abusive father who'd inflicted it, we hadn't talked much about our personal lives. And that seemed to have suited us fine. The sex alone had been enough of a diversion from the ugly world we inhabited. Perhaps that kind of relationship, shallow and functionary, was what I was best fitted for.

I crossed the street and was ready to catch the door when the last worshipper exited. The man, shivering and practically toothless, grinned at me as he popped a biscuit into his mouth and worked it busily around his gums.

'S'all over,' he garbled. 'You're too late to be saved, matey.'

'Tell me something I don't know,' I said, and pressed a tenner into his hand. 'So what do you think of the preacher here?'

He winked, pocketed the money, and running his finger under his lip to make sure he'd got the last of the biscuit, said, 'You a copper?' When I shook my head, he shrugged. 'Preacher man's a fucking loon, but then most of them are. Long as you play along with their claptrap, you get to warm your bones awhile and there's usually something to eat at the end. This one only hands out weak orange drink and broken biscuits, but considering he looks half-beggar hisself, what can you expect? One thing I'll tell you for free.' He motioned me closer and I decided to brave the halitosis. 'There's something not right with him. Not tonight anyway. Been jabbering on more crazy than usual and clutching hold of that good book till his knuckles turned white. Proper loon, like I said. Still, the biscuits weren't half bad.'

I thanked my informer and stepped inside the chapel.

Cloade stood with his back to me, fussing over something at the altar – a simple plank of wood covered with a white cloth and supported on breeze blocks. At the sound of the door, he gave a shrill cry and swept around. I managed to catch sight of a white paper bag, blotched at the bottom with large, reddish-brown stains, before it was thrust into his jacket pocket.

'The evening service is over,' he trilled, stalking towards me. 'If you come tomorrow then—'

'Do you turn sinners away so easily, Christopher?' I asked.

He jerked to a halt. 'Mr Jericho? I ... I'm sorry. I didn't recognise you for a moment. The light in here isn't good. And I fear ...'

I nodded. 'I can see that, Pastor. I think you fear a lot of things. Why don't you tell me about them?'

He lifted a shaking hand to his mouth and twittered like a bird. Meanwhile, those bulbous eyes, red-rimmed and etched with veins, stared at me from behind the broken Cartier frames.

'She's haunting me,' he whispered.

'The little girl you hurt?' I suggested.

He shook his head and clucked. 'No, no, not her. God wouldn't allow her to haunt me. I've prayed and done enough penance to wash that sin clean away. In any case, she isn't dead. Not like *her*.'

'You mean Genevieve Bell? But why would she haunt you?'

'How do you know about me and Genevieve?' He stared at me, then laughed and waved his hand. 'I don't know why she haunts me. All I wanted was to bring her the comfort and solace of the Word. Now I see her everywhere. In my dreams, in the street, outside my window at night, even here in the sanctity of His house. She had no respect for His laws in life and so has none in death. "There shall not be found among you any one who useth divination, or an observer of times, or an enchanter, or a witch." Deuteronomy.'

'Then why don't you cast her out, Christopher? As a man of God, isn't that within your power?'

'I am weak,' he said, leaning in as if to share a confidence. 'And so the right is denied me. Would that I had the strength of that trumpet that felled your walls, O Jericho.'

'I don't think she's haunting you at all, Mr Cloade,' I told him. 'I think it's just good old-fashioned guilt. You tried to con her out of money, didn't you?'

'Those were the wages of sin,' he insisted. 'Earned through foolishness and falsehood. She told me so.'

I nodded, guiding him over to one of the folding chairs that stood before the altar and sitting him down. I then knelt beside him – an old interview technique I'd used with skittish suspects to make them feel as though they were in control by assuming a submissive posture. It also allowed me to get closer to that pocket containing the stained paper bag.

'Why don't you tell me how you first met her?' I said. 'I know you went to Cedar Gables not long after Genevieve's podcast with Dr Gillespie.'

'*Him?*' A puritanical lip was curled. 'He's as damned as she ever was. A materialist putting his faith in the false idol of science. They will all burn, you see? Just as Judas burns in perpetuity for his betrayal and despair. He hung himself high but as the last breath left him, so his soul was dragged down deeper than any.'

'Hanged and then burned, eh?' I nodded. 'Like the witches once were?'

He clapped his hands and stamped his feet like a delighted toddler. 'Yes, yes, well said! She should be burning now, of course, but somehow her soul has escaped perdition. I knew she was a wily one, even when I visited her after the podcast and held out the chance of absolution. She sounded so contrite after her tricks were exposed. So pliable. So broken. I thought she might require my ministry to mend her foolish ways.'

'You thought her a fool, did you?'

'A disciple of the first deceiver. Yes. But ...' He suddenly looked unsure. 'I found her so very weary. A grey-haired woman of forty, not the Delilah I'd expected. Yet she seemed open to reform and redemption. She gave me a contribution to my church and said we should talk again, but afterwards she wouldn't return my calls.'

'And did that make you angry, Pastor? No more money for your mission, no celebrity to endorse your cause?'

His overlarge eyes narrowed. 'She ought *not* to have rejected His beneficence. But she ...' He turned in his chair and gripped my hand in a clammy fist. 'She frightened me, O Jericho. She frightens me still.'

I pulled my hand away. 'What have you got in your pocket, Christopher?'

His startled scream shattered the stillness of the old schoolhouse. It was like the cry of a child scalded with boiling water. What happened next was over so quickly I barely had time to register the pain before I heard the scrape of his chair, his running footsteps, and the chapel door slamming shut behind Christopher Cloade.

Chapter Twenty-Five

I'D BEEN REACHING FOR THE edge of that paper bag protruding from his pocket when I caught a flash of movement. Later, I'd realise that he'd snapped off the broken arm of his glasses and then used the exposed metal prong to stab at my left eye. Fortunately, the man of God had misplaced his aim. The makeshift weapon had pierced the skin of my temple and scraped along the bone, opening up a gash that ran into my hairline. A nasty cut but my sight was saved.

A second after the door slammed, I was on my feet. I'd almost made it out of the chapel when a wash of blood spilled off my brow and into my eyes. Using the cuff of my coat, I cleared my vision, and on seeing that slick, red mess, felt a cold fury unfurl in my chest. Back at the altar, I ripped away the sacred cloth and tore off a strip of material, winding it hastily around my head. Almost at once, I could feel the throb of blood pulsing through the layers.

Outside again, the night air made my senses reel. I doubled over, grabbed my knees, sucked down a huge breath, and looked up. I was certain I must have lost Cloade. But there, at the corner of the street, I saw my toothless informer. He was pointing excitedly towards an alleyway that ran between an off-licence and a chip shop. Fighting back the urge to hurl my guts onto the pavement, I set off in his direction.

'Running like the devil's after him!' my new friend cackled. 'Better catch him before you bleed to death.'

Wheeling into the alley, I glimpsed Cloade as he disappeared through a distant gap in the wall. Men and women appeared to be lounging either side of this spot, the glow of their cigarettes igniting like fireflies in the dark. A few had noticed the raggedy preacher as he passed them and now stood hooting after him. Meanwhile, my footfalls echoed from wall to wall while the fury prickled under my skin.

I'd reached the gap in the wall – the rear entrance, I now realised, to a pub's crowded patio area. Over the heads of the drinkers and smokers, I saw Cloade shoulder his way through a back door and into the heaving bar. I tried to follow but one of the men who'd been hurling catcalls after the preacher suddenly seemed to have a change of heart. The terrified scarecrow in the charity shop suit was clearly the victim here and needed both his and his friends' protection. When I tried to pass, he snatched hold of my collar.

'Hold up, son! Hey, I said, hold up!'

'Take your fucking hands off me,' I grunted.

Not the most diplomatic of responses, it led to Cloade's champion and three of his mates attempting to pin me to the wall. I'd probably lost a quarter of a pint of blood by this stage, but I'd been throwing harder and soberer men than these off fairgrounds since I was fifteen years old. I didn't even need to dig into that bag of bareknuckle tricks my father had taught me. The back of my head shunted into the champion's nose and he slid to the cobbles like a puppet whose strings had been cut. My left elbow then found a yielding cheek. My right, a soft stomach and a ladder of ribs. Turning around, I was confronted with three men on the ground and one still upright, a stray house brick in his fist. He appeared to conduct a short debate with himself, glancing between me and the brick before finally throwing it down and claiming that he 'wasn't looking for any trouble'.

Following Cloade's example, I shouldered my way across the patio. Not that much shouldering was now required. Practically everyone made a path for me and even the bouncer held open the back door.

'He's legged it through the front and into the street,' he said. 'Could tell he was a weirdo, just by looking at him. You a cop or something?'

'Or something,' I agreed.

Just as the cold had set my senses reeling, now the heat of the bar sprang a sickly sweat across the nape of my neck. Customers gawped and glared at me from their tables, a carousel of expressions that blurred into a single hideous leer. By the time I reached the exit, the back of my shirt was drenched and the blood was in my eyes again.

I cannoned into the street, cuffed my face, and gulped down the icy air as thirstily as any drinker back at the bar. Luckily, it seemed I wasn't the only one suffering a disadvantage. The pub let out onto a cobbled hill that ran steeply down towards the riverside. Staggering on his way, pinballing almost from pavement to pavement, the preacher appeared to be running out of steam. I watched for a second as his hands clutched for the support of lampposts and parked cars. And then I saw the broken glasses with their thick lenses in the gutter at my feet and understood that Cloade was running practically blind.

I took off again. Antique shops and chintzy tearooms flashed by, the kind of picture-postcard establishments that tourists delighted in. Now closed for the day, I wondered what their clientele might have thought had they looked up from their Darjeeling to witness a blood-soaked madman hurtling past the window. As it was, there was no one to see as I began to make up the distance that separated me from Cloade.

A blast of car horns, a screech of brakes. The preacher stumbled into the busy road that intersected the bottom of the hill. I followed, dancing around bonnets, glimpsing my Halloween mask of a face in the mirror of windscreens. Then the safety of the far pavement, where the oaths of motorists were drowned out by the roar of the river.

Cloade's head whipped about when I called his name. At first, I wondered if he was going to climb up onto the low concrete parapet and hurl himself into the torrent beyond. Swollen by the recent rains, the black ribbon of the river churned and eddied, whitecaps chasing each other into the vanishing dark. But then I saw him drag the paper bag from his pocket, and pulling back his arm, prepare to launch it over the wall.

My rage overwhelmed me. All the grief and horror and frustration of the past twenty-four hours tearing out of my heart and into the iron grip that closed around the preacher's elbow. I wrenched his arm with such force I was certain I must have dislocated it. The whole limb seemed to slacken and become boneless in my hand, like a stunned fish on the deck. In the end, it was this same force that sent the bag flying from his grasp. Cloade's entire body had surrendered to my attack so that the momentum twisted him back around to face the river where, released from nerveless fingers, the bag tripped lightly across the parapet and dropped into the swell.

Letting go of Cloade, who fell moaning to the pavement, I leaned far out over the wall. The yellow glow from a nearby lamppost helped me locate the sodden pulp of the bag, already disintegrating under fists of water. But this wasn't the sight that held me. Thrown clear of the bag, its contents were drifting like sinuous eels in the sweep of the current, snaking together before finally being pulled apart and separated forever. Black, gleaming, gone: the long lace gloves given to Genevieve Bell by Tilda Urnshaw.

Bloodstained, if those marks on the bag were anything to go by.

I turned back to Cloade.

'She left them for me,' he wept. 'She haunts me, you know.'

Pulling out my phone, I called Tallis.

'I've spoken to our marine unit,' the DCI said. 'The divers are going to give it a go in the morning when the level's down, but they don't hold out much hope. This is a tidal river and it flows fast back up to the Wash. Even before it reaches the sea, there are a hundred different arteries and tributaries and inlets and whatever else.'

'Needle in a haystack.' I nodded and winced.

The paramedic gluing my head back together at the roadside told me not to be a baby. When he was done, I stepped down from the ambulance and wandered with Tallis over to the parapet. There, we looked into the boiling rush.

'There won't be any forensic evidence left anyway,' I said. 'Probably not worth the public expense.'

'Let me worry about that,' Tallis grunted.

'What has Cloade said about it?' I asked.

The preacher had been taken to hospital before being formally interviewed, just to be on the safe side. Despite what I'd initially thought, it appeared his arm remained fully intact. I wasn't sure whether I was glad about that or not.

'Not much. Just that he believes the ghost of Genevieve Bell left her gloves for him in a bloodstained bag on his altar. He's convinced they were hers, by the way. Said he recognised them from his visit to Cedar Gables.'

'But why does he think she'd leave them at his church?' I asked.

'To torment him, he says. "Like the demonic witch she is."' The chief inspector took a pebble from the parapet and sent it skipping across the river. He looked more boyish than ever. 'But why would the killer leave them for Cloade in the first place? Unless *he* is the killer, of course.'

'He's got the conviction but not the brains,' I said, shaking my head. 'It seems to me there are three options here. The killer is playing with Cloade; someone is trying very clumsily to frame him; or else he's working with the murderer.

'In the first two scenarios, the killer must have been at the chapel tonight, disguised as one of the homeless worshippers perhaps. It was dark in the street, so I wouldn't necessarily have recognised anyone if they'd put some effort into their disguise. If it's an attempt to frame him, it was a ridiculous one – they had no guarantee he'd be discovered with the gloves. So that leaves the third scenario, that he might be an accomplice, perhaps helping to divert suspicion.

'Despite what he believes about his ministry, Christopher Cloade is a follower, not a leader. If he could be convinced that his salvation depended on it, there's nothing he wouldn't do.'

'I agree.' Tallis nodded. 'By the way, what do you feel about pressing charges against him for assault?'

I shook my head. 'I'd rather have him out and about. He might lead us to something.'

'Or he might end up killing someone,' Tallis sighed.

'Even if you arrested him, he'd be out on bail soon enough,' I said. 'I can't see that it's worth the effort.'

'All right,' the inspector agreed. 'But I'll still need an official statement from you. Feel up to coming back to the station with me now? I can drop you back to your car later.'

I nodded and we made our way over to Tallis's gleaming Volkswagen Golf. Through the passenger window, I could see an interior as forensically spotless as the car's unblemished bodywork. I even felt guilty about smearing the door handle with my fingerprints. I was about to ask if he was sure he wanted to risk my slightly bloodied trench coat on his upholstery when I caught sight of Haz.

He was coming out of an Italian restaurant across the street. Smiling that warm, open Haz smile as a young man in a dark overcoat helped him on with his jacket. I watched as he turned to thank the man, his hand resting against the stranger's arm. An intimate, trusting gesture. Good-looking, well-built with wavy blond hair and kind eyes, the man then said something and Haz laughed. I hadn't seen him laugh like that in weeks.

'Jericho?' Tallis frowned. 'Everything all right?'

I nodded and opened the passenger door. 'Just laying to rest a few ghosts of my own.'

Chapter Twenty-Six

'*So anything you can't touch and observe and evaluate is a lie? Even love.*'

I woke with only the fragments of the dream still before my eyes. Haz's words and the fading image of him standing with a stranger, the road that divided us expanding and liquifying until it ran like a river. A torrent littered with bloodied gloves and tarot cards and the bloated corpses of the chattering dead. Toothless mouths agape, calling to me with ringing voices ...

My eyes snapped open. Without thinking, I rolled across the bed and pulled my phone from its charger. I didn't even glance at the caller ID before thumbing the screen.

'Huh-ello?'

'Scott, I hope I find you well and ready to talk at last?'

I sat bolt upright. 'No, Peter. You don't.'

Garris sighed. 'I happened to call your father last night, just for a social catch-up. He wondered if we'd had some kind of falling out, not having seen me since Bradbury End. Sharp as ever, your old man. Anyway, he told me about poor Tilda Urnshaw. I'd guessed something of the sort must have happened after seeing the news yesterday morning. I know you won't believe me, but for what it's worth—'

I gripped the phone until the casing squeaked. 'Do you get a kick out of this, you sorry old sack of shit? Pretending you actually have the emotions of a real human being? You're a psychopath, Garris. A fucking soulless monster. We both know that this is just you wanting to wheedle your way back into my head. And you know what? I'm actually tempted to let you in. Maybe it would take someone as twisted as you to make sense of that rat's maze I've got between my ears. But . . . no. I don't think I'm going to tell you anything.'

A beat. I could hear him breathing lightly at the end of the line. 'I could make you tell me,' he said slowly, deliberately. 'I still have the recording, remember? The one where you describe what Harry did to his father.'

I felt the phone casing crack under my hand. 'If you want to hurt anyone, you come after me. Do you hear what I'm telling you? If you so much as look sideways at Harry Moorhouse, then I swear to God, I will make you suffer beyond anything even your diseased mind could invent. Haz deserves . . .' I swallowed hard. 'He deserves his chance to be happy.'

'He deserves his chance,' that neutral voice echoed. 'Something's happened between you, then? Scott, I am truly sorry if—'

I turned off the phone and threw it to the end of the trailer.

Then, my head still pounding, I staggered over to the sink. After making my statement to Tallis at the station last night and him driving me back to my car, I'd asked the inspector if he fancied a drink. It wasn't some desperate rebound thing. I didn't particularly fancy him and I wasn't even sure Tallis swung my way. I just didn't feel quite ready for my own company. Anyway, he'd politely declined and I was soon back at the fair where, after a heroic ten-minute battle, I surrendered to the half-bottle of Scotch and a couple of sleeping pills I'd been saving for just such an occasion.

Now, I poured a bowl of cold water from the canister by the sink and splashed my face, careful to avoid the surgical glue that held my forehead together. My physical pain, at least, seemed to be centred there. A sharp, hot throbbing that made me wonder if the wound was infected. I slapped my tongue against the roof of my mouth, tasted the metallic residue of the sleeping pills. With the waning effect of the drug still in my system, I knew my thoughts would be sluggish for the rest of the day. Some way to catch a killer.

'Selfish bastard,' I muttered to myself, and went in search of my phone.

Two forty-three p.m. The time and a text alert from Tallis glared up at me almost accusatorially.

The message ran:

Nothing more from Cloade. He still insists he found the bag on the altar after the evening service. Refuses to give names or even descriptions of his congregation. The homeless man you mentioned is known to us and I managed to have a word with him this morning. He thanks you for the tenner. Says those attending the church come and go – no particular regulars and he doesn't know all of them. No one stands out in his memory. First sweep by the marine unit has come up empty-handed – no sign of Genevieve's gloves . . . I'm sorry, btw, if I seemed standoffish last night. Maybe a friendly drink when the case is done. All for now. Tom

I washed and dressed quickly, pulling a beanie hat over my wounded forehead before stepping outside. I had some thought of checking the communal post box by the gate to see if my copy of *Hearing the Dead* had arrived ahead of schedule when Sal ran into my path. She'd been playing a chase game with Jodie and the other chavvies. Her expression darkened when she saw me. The munchkin herself squealed and started to dash over, asking breathless questions about Haz. 'Did you hear our song for Aunt Tilda? Is Uncle Haz coming back again today? Can we go and see him if not?' Sal ordered her away and I could see the tears start in Jodie's uncomprehending eyes.

'What the hell have you done now?' Sal demanded when her daughter was at a safe distance. 'I called him this morning and he sounds devastated, Scott. Just bloody devastated. Of course, he'd never say a word against you, but I could tell—'

'Enough,' I said. 'Sal, I mean it. *Enough*. What goes on between me and Haz is none of your business.' When she started to argue back, I shot her a look I would later regret. 'I don't want to hear any more about it. Not from you, not from anyone. Are we clear?'

'You're on something again,' she said in a brittle, cracked voice. 'Pills or booze or both. Is that why he left?'

I felt my lips twitch into a hard smile. 'Whatever you think he sounded like this morning, he's most definitely *not* devastated. He's got someone else, OK? I've seen them together, and you know what? I'm happy for him. Genuinely. And you and Jodie and everyone else who's fallen in love with Harry Moorhouse on this fair should be happy for him too. I was never worthy of being loved by someone like that.'

Sal's face crumpled at my words. 'Scott. No. What are you saying? Of course you're worthy—'

I pushed her hands away when she tried to reach for me. 'I don't want to hear it. If you ever speak to me about him again, Sal, that's it. We're done.'

I left her on the side ground and made my way towards the forest road. I already felt sickened by what I'd said, but I couldn't bring myself to turn back and start making apologies. That would only lead to more discussion on a subject that made my heart ache. Fortunately, a diversion was ready and waiting on the driveway to the rectory. Everwood's Bentley appeared to have suffered another puncture and he was standing to one side of the car with Deepal Chandra while a furious John Chambers screamed in his face. Meanwhile, Mrs Chambers hovered behind her husband, making ineffectual attempts to pull him away.

'Do you have the slightest idea what you've done to us?' Chambers asked, a spray of spittle flying from his lips. 'To our family? To my *wife*? Show him, Anne.' When Anne Chambers tried to resist, he dragged her forward so that she stood almost toe to toe with Everwood. The psychic shrank back. 'Go on, show him.'

Both Everwood and Deepal looked on, horrified as the grieving mother's coat sleeves were pulled up and her scarred forearms displayed. Even from a distance, I could see those intersecting tracks glinting in the pallid autumn daylight. Mrs Chambers flinched while her husband raged on and Deepal took out her phone.

'You ripped our hope away,' he shrieked. 'Tore out the last of it so we had nothing left. Even if we didn't believe what you said about Debbie, everywhere we looked – the papers, the telly, the internet – there you were, insisting over and over: she's dead. Dead, dead, dead, *dead*! No one should *ever* do such a thing to people who are suffering like we are. People who've lost something so precious. It's cruel. Inhuman. And why did you do it, eh? For a few column inches, for another scrap of attention to feed your fucking ego? You deserve to burn in hell for that, Darrel Everwood.'

Chambers started to lunge forward, and reaching the group at a run, I caught him under the arms and hauled him back. He was a small man, almost weightless, and I wondered if the stress of the past six months had eaten away not only at his nerves, but his body. He felt like a bundle of loose bones under that waterproof jacket, a frame on the point of disintegration.

Dragging him towards the car park, I shouted back at Deepal, 'Don't call the police. Let me handle this.'

Anne Chambers threw the PA a pitiful look. 'Please. It won't happen again, I promise.'

Meanwhile, Everwood appeared to be watching me closely.

Near the opening to the avenue of trees, I released John Chambers. He spun around to face me, almost tripping over his own feet so that I was forced to catch him again before he fell into the mud. It made me ashamed to do it. As if I'd stripped away some vital last layer of his dignity. Anne hurried to his side and clutched at his arm, pulling him back when he tried to confront me.

'Who are you?' he demanded. 'What gives you the right to—?'

'My name's Scott Jericho,' I said. 'And believe me, Mr Chambers, I have no sympathy for Darrel Everwood, but nor do I want to see you arrested. I used to be a detective and I'd like to help you, if I can.'

'You know our story?' Anne looked at me with such hope in her eyes I almost had to turn away. 'Do you think our daughter could still be alive?'

'I think ...' These broken people – they'd been tormented for so long by a psychic's guesswork – I at least owed them the truth. 'It's very unlikely.' I sighed. 'But you'll have been told all the statistics. Keeping Debbie alive this long would have become too much of a risk for whoever took her. I'm so sorry.'

As her husband crumpled against her shoulder, Anne turned a defiant gaze upon me. Despite initial appearances, she was by far the stronger of the two. I could hear that inner steel ringing in her words.

'You're wrong,' she said. 'I know you are. She told us that our girl was alive and that, if we could only hold on a little longer, we'd see her again.'

'Who told you?'

'The fortune teller.' She lifted her face to the ash-grey sky and her smile became so radiant I thought I caught a glimpse of the young mother she'd once been. 'She asked us to call her Aunt Tilda. She promised that I'd hold my little girl in my arms again. That on All Hallows' Day, Debbie would find her way back to us, through water and wood, until the red eye guided her home. She wanted us to know that Darrel Everwood was wrong about Debbie – wrong about everything.'

Anne looked over to where the psychic remained, staring back at us.

'The dead do speak,' she insisted. 'But not to him. They never did.'

Chapter Twenty-Seven

Standing there, looking at Debbie Chambers' shell of a father and her somehow still hopeful mother, I remembered Everwood's accusation that this couple had murdered their daughter and that their subsequent hounding of him was simply a campaign designed to divert suspicion. I'd met many child-killers in my time on the force. They ranged from the worst sadists imaginable to the most devoted of parents who, nursing a terminally ill infant, had been unable to bear its suffering any longer. But in the Chambers' pain, I didn't sense the callous inhumanity of the former, nor the poignant peace that had settled over the latter.

These people were tortured with doubt, with questions, with what-ifs, with shadows on the wall that wouldn't let them rest. Just like Miss Rowell seemed to project her sense of anger and betrayal onto Darrel Everwood for the sins of her husband, so the Chambers used him as a target for their guilt. He was their poppet, if you like, an effigy they could stab at when the trauma of what they'd done became too much. That he deserved all of their venom wasn't the point.

'It wasn't your fault,' I told them gently. 'You couldn't have watched her every second of every day. John, Anne, listen to me. I've known depraved men like the one who took your daughter. He'd have become fixated on her, stalked you as a family, learned your routines. He'd have found his chance sooner or later. You can't go on blaming yourselves.'

John blinked at me as if coming out of a daze. 'Not my fault?' he said through clenched teeth. His body started to shake, tears flicking from the corners of his eyes. 'She was *my* daughter. It was my job to watch her, always.'

'No.' I took hold of his arms, steadying him. 'It was your job to care for her and love her, and you did that. You're still doing it, both of you. But chasing after Darrel Everwood, trying to make him pay for the shitty thing he did, that isn't helping Debbie or yourselves.'

Anne smoothed her husband's hair from his brow. 'Listen to him, love.'

'But we *should've* been watching her,' John insisted. 'It was me who told her to go and play outside. She didn't even want to. She said she was enjoying playing tea parties with her teddies in her room. But she was such a demanding girl and we'd hardly any time to ourselves and I only—'

'We were having sex when Debbie was taken,' Anne said, her tone flat, her eyes glassy. 'For the first time in weeks. Just a moment to ourselves, and then afterwards . . .'

I nodded. In their minds, the act that had brought their daughter into the world had then taken her from it. I could easily picture the days and weeks that followed. I'd seen it a dozen times in similar cases – a storm of unspoken recrimination battering at what they had imagined to be the solid walls of their marriage. When the diversions of police and media interest had faded, the Chambers had found themselves strangers, pottering around in a house full of ghosts. Then all it had taken was a frosty word, a misinterpreted look, a misjudged smile perhaps, gestures that could easily insinuate themselves into tiny fissures until slowly, slowly those once-sturdy walls began to break apart.

And then the mixed blessing of the psychic had exploded into their empty lives. The little candle they'd passed between each other, sheltering it even as they drifted apart – the hope that one day their daughter might return to them – Darrel Everwood had threatened to blow out that light for good. To leave them scattered in the dark and utterly alone. And for a time, he had succeeded.

Without a word, one morning Anne Chambers had handed over the safe-keeping of that fragile flame to her husband. She'd seen him off to work and then, perhaps taking one last look inside her daughter's bedroom, had gone and drawn herself a hot bath, removing a blade from her husband's razor and laying it on the side of the tub. I didn't believe that John had accidentally forgotten his briefcase and returned home just in time. Where the people we love are concerned, we're all detectives, to a greater or a lesser degree, and sometimes, just sometimes, we're lucky too. I think John Chambers had noticed something that morning before he left for work – a passing clue that had made him turn back. A word, a look, a movement that he could probably no longer recall but which had ended up saving Anne's life.

'You told her that this was your fight now,' I said, turning from a stricken John to his wife. 'To hold Darrel Everwood to account, to challenge him publicly whenever you could, to make sure no one suffered again like you had suffered. It was a project you could work on together, a mission to live for. And a way to unload a little of that awful guilt you carry.'

'And I'm tired of it, John,' Anne told him. 'We have our hope again, don't we? It's enough.'

'But I don't believe it,' the man cried. 'That old woman, how could she know anything?'

'You visited my aunt on the night she was killed,' I said. 'Do you remember what time that was?'

'It was just after eight o'clock,' Anne said. 'That bodyguard of Everwood's had thrown us off the fairground earlier but we came back.'

'Why?'

'Because I'd read an interview with Darrel Everwood's ex-fiancée, the one in which she said he was a fraud. She mentioned a book about a celebrity psychic from years ago that had prompted him to get into the racket. That was the word she used, "racket". She said he'd had no interest in the paranormal until he read about this woman's life and saw how much money she'd made from it. He knew he could use the skills he'd learned as a magician to replicate most of the psychic's tricks.

'Anyway, the interview piqued my interest. It took a while, I had to do a little digging into old newspaper articles, but eventually, I found the name of the woman and the book – *Hearing the Dead: The Story of Genevieve Bell*. Again, it took some time, but I finally tracked down a copy and saw the name of your aunt mentioned in one of the early chapters. We thought—' she glanced at John '—*I* thought, if we could consult the medium who'd inspired the original Genevieve Bell then we might get a real psychic's opinion on what had happened to Debbie.'

'The original Genevieve Bell,' I murmured. 'Did you try to contact her too?'

Anne shook her head. 'We tried writing but she never answered. By the time we thought of actually just turning up at her house, she was dead.'

'How did my aunt seem to you during the reading?' I asked.

'Very calm. Very kind.' Anne frowned. 'But resigned, in a way. As if she'd made up her mind to accept something.'

I nodded, recalling Tilda's words from the night before her death. *Whatever happens, it's nobody's fault. I want you to remember that.* Had she known what was coming for her? And if she had, might she have accepted her fate as some kind of justice?

'Did you notice anything unusual in the tent or outside it when you left? Anyone hanging around, maybe?'

John shook his head. He seemed more composed now. 'I don't think so. But then almost everyone except us was in costume – vampires, werewolves, ghosts, Frankenstein monsters, superheroes – we would've been the ones who stuck out like a sore thumb. Might even have saved us a few quid on the gate if we'd bothered to dress up.'

'My dad announced the half-price costume concession that morning,' I said slowly, then turned my attention back to the Chambers. 'And afterwards, when you heard about the murder?'

'We were terrified,' Anne said. 'After Debbie's disappearance, we'd naturally come under police suspicion. All parents do in such cases, I believe. Plus, we'd heard that Everwood was spreading a rumour that we'd had something to do with it. I had an entire search history on my computer at home, full of stories about Genevieve Bell and Darrel and Tilda Urnshaw and fake medium exposés. And there we were, two apparently unhinged parents visiting a fortune teller just minutes before she was brutally murdered.'

'And Genevieve's book?' I said eagerly. 'Do you happen to have your copy with you?'

'I'm sorry, no. We're staying at a local hotel and the book is back at home.' She turned to John. 'Which is where we should be. Not persecuting that ignorant, stupid man, but waiting for Debbie to come home to us. Just two more days, John, and we'll see our girl again.'

He looked me square in the face. 'Do you believe that, Mr Jericho? That your aunt could really see such a thing?'

I thought back to my childhood, to those short years of unquestioning belief before all the monsters and miracles are stripped away from us. Back then, I had believed without question in my mother's bedtime stories, in my father's invincibility, in Aunt Tilda's third eye that could see into veiled worlds and futures yet to come.

'It doesn't matter what I believe,' I told them. 'But if you feel you need my help at any time, please call.'

I pulled a page from the notebook in my back pocket, scribbled my number, and handed it to Anne Chambers. Together, they then turned and walked away down the forest road.

I watched until they disappeared among the trees. Something they'd said about their visit to Tilda's nagged at me. Not the extraordinary claim that their daughter would soon return to them, but a detail so bland in comparison it was difficult to draw it from my memory. It seemed to link up with a comment someone else had made in recent days. Not about the case itself – or at least not obviously – just a stray passing remark.

It was no good. Maybe if my brain hadn't been so fried with last night's booze and sleeping pills, I might have realised the significance of what the Chambers had just told me. Would it have saved lives in the end? I'm not sure. I might have dismissed it anyway as a flimsy coincidence. Suggestive perhaps, but no more than that. In any case, I now had to roll the dice with Darrel Everwood.

Chapter Twenty-Eight

WALKING BACK TOWARDS THE MEDIUM and his PA, I considered my reaction to what had probably been Aunt Tilda's final prediction. It had come from a kinder, more generous place than Darrel Everwood's pronouncement of death – I doubted Tilda had even taken any money from the Chambers – but in its effect, it could prove even more devastating. Every hope of these shattered people now rested on an old woman's conviction that their daughter would somehow return to them. When that failed to happen? I didn't like to think about the consequences.

'Well?' Everwood asked as I approached.

'They've had their say,' I told him. 'I think they'll stay away from you from now on. No need to involve the police.'

I could see him visibly deflate. 'Thank Christ. I told you we should have sorted a face-to-face with them months ago,' he shot at Deepal. 'But no, you thought that would just "inflame interpersonal tensions" or some such PR drivel. And now look what's happened – they've vandalised my bloody car again.' He strode over to the Bentley and kicked a monogrammed cowboy boot against his punctured tyre. 'I told Benny I was sure they'd done the first one, but he wouldn't have it. Said it was just a stray nail on the driveway.'

'Where is your bodyguard?' I asked.

'I sent him on an errand,' Everwood grunted. 'Never around when I need him. Anyway, I'm very grateful for what you did, Mr . . . ?'

'Jericho.'

'Jericho from the fair?' He frowned. 'I thought you'd be older.'

'You're thinking of my dad. I've been waiting for an opportunity to talk to you, Mr Everwood. It was my aunt who was killed the other night and I wondered if I could get any insights you might have into the murder. She was a psychic, too, you see? A fortune teller. I don't know much about these things personally, but wouldn't gifted people like yourselves have an intuition about each other? If something bad had happened while you were in the same vicinity, you might feel the passing of their soul or whatever?'

'Not intuition,' Everwood objected. 'Knowledge, Mr Jericho. Accurate, professional knowledge. So Tilda Urnshaw was your aunt?'

'I'm not sure this is a good idea,' Deepal interjected, throwing me an annoyed glance. 'I'm certain that Mr Thorn would have something to say about it.'

'Seb's my manager, not my employer, whatever he might think,' Everwood said, cutting her dead. 'I can make my own decisions about who I talk to. It would be my pleasure to meet with you, Mr Jericho.'

'Do you have a spare five minutes now?' I suggested. 'I mean, unless your personal assistant has any objections?'

The psychic took the bait. 'She certainly does *not*. Deepal, you wait here for Ben and then get him straight to work on that fucking tyre.' He threw his arm around my shoulder and I almost choked on the reek of expensive cologne. 'Me and my new mate are off for a chinwag. Do not disturb.'

'But Mr Thorn won't like it,' Deepal called after us.

'Mr Thorn ain't here,' Everwood shouted over his shoulder. Then, in a softer tone, 'That old bastard is never around when I need him.'

Keys clearly being for lesser mortals, Everwood's trailer was accessed by a palm-print reader. His biometrics scanned, the medium tripped up the stairs and into an almost absurd level of luxury. Granite countertops, illuminated makeup table, crocodile leather upholstery, an entertainment system that took up a third of the floorspace, even a low-hanging chandelier to crack your skull against. Everwood waved me onto the couch while he flicked the switch on a complicated-looking coffee machine.

'Can I get you one?' he asked, that stage cockney accent slipping already.

'No, I'm good,' I said, my gaze playing around the plush interior. 'So your manager isn't on the scene very much then, Mr Everwood? Even when you have a big show coming up?'

'The media event of the century,' Everwood muttered. 'Have you seen the socials? They've been blowing up for weeks now. Seems like the world can't talk about anything else except this Halloween gig of ours. The great ignorant British public. If only they knew ...' He blinked hard. 'But you were saying something about Seb? No, he never shows up in the days before a broadcast. Not his style. Don't get me wrong, he's been good for me. Built my career, gave me my first shot, kept me sane. Well, more or less. And there's no one better in the business when it comes to negotiating a new deal, putting the thumbscrews on the money men, cleaning up a mess, that sort of thing. But he's not one for the limelight. That's my department, so he says. Seb's more comfortable down in his mansion, pulling all our strings from afar like the controlling puppet master he is. Or thinks he is ... Anyway. You wanted to know something about, what was it again?' His brow corrugated, as if he'd already forgotten who I was and what I was doing there.

'I happened to catch sight of you on the night my aunt died,' I told him. 'Part of my job is fairground security, patrolling the site, keeping everyone safe. I was passing when Deepal told you what had happened to Tilda. You seemed upset.'

'Did I?' He pulled the little espresso cup away from the tray, downed its scalding contents without flinching, and immediately refilled. 'Well, it was a shock, I suppose.'

'Did you know my aunt, then?'

'Know her?' The machine clanked, gurgled, dribbled into the cup. 'Not personally. I'd heard of her, of course.'

'From where?'

Throwing back the coffee, he moved to the rear of the trailer, returning a few moments later with a tattered, well-loved paperback. I recognised the book immediately – a dandelion-yellow cover with black, curling font and a photograph on the front of a teenage girl, her gloved hands raised in a defensive posture. Everwood handed the book to me almost reverently.

'You know what my ex has been saying about me?' he asked, dropping into a chair. 'Well, the only part of her bullshit story that's even vaguely true is that I *did* read Genevieve Bell's book, and yes, you could say it inspired me. Not to fake my psychic abilities, but to help people. That was what Genevieve did, right up until the day she died. Used her God-given gifts to comfort grieving families and to let them know there is something beyond all this pain and misery.'

'So you were never a children's party magician?' I asked, slipping the book into a gap between two crocodile-covered cushions.

'I was, as it happens. And so what if I once made a living entertaining a load of snotty-nosed brats? I was too young then to realise I already had a gold mine up here.' He tapped his temple. 'I'd always heard voices, you get me? Right from when my mum kicked me down the stairs when I was a nipper and I hit my head on the banister. Concussion, two days in hospital. After that, our flat was spook central. Saw me granny first, sitting in her old chair by the window, smoking them little Russian cigarettes that had ended up killing her three years before. I could even smell the fucking things, so don't tell me I've made all this up. You ask Deepal, ask Ben, ask Seb Thorn, ask any of them.'

The espressos were clearly having an effect. I held up a soothing hand. 'I believe you, Darrel. Don't forget, my aunt was a psychic too.'

Mollified, he shuffled back into his chair. 'Sorry. No offence. It's just, when you're surrounded by haters, it's hard to relax. What was I saying?'

'About how the book inspired you?'

'Right.' He rubbed his hands together. 'So my mum died when I was eighteen – drunk herself to death at last, the vicious cow – and from then, I was pretty much on me own. The magic stuff was ticking along, nothing special. Then I read the book, and I saw how this little girl, who could do the same things I could, had made a mint out of it. I started making notes, following things up, putting out feelers, and before you know it, I've got my first psychic gig lined up. I signed with a manager, and within a year or two, I'm packing theatres up West and there's even talk of my own TV show.' He started laughing – a high, hysterical, hyena-like chuckle. 'You know something, Mr Jericho? I bless the day my mother booted me down them stairs. Must have dislodged a psychic screw, so Seb Thorn says.'

I wondered if Thorn, the ruthless absentee puppet master, knew very well what effect that injury might have had on his client. Almost every psychopath I'd ever met had suffered some form of head trauma in their early years. Hearing voices wasn't an unusual symptom.

'The one thing I didn't cotton onto was how it all ended for Genevieve Bell,' Everwood went on. 'How the public attention got too much for her and she had to hide herself away. There was a lesson there, if only I'd listened.'

'And it was in the book that you first heard about my aunt?'

He nodded. 'Tilda Urnshaw. She was like the Obi-Wan to Genevieve's Luke Skywalker.' He cackled. 'I was looking forward to meeting her.'

'You knew she travelled with us?'

'I'd looked up the fair's website when we did the deal with your father. The show's going to look spectacular, by the way. Introductory drone shots of the fair, then zooming in on the house, the *Ghost Seekers* theme kicking in. Always something creepy about a carnival, isn't there? And then a haunted house is the Halloween double-whammy. Anyway, I saw Tilda's name and photograph on your website. Recognised it straightaway from that chapter in *Hearing the Dead*. I was even thinking of paying her a visit the night we arrived, just as soon as Ben got back from his patrol.'

'But you didn't?'

'Course not. She was dead or dying by then, wasn't she?'

'But you didn't know that,' I said. 'It was roughly another hour before the police arrived. You could've got Ben to walk you over to the tent.'

'Had second thoughts, didn't I?' Everwood sniffed. 'It was bloody cold out.'

'Why did you come here so early?' I asked. 'I saw you and Deepal paying a visit to the rectory the other night, way ahead of schedule. The rest of the production team aren't supposed to arrive until tomorrow morning, are they?'

'I ... I always show up before the ... before the rabble descends,' he said, faltering a little. 'All the noise and confusion and radio signals from the crew interfere with my psychic frequencies. I like to attune myself to the haunting before the show goes live.'

I didn't detect any obvious play-acting on Everwood's part. I wondered, hammy as his on-screen persona was, did he actually believe all this? Just because Dr Gillespie was convinced that, unlike Genevieve, Darrel was a conscious fraud, that didn't mean his assessment was accurate. It may have started that way, but as Evangeline had described in her sister's case, a psychic's idea of themselves can change over time. It might even be psychologically necessary to protect their sense of self-worth.

'Going back to your reaction to Tilda's death,' I said. 'You certainly looked very distraught.'

'I was.' He said it in a wondering sort of tone, as if he couldn't quite believe the reaction himself. 'I don't know. Someone killing her after she was part of the same story that made me what I am. It felt personal.'

An echo of what Tilda had said about the poppet resounded in my head. To her it felt haunted, *But not by spirits. By a living person's spite and wickedness. It feels . . . personal.* That intimate thread, perhaps, connecting the life of Genevieve Bell to the fates of those she'd touched.

'Did you ever meet Gennie?' I asked.

'Who?' He shook his head. 'Sorry, I've never heard her called that. Stupid of me. No, I . . . I didn't get the chance. I'd have done anything to, of course. I mean, her powers when she was a kid were off the scale – mediumship, telekinesis, precognition, apportation, automatic writing, telepathy – almost the entire paranormal set.'

'But she didn't believe in those gifts herself,' I said. 'Not in the end.'

Everwood's expression soured. 'That bastard Gillespie wormed his way into her thinking. That man's like a cancer, you know. He eats away at all that's pure and good.'

'Great minds,' I said. 'He recently described you as a cancer too.' I sat forward on the couch. 'Tell me, why were you afraid to come to Purley Rectory?'

He jerked away as if I'd threatened to strike him. 'Who told you that?'

'Are you afraid?' I pressed. 'Maybe you've received some kind of threat you haven't told Deepal or Ben about? Something personal you wouldn't want leaking to the press, especially with everything going on with your ex.'

He licked his lips. 'Why should I trust you?'

'I'm Tilda Urnshaw's family,' I said. 'I want this killer caught.'

His eyes darted to the trailer door. 'You know what they think, don't you? My manager and the producers. That I can't stand the pressure anymore and that I'll say anything to get the event called off.'

'And would you?'

'Maybe I would have. I was frightened that I'd crack up live on-air and that my career would be over. That would have killed me, sure as anything. But then I had my eyes opened to the truth. An incredible truth.' He looked down at his hands and smiled. 'But I'm not going to say anything. Not until the time's right. Then the world is going to know exactly what's been going on here, and all the doubters will see just how wrong they've been. Trust me, Mr Jericho.' His smile became almost dreadful. 'It really is going to be the media event of the century.'

Chapter Twenty-Nine

THE DOOR BURST OPEN AND Ben and Deepal stormed inside.

'That's it,' the PA ordered. 'We're done here.'

I looked at Everwood and saw immediately that I'd get no help from that quarter. It was as if he'd taken a handful of those sleeping pills that had knocked me out the night before. His eyes had an unfocused, foggy look and he gazed back at me as if I was a complete stranger. During my short interview with him, I'd noticed how his attention would wander, sudden flares of intensity lapsing into virtual incomprehension. Whatever substance issues he might have, he seemed to be in the grip of a genuine persecution disorder. One in which he now believed he was about to turn the tables on his enemies and prove to them, once and for all, that his powers were real. I wondered who'd implanted such an idea in his head and why?

'I've just got off the phone with Sebastian Thorn,' Deepal said, more to me than to Everwood. 'He says that, unless Mr Jericho leaves immediately, the *Ghost Seekers*' legal team will seek full damages against Jericho Fairs for breach of contract. It was stipulated in the deal with EverThorn Media that there should be no direct contact between any employee of Jericho Fairs and Mr Everwood.'

Sebastian Thorn, the puppet master reaching out again. Was there something in that? A distant, unknown personality pulling all our strings and setting us to dance? But what would be Thorn's motive in the ritual slaughter of strangers? Unless it was personal in some way. Was this like Peter Garris and the Bradbury End murders? Was Thorn enacting some kind of gruesome, elaborate farce? If so, why? I glanced at the nervy, distracted Darrel. Perhaps to drive his fragile client out of his mind. After all, I didn't know anything about the history between the two men, the resentments, the slights, the animosities that might have grown up over the years of their partnership. Even if Darrel was Thorn's cash cow, could there be some festering motivation that overrode mere money? I mentally shook myself. This theory of an unknown factor didn't feel right. I was fairly certain that I had all the major clues and suspects in front me, I just needed to understand the pattern in what I had already seen and heard.

While Deepal had been reading me the riot act, I'd discreetly claimed Darrel's copy of *Hearing the Dead* from among the sofa cushions. More necessary for a private detective than keen eyes and brilliant deductions was a coat with capacious pockets. Now I held up innocent hands and moved with Ben to the door.

'No harm done,' I assured her. 'Thank you for your time, Mr Everwood, and good luck with the show.'

He blinked and grinned after me. 'Be sure you tune in from the start. You wouldn't want you to miss the big reveal.'

'The media event of the century, so I hear.'

He laughed and clapped his hands, a little like Christoper Cloade had done a few moments before he'd tried to impale my left eye. 'That's right. Who told you?'

Back outside with the door closed behind us, I turned to Ben. 'What the hell are they thinking?'

He shrugged, feigning ignorance. 'Don't know what you're talking about.'

'Come on.' I gestured towards the trailer. 'He's barely holding it together. Look, what Everwood did to the Chambers proves that he's a self-obsessed piece of garbage, but he's also very clearly not well. They can't seriously be thinking of putting him on live television tomorrow night?'

Ben made a hushing gesture, and planting his palm in the small of my back, directed me to the rear of the rectory. Here, the hibernating forest bustled up against the house, its naked fingers dreamily caressing the stone and glass of Purley. In the failing light, Ben clasped and unclasped his hands, the burn his father had branded him with appearing and vanishing like a marked card in a conjurer's deck.

'Darrel's losing it, I know,' he said in a fretful whisper. 'We all know. But what do you think any of us can do about it? When he isn't throwing espressos down his throat, one after the other, it's the booze or the uppers or the downers. Our old pal Mark Noonan would've made a fortune off him. Anyway, I overheard Deepal talking to Thorn. The plan is to get him shipped off to some kind of detox retreat as soon as the broadcast is over. But they've all got too much riding on this to let him pull out now. They've sold the advertising space, spent fortunes on marketing and publicity. He just has to get through it.'

'And if he doesn't?'

Ben blew out his cheeks. 'Then he's fucked. And Deepal's fucked, and I'm fucked, and anyone who works for him is fucked.'

'At least he isn't afraid anymore,' I said. 'He even seems to be looking forward to the show. When did that happen?'

'Sometime last night.' Ben scratched the nape of his neck. 'It was weird. Up until then, he kept saying the same stuff about how coming to Purley was going to be the end of him.'

I nodded. 'It fitted in with the paranoia he'd built up following his fiancée's attacks and Gillespie's campaign against him. His whole professional and personal existence is on the line. His reputation, his wealth, his own idea of himself. If he fails here, that life – the only life he sees any value in – could be over. A reality so terrifying he might even have considered cancelling the event. But suddenly it's like he's got an ace up his sleeve. Some huge revelation that will redeem him in the eyes of the public, perhaps even convince mockers like Gillespie.'

'All I know is, he got a call just before midnight,' Ben said. 'Unidentified number on his personal mobile. I only caught the beginning of the conversation. At first, Darrel acted like it was a prank. "That's some sick shit you're talking," he said. "How dare you even pretend to be . . ." And then his mouth clamped shut. Honestly, Scott, the look on his face – it was like someone had reached down that phone and shown him that every nightmare and every dream he'd ever known was real. He couldn't get me out of the trailer fast enough.'

'Did you tell Deepal and Thorn?' I asked.

'Darrel swore me to secrecy,' Ben said. 'Promised I'd get a raise if I kept my mouth shut.'

'And that's all you know about the call?'

'Pretty much. But from that moment, his attitude towards the whole broadcast changed. I think he actually can't wait for tomorrow night.'

Movement high up in the house suddenly snagged my attention. Framed like a human spider in the dusty web of an oculus window, Miss Rowell looked down upon us. Whether or not she could have overheard what we'd been discussing, she shrank back when she caught my eye, like a guilty thing startled.

I said goodbye to Ben and traipsed back through the fair to my trailer. Funny how quickly that possessive 'my' had slipped back into how I thought about the place – until yesterday it had been 'our trailer'. The thought almost winded me but I shoved both it and Haz aside. I had a good few hours of reading ahead of me and I needed to stay focused.

After throwing together a quick sandwich and downing a pint of water with two paracetamol, I peeled the beanie from my forehead and examined the wound Cloade had inflicted. It looked red and felt hot to the touch. I'd have to get some antibiotics or something in the morning.

Pulling the book from my coat pocket, I settled myself on the bed and began to read. Despite its fantastical subject matter, *Hearing the Dead* wasn't the most absorbing of biographies. The ghostwriter – had that job title ever been more apt? – made plodding work of the early life of Genevieve Bell, repeating the bare facts and figures from her birth certificate, school reports, childhood illnesses, locations and durations of holidays, placings in sports day events, a prize from a local drama competition. It was exhaustive, colourless, and without any emotional detail. My eye started to skim over the pages.

I was disappointed. I had thought some clue might be waiting for me here. A key that would unlock the mystery of why anyone would centre a pathological hatred for psychics on Genevieve Bell. Pretty much all of it I already knew, either from my research or from what Evangeline had told me. Obviously, the reality of the supernatural was never questioned in this account. No suggestion here that it had all begun as a game between the two sisters. Gennie's powers were demonstrably genuine and had been honed and nurtured by the kindly fortune teller, Tilda Urnshaw. Three mentions in total for Tilda. I wondered if she might still be alive had the ghostwriter left her out of the narrative.

In the end, *Hearing the Dead* seemed to work just as well as my knock-out pills. After a short, dreamless sleep, I jerked awake not to the roar of the fair but to its silence. Tossing the open book from my chest, I stood up, stretched, and poked my head out of the trailer door. A bracing gust of night air greeted me. Out across the fairground, generators were whirring to a stop as the lights on the rides winked into darkness. I checked my phone – ten past midnight.

Halloween and the day of the broadcast had arrived.

Away to my left, an engine started and a wash of headlights swept across the forest. Illuminated, I saw a couple of Tallis's constables stationed near the car park wave down the driver. It was Ben, pale-faced behind the wheel of the Bentley. I dragged on my coat and hurried over, just in case he needed someone to vouch for him.

Caught by the breeze, I heard his voice as he explained, 'Mr Everwood wants me to check on something. I should be back in a couple of hours.'

The officers tapped the roof and the Bentley moved on. Probably just another of the medium's eccentric whims, I thought.

I finally finished *Hearing the Dead* just before 3 a.m. It had taken the story of Genevieve right up to the moment that her fame had reached its zenith. I knew from my research that not many months after publication, Gennie had begun her long retreat from the spotlight. Again, I felt frustrated. There was nothing here that could help me identify the killer, or any future victim. Just a catalogue of names, dates, instances of absurd paranormal phenomena drily recorded . . .

I stopped dead. I had been flicking idly through the book when I saw that the title page had become stuck to the inside cover. The paper was brittle, crinkled, and I imagined something sticky must once have been spilled over it. Carefully, I edged a thumbnail between the leaves and began to tease them apart. Most of the page came away undamaged, so that I could make out an inscription scribbled in faded blue ink beneath the title:

For Darrel, in the hope that I can do the same for you as I did for Genevieve. Here's to the future, kid! Seb Thorn.

What had Darrel said he'd done after reading the book? *I started making notes, following things up, putting out feelers . . . I signed with a manager, and within a year or two, I'm packing theatres up West . . .* An ambitious young man, he had wanted to emulate Genevieve Bell, and so of course he would have sought out the publicist who'd made her famous. Sebastian Thorn, now one half of EverThorn Media and co-owner of global TV sensation *Ghost Seekers*. Gennie Bell's original manager. An experienced promoter and enabler of psychics.

And in the mind of a killer perhaps, a creator of witches.

Chapter Thirty

THE FACE OF HER SISTER'S former publicist was before me when Evangeline Bell answered my call. She sounded exhausted. I wasn't surprised. It was almost four in the morning.

'Yes? Who is this?'

'Miss Bell, I'm sorry to disturb you. I wouldn't have called if I didn't think it was important. This is Scott Jericho.'

I heard a rustle of covers, the click of a lamp. Evangeline cleared her throat. 'Mr Jericho. Has something happened? Please don't tell me another—'

'I hope not,' I said. 'I'm connecting a couple of dots here and I need your help. You told me that, after Gennie started coming to the attention of the press, the family was contacted by a publicist. You said his name was Rose?'

'Oh,' she sighed wearily. 'Something like Rose. A smart, smooth-talking, oily sort of man in his forties. My mother said he reminded her of one of those sharp-suited spivs you see in old war movies. He ditched Gennie as a client as soon as she started to withdraw from the big public events. I haven't thought about him in years.'

'Might his name actually have been Thorn?' I said. 'Sebastian Thorn?'

There was indeed a touch of the old-fashioned spiv in the man smiling back at me from my laptop. Thorn's photo on the EverThorn Media website showed a jowly, hawk-faced sixty-something, receding hair slicked back, a white pencil moustache, teeth almost as luminous as his younger partner's. But despite the twinkle, there was a hardness in those eyes that made me think of Ben's description. *That guy's like a bulldog protecting his pup*.

'Thorn, of course,' Evangeline muttered. 'A creepy, bullying old man, although I suppose back then he wasn't all that old. But naturally, anyone over twenty-five is ancient to a pair of teenage girls. He seemed to like getting in between the two of us and wrapping his arms around our waists. "A thorn between two roses," he'd laugh. I suppose that's how I got the name mixed up. God, our mother just used to sit there tittering as he did it. She'd never say a word against anyone who brought money into the house.'

I thought of that confused, bedraggled woman emerging from the bushes of Cedar Gables, wittering about her missing scarf and bedsheets and underthings. Whatever the faults of her past, Patricia Bell's dismantling mind seemed punishment enough.

'How did he first hear about Gennie's abilities?' I asked.

'Word had started to get out by then,' Evangeline sighed. 'First through our cousin's spiritualist friends, then the internet chatrooms, then pieces in the local paper that were eventually taken up by the national press. I remember it was around that time I really started to get frightened. Things were getting out of hand, you see? Our silly game had taken on a life of its own. Of course, when he turned up at the house, Thorn denied he'd heard of Gennie through any of those sources. He said her name had been passed to him by his contacts in the spirit world.'

'Wait,' I said. 'You mean he claimed to have psychic powers of his own?'

'That's how he started, I believe,' Evangeline said. 'As a medium.'

So not only a creator of witches, I thought, *but a witch himself.*

'He was furious when Gennie finally said she wanted to stop. As far as he was concerned, she was the goose that laid the golden egg. But, as fragile as she seemed, my sister could be remarkably obstinate when her mind was made up. Not even our mother could move her.'

'And what about you?'

'Truly, Mr Jericho? With all that publicity and press attention, I was just glad that she'd never been found out. She had at least twenty more years of blissful ignorance before Dr Gillespie tore that fantasy away from her.'

'Just one more thing and I'll let you get some rest,' I said. 'Would your sister have kept Sebastian Thorn's home address?'

'I shouldn't have thought so. After the Gillespie podcast, Genevieve seems to have thrown away every reminder of her old life, but if you'll hang on a moment . . .'

I heard the phone clatter onto a table and then the muffled sound of bare feet on carpet. Then nothing for a long time except the buzz of the line. I'd just started to feel my eyes droop when a shriek cut through the stillness.

'Eve! *Eve!* Where have you been? The birds are back in the cellar, peck-peck-pecking all the live-long night. You said you wouldn't leave again. Can't you hear them? Enough to wake the dead.'

And then Evangeline's voice, hoarse with weariness: 'I'm here, Mother. I haven't gone anywhere. Now get back to bed and I'll bring you a hot drink.' A clump, a cough. 'Mr Jericho, are you still there?'

'I am. And I'm sorry, Miss Bell, it sounds like you get little enough sleep without strangers calling you at all hours.'

'I don't know how Genevieve coped with it.' She sighed. 'I suppose eventually I'll have to start looking into some kind of home for her. It's hard to admit, but I'm not the dutiful daughter my sister was. Anyway, I'm sorry but I can't find Thorn's contact details in any of Gennie's papers.'

'Never mind,' I told her. 'Thank you for looking.'

'Do you think he could be in danger?'

'I think . . .' I raked fingers through my curls, inadvertently catching the hot tenderness of my head wound and wincing. 'It's possible. Another quick thing before you go. Did your sister continue to wear her gloves even after the podcast?'

'Funny you ask,' Evangeline said. 'That was one of the last conversations I ever had with her. Even though by that stage she'd accepted she didn't have any psychic powers – certainly not the touch ability of psychometry – she said she'd become so accustomed to wearing them that she couldn't shake the habit. Why do you ask?'

I thought of the bloodstained bag Cloade had tossed into the river. Gennie must still have been wearing the gloves when her hands were removed by the killer. And then there was the almost total absence of her fingerprints in her own home. She must have practically slept in the things.

'Doesn't matter,' I said. 'Thank you again, Miss Bell.'

I glanced at the time: 4.16 a.m. Even if it wasn't the early hours of the morning, I knew that banging on Everwood's door and demanding Thorn's address wouldn't go down well, especially with his PA. There was only one option. I picked up my phone again and hit dial. This time the voice that answered was sharp and alert.

'Thorn fits the victim profile almost too well,' I said, having updated Tallis on my discoveries. 'He's a solid link between Genevieve and Darrel Everwood, he was a psychic himself before becoming a celebrity publicist, and without him, Gennie might never have reached the level of fame she did.'

'OK,' Tallis said. 'Let me look into it. I'll get back to you as soon as I have any news.'

'Thanks. And there is one more thing before you go.'

'If this is about going for that drink, I'm a real ale man,' he chuckled. 'But it'll have to wait until we've caught our killer. In any case, I should probably tell you that I'm—'

'No, it's not that,' I said. 'Sorry, I was just going to say that Darrel Everwood appears to have had a dramatic change of heart. He's no longer afraid of Purley Rectory or the consequences if this live Halloween broadcast goes to hell. I spoke to him earlier and his mood was practically manic. Someone called him the night before last, and from the sound of it, they've shared a psychic revelation that will astound the world.'

'Really?' Tallis yawned. 'Well, that should bump up the ratings.'

'I think it was the killer,' I said. 'Toying with Darrel just as he used Genevieve's gloves to toy with Christopher Cloade.' I thought about what Evangeline had said regarding the taking of her sister's hands, the murderer thereby denying her power of touch-telepathy, and then the marking with blood of The Fool card in Aunt Tilda's tent. 'He enjoys laughing at them,' I went on. 'Mocking what he sees as their ridiculous beliefs. Desecrating their altars, dismembering talented limbs.'

'Sounds like someone who despises all faith and spirituality,' Tallis said suggestively.

'Gillespie.' I nodded to myself. 'Perhaps.'

'So you think someone is setting Darrel up for a fall live on-air? Promising him a big reveal and then making him look ridiculous in front of the entire nation?'

'I hope it's only that,' I said.

'What a case,' Tallis sighed. 'Well, I'll get straight onto tracking down Sebastian Thorn. In the meantime—'

'Yes, Inspector. I'll keep my nose clean and report back anything I find.'

'Very public-spirited of you. And from what I've seen so far, completely out of character. Do try to play by the rules, won't you, Mr Jericho? After all, it's not just your balls on the line, it's my career.'

This was the part of an investigation I had never coped with particularly well. Developments were in the hands of others. All I could do was sit and wait. I settled back onto the bed, tried to grab another couple of hours' rest, and found myself rolling into the scent of Haz's pillow. I grunted, sat upright, threw the thing away from me, and then instantly, and absurdly, regretted it. I don't know how many minutes I lost, staring at that pale shape snagged on the edge of the settee. Tomorrow, I'd wash all of the bedding, exorcise what lingered of Harry Moorhouse from the trailer, and then phone him to say goodbye. A proper farewell this time, final and absolute. He was better off without me. Safer, anyway.

It was still dark outside. Nevertheless, I couldn't sit there any longer. After pulling on my coat and boots, I shut the trailer door behind me and headed into the trees that encircled the clearing. Just like on the night Haz, Webster and I had walked the perimeter, the forest stretched out around me, cold and unmoving. Not even the branches stirred. Thick, gnarled limbs that, to a certain mind, might have been carved by God Himself for the sole purpose of hanging witches.

I walked aimlessly, my footfalls muffled by damp leaves. It wasn't until I saw the ocular window blinking back at me that I realised I'd reached the rear of the house. Was there a light at that window? With the moon reflected on the pane, it was difficult to be sure. What I could definitely see as I moved around the side of the building, however, was the hunched form of Miss Rowell hurrying to the steps of Darrel Everwood's trailer. She kept casting furtive glances over her shoulder, as if the spirits whose home she tended were spying on her. Or perhaps even egging her on. I had concealed myself at the corner of the rectory just as the housekeeper stooped to leave her gift on Everwood's topmost step. She then scurried back to the safety of the house, a strange smile on her lips.

I came out of the shadows and headed for the trailer. I could see Miss Rowell's gift perched on the step, pink and eerie in the moonlight. Even before I noticed her fingerprints in its soft, pliant flesh, its presence alone confirmed my suspicions. I had already made up my mind about the crime Miss Rowell had committed on the night of the murder. Now, picking up the little wax poppet she'd left for Darrel Everwood, I knew for certain.

Chapter Thirty-One

I THREW THE DOLL ONTO THE table and Miss Rowell spun around, her hand flying to her throat.

'Don't worry,' I told her. 'I'm not one of your ghosts. But I think you know that.'

It was the first time I'd stepped inside Purley Rectory. With its Gothic flourishes and chaotic architectural design, the exterior enhanced the house's haunted reputation. Even its stained-red brickwork gave the idea of a living thing, organic, malevolent and tumorous. But beyond the threshold, this spell was abruptly broken. A draughty, dank, sorrowful place, fussy as a grandmother's parlour with every surface covered in knock-off knick-knacks. I doubted any reputable ghost would care to haunt it.

I was certain that the success of Purley as a supernatural attraction was down entirely to the formidable Miss Rowell. Her energy, her commitment, her sacrifice were the living heart of this place. And what a sacrifice it had been. She looked at me now, a shadow of her old pride and defiance still clinging to her.

'What do you mean by this intrusion?' she snapped. 'The house won't be open to the public until—'

'Not for many hours,' I agreed. 'No ghost tours for you to guide at this time of the morning, eh, Miss Rowell?'

We were standing in what I assumed was Purley's main sitting room. Maroon brocade curtains hung in the window while the floor was covered in a Persian rug so faded it was difficult to make out any of the original pattern. Cheap china dogs and imitation Dresden shepherdesses watched us with painted eyes from the mantelpiece. A tasselled lamp stood in one corner, casting a greasy shimmer over the dark lacquer of a worn-out writing bureau. Yet, some of the cheapness may have had a purpose.

Moving to the fireplace, I ran my hand under the mantel until, catching a hidden switch, I sent a shepherdess leaping to her destruction. Miss Rowell immediately went to her knees and started gathering up the broken pieces.

'What do you use on the front garden?' I asked.

She kept her face turned away. 'A mixture of bleach, vinegar, and rock salt. After all these years, the soil's saturated in it. Nothing ever grows. The china and crockery I get as a job lot off the internet.'

'You've got similar tricks set up all over the house?' I asked.

'Not as many as you might think,' she said, straightening up and disposing of the shattered shepherdess in a wastepaper basket. 'The punters, as you would call them, do half the work for me. They wander around claiming they feel cold spots and pressing their ear to the walls saying they hear voices. I just add a little set dressing, that's all.'

'Set dressing?' The phrase brought me up short. I shook my head. 'I'm assuming Lord Denver knows about all this?'

'He may, he may not. He bought Purley almost twenty years ago and I'm the only person in his employ who has ever worked here. Those things like the secret switch on the mantelpiece, I discovered when I arrived. It seems that the rectory has had a long and very undignified history of paranormal fraud.'

'A history you're a part of,' I said.

'To my shame.'

'It must be very hard for someone who values honesty so much to sacrifice her principles every day. You'd been happy up in Lincolnshire, working for Lord Denver at his ancestral estate?' She nodded, her lips forming a wistful smile. 'A hard-working, proud, and efficient housekeeper in charge of such a prestigious property. But there was a problem, wasn't there? Your husband.'

'Lord Denver had always trusted me implicitly,' she said. 'But he was no pushover. He knew what kind of man I'd married. Steven Manders was never given so much as the key to the tool shed. I don't mean to sound arrogant, Mr Jericho, but it was a testament to the value his lordship placed in me that he even allowed Steven on the property. However, it was a mistake he'd come to regret.

'One night, Steven returned home from the pub with one of the grooms who worked in the stables. They'd both spent the day drinking and plotting. This man had a friend in London, he said, who could fence easily identifiable goods. He and Steven had their eye on a painting and a tiara in Lord Denver's collection, but they needed my help to get access to the house. When I refused to hand over my keys, they beat me so badly I was in hospital for a month.'

She stated it as a plain matter of fact, not a trace of self-pity in her voice.

'His lordship was kind enough to visit me after I'd regained consciousness. He said that no one held me responsible for what had happened and that my job was secure. But I couldn't face the family. Not after I'd failed them. They'd reposed their trust in me and the consequences had been disastrous.'

I thought back to that sneering, cut-glass voice on the phone to my dad. How Denver had called Miss Rowell his 'loyal dog'.

'You were beaten and abused,' I said. 'No one would describe that as a failure.'

'I knew what he was before I married him,' Miss Rowell said sharply. 'And I still brought him onto the estate that it was my duty to protect. His crime was made possible by my weakness.'

'And so you decided to serve his sentence?'

'*My* sentence,' she corrected.

'You're very hard on yourself, Miss Rowell.'

'It's because most people aren't hard enough on themselves that the world is in the state it is. Duty, responsibility, honesty, integrity. Values that I hold dear and that are now laughed at as stuffy and old-fashioned. In any case, Lord Denver had recently bought this place and needed someone to run it, perhaps even see if it could turn a profit. It was a descent in terms of status but that was no more than I deserved.'

'But this placed you in a dilemma, didn't it?' I suggested. 'Those values you just spoke of. After your husband's betrayal, your commitment to truth and integrity must have deepened. A rejection of him and all he stood for. But to make a success of Purley, you would need to embrace deception yourself.'

She threw back her head and laughed. I doubted that it was a sound Miss Rowell made very often.

'The ghosts of Purley.' She swept the bland sitting room with a contemptuous gesture. 'The *personalities* with their quirks and curses. I have lived and breathed this house for twenty long years, Mr Jericho, and one thing I know beyond any doubt: there is no such thing as ghosts.'

'And yet there had to be,' I said. 'To repay Lord Denver, you were forced to tell a hundred lies a day. A conflict that couldn't be borne without some kind of punishment. May I?'

She consented with a nod and I unbuttoned the tight sleeve around her wrist, drawing the material back. The always-present elastic band hung there, seemingly innocent enough. What had she said it was for? An aide-mémoire to remind her of certain tasks. I doubted Miss Rowell had forgotten a task in her life. The band's real purpose was revealed in the old scars, the broken skin and weeping welts that covered her forearm. A snap and a lash for every lie that passed her lips in the service of Lord Denver and her conscience.

'You don't only see your husband in Darrel Everwood, do you?' I said. 'You see an aspect of yourself.'

She drew down her sleeve and refastened the button. 'A wilful deceiver.'

'But one who, unlike you, doesn't feel the need to punish himself. And so you decided to give him a little of what he deserved.' I went to the table where I'd thrown the wax doll, and retrieving it, handed the housekeeper her poppet. 'You're upping the stakes, Miss Rowell, but believe me, this isn't a game you want to play. Where did you hear about the dolls?'

For the first time, her composure broke. 'I'm sorry. I heard the woman who died was a relative of yours. I shouldn't have used something like that to try and frighten him. As to where I heard about it, the news seems to have gotten around. A killer planting wax effigies at his crime scenes.'

'Not enough detail in the gossip, though,' I said. 'Your doll is a pretty shade of pink, not the pure white of the murderer's efforts. You're also lacking one or two of his more gruesome additions. Oh, and perhaps when you're shaping your revenge effigies, it might be an idea not to leave your fingerprints in the finished product.'

'Careless of me,' she said. 'Pink was the only candle I had to hand. There were a couple of small white prayer candles in the cellar, back from when this was a real rectory, I suppose, but not enough to shape a figure with. In the end, I had to bring one from home. Ridiculous, I know.'

'Ridiculous just about covers it,' I agreed. 'So I guess that inconveniencing Darrel by puncturing his tyres had become a bit old hat? You wanted to give him a proper scare.'

'How did you know about the tyres?' she asked.

'I saw you on the night of the murder, remember? Hurrying away from Purley, desperate to catch a bus, wasn't it? The first time committing a crime is always the most nerve-wracking. It was the hem of your skirt that gave you away – muddy from where you'd bent down to hammer the nail into his tyre.' I thought back to my early suspicion that the marks in the earth outside Tilda's tent had been made by Miss Rowell as she'd knelt to secure the door. However, her venom had never been focused on psychics in general, but on one specific huckster who, suddenly invading her world, had so poignantly reminded her of her own failings.

'I found a couple of nails on the drive just after I saw his car pull up,' she said. 'It was almost as if they'd been left there for me. I came back to the house to get a hammer and the rest you know.'

'Did you see who dropped the nails?'

She frowned. 'I thought I might have seen something white fluttering in the trees nearby, but I'm not sure. It could have been anything.'

'Miss Rowell, you value the truth. I need you to answer my next question with absolute honesty. You've vandalised his car, tried to scare him with the doll, have you also telephoned him recently? Perhaps played on his paranoia, impersonated someone, made up some story so that he'll embarrass himself during the broadcast?'

She shook her head. 'Even if I wanted to, short of trying to speak to the man in person, I wouldn't know how to get in touch with him.'

I believed her. In the pattern of her escalating persecution, she would naturally have used the doll before trying anything as direct as a phone call.

'This stops right now,' I told her. 'I won't report what you've done, but if you continue, your actions could confuse an already complex investigation. Are we clear?'

'Perfectly. And I am sorry, Mr Jericho.' Her fingers went to her wrist, hovering over the old scars and fresh weals made by the band. 'After two decades of lies and self-loathing? I don't know. Looking back on these past few days, I can't believe it was really me who did those things.'

'Almost as if you'd become another person ...' I murmured.

My phone broke into the pause.

Tallis started speaking as soon as I picked up.

'You were right,' he said. 'I've just got off a call with the local police. Sebastian Thorn was murdered a couple of hours ago. But this one's different. Jericho, are you there? I think you need to see this with your own eyes.'

Chapter Thirty-Two

Dawn flared across the horizon of two English counties as I reached the midpoint of the bridge. It painted the estuary landscape of Essex and Kent a liquid red, transforming the turgid ribbon of the Thames into a single pulsating artery. Down this bloody channel flew clots of darkness, defining themselves momentarily into seabirds that soared between the stanchions of the bridge before flowing on into the great heart of London.

At the far side of the Dartford Crossing, I lost the light and passed into the shadows of the motorway. Tallis had given me few details regarding Thorn's murder, saying only that he'd meet me at the dead publicist's house, just outside the town of Tunbridge Wells. Despite hardly having slept, I was filled with the nervous, skittish energy that always came in the closing hours of a case. So much remained unclear but still I sensed that, whatever the killer's ultimate purpose, the final threads of it were being drawn together. I only hoped that Ben Halliday wouldn't find himself enmeshed in the web.

Before setting out from Purley, I had run into Deepal in the car park. I'd thought she might still be annoyed with me for having tricked my way into an interview with Everwood, but the PA looked as if she had other things on her mind. Her hair was back in that severe bun and there were already coffee stains on the sleeve of her jacket.

'You're up and about early, Miss Chandra,' I said.

She glanced towards the *Ghost Seekers*' production trailers. 'The whole crew will be arriving in a couple of hours, then the chaos will really begin. I'll need to touch base with your father, by the way, just to make sure he knows the timing for when we go live. It's looking like our catering has hit a snag, so we might need to commandeer some of your food trucks. Oh, and now Darrel's insisting he needs time alone before the broadcast to "attune with the spirits". God give me strength. Makeup is going to just love that.'

'If you don't mind me saying, it doesn't sound like you enjoy your job very much,' I said. 'I wonder why you do it?'

Deepal looked at me curiously. 'You see a lot, Mr Jericho, but I promise you, I take my work here very seriously. I only wish others did the same.'

'What do you mean?'

'Seb Thorn, Darrel's manager for one. The night before the biggest broadcast in *Ghost Seekers*' history and he wasn't answering his phone. Darrel started fretting about some production detail or another and needed the old man's reassurance. In the end, things got so stressed I suggested sending Ben over to Seb's to see what was going on.'

I nodded, remembering Ben being flagged down by the constables in the car park at around midnight. Glancing over at the driveway, I now saw an empty space where the Bentley was usually parked.

'Ben's still not back?' I asked.

'No, and now he's not picking up any of my calls either,' Deepal sighed. 'Still, I suppose if he got to Seb's and couldn't get an answer at the door, he might simply have turned around and started back. If so, he could be here any minute.'

We both looked towards the forest road as if the Bentley might reappear by magic.

'But you say you've been calling him?'

'The hands-free system in the car has been glitching.' She shrugged. 'He might not be able to answer. It also doesn't help that Seb is deaf as a post. He could have fallen asleep before twelve and not heard Ben banging at the door.'

I kept my mouth shut. It wasn't for me to tell her that the co-creator of *Ghost Seekers* had been ritualistically murdered sometime in the past few hours. I doubted it would improve her stress levels anyway. What concerned me from that point on was the consequences for Ben. He'd been desperate to shrug off the shadows of his former life and make a new start, far away from the jealous, violent clutches of mobster Mark Noonan. For Ben, I think this had been more than just a break with the immediate past. In the form of Noonan, he had discovered another possessive, abusive parent figure to replace the father he'd escaped back in Hull. Wanting to finally end that toxic cycle for good, he'd begged me not to expose his background to Everwood. I now worried that Ben's choice in the matter may have been taken from him.

The rush hour traffic was starting to hit gridlock when I eased off the motorway and passed into Kent's leafy suburbs. Even in deepest autumn, the county clung to its reputation as the Garden of England. Fields and churchyards bustling with maple and rowan, blueberry bushes crowding against a gatepost, the light on their leaves reminding me of the marigolds in Garris's garden. The only marker for Lenny Kerrigan's grave.

I had parked at the end of an isolated lane and got out of the car when my phone pinged with a message. It was from Sal.

Where are you? Look, Scott, even if this means you never talk to me again – you MUST call Harry. I've spoken to him – told him what you told me yesterday. There's so much you don't know, so – call him!

'Jericho? Thank you for coming.'

I looked up to find Tallis striding towards me. Shoving my phone back into my pocket, I shook his outstretched hand. Whatever Sal was going on about, it could wait.

'So you've been inside already?' I said, looking to the house at the end of the lane.

The home of Sebastian Thorn was as impressive, in its way, as that of his old client, Genevieve Bell. However, the styles were very different. Instead of a modernist mansion of steel and glass, Thorn's residence was a Tudor fantasia complete with a thatched roof, a jutting timber frame to support its overhanging first floor, and small lead lattice windows. It stood by itself in acres of almost treeless land, no neighbour in sight.

In a SOCO tent outside the front door, Tallis and I donned protective Tyvek suits and the rest of the forensic paraphernalia before signing our names into the scene log. I could see that Tallis's sergeant wasn't best pleased by my presence, but a look from his senior officer quelled any objection. As we passed into the stone-flagged entrance hall, the DCI gestured towards my forehead.

'That wound you got from Cloade still looks nasty. You should get it seen to.'

'I will,' I muttered. At that moment, all I could feel was a dull ache. 'Any news on him, by the way?'

'Seems to be hunkering down in his church,' Tallis said. 'One of my DCs looked in on him last night. Found him flat on his face before his altar, begging God to deliver him from evil spirits.'

'He should do the tour at Purley,' I said. 'The housekeeper there would soon set him straight.'

Tallis might have asked what I meant, but by then we'd reached the great staircase with its dark-oak banister and the faceless man sprawled across its steps. A photographer had just finished filming the corpse in situ when Tallis begged a moment before the waiting forensics team swept in.

'Keep your distance,' he told me. 'If you need any details confirmed, I'll get one of these guys to take a closer look.'

I was pretty sure that wouldn't be necessary. The morning light streaming through the gallery windows above our heads illuminated the scene better than any floodlight. I could see from the angled stain on the newel post – thick with blood at the top of the cap, tapering into a light smear as it ran downwards – that, like Genevieve and Tilda, Thorn had been struck from behind. A spot or two of unsmeared blood on the flagstones as he staggered to the staircase. Then, his right hand automatically going to the wound before he grabbed the newel cap for support, he had finally fallen, twisting around as he clung to the post. He had landed on his back, the blood flowing freely onto the step pillowing his head until his heart had stopped.

'He knew the killer,' I said, explaining my reasoning to Tallis. 'Let him in just like the others.'

'Except this one isn't quite like the others,' Tallis observed.

Those words from Mozart's 'Lacrimosa', the requiem Haz claimed he'd been practising with his fictitious choir, replayed in my head. *Full of tears will be that day; When from the ashes shall arise; The guilty man to be judged.* Well, Sebastian Thorn had certainly been judged guilty by the killer. In this latest recreation of the witchfinder's execution methods, we had reached the hanged witch. After death, a coarse rope had been knotted around the victim's throat and, drawn taut, lashed to one of the staircase spindles on the landing. Just as with the drowned doll and the pricked doll, a wax effigy had been left beside the corpse.

But Tallis was right. There were differences here in the killer's MO, ones that had already been suggested in the murder of Tilda Urnshaw. For a start, although his doll was faceless, my initial impression of Thorn's injuries had been mistaken. His features masked with blood, I hadn't realised that most of them remained intact. His hands, too, had been spared, though the effigy's had not.

'Most serial killer rituals evolve over time,' I said slowly. 'They become ever more detailed and elaborate, the intensity of the carnage more marked. But our murderer seems to be *de*volving, losing his enthusiasm for the trademarks of his slaughter.'

Tallis nodded. 'And yet he persists.'

'I wondered with Tilda if there was something half-hearted about it all,' I said. 'As if the ritual itself wasn't crucial to the killings. That it could become almost an afterthought ... Have his teeth been taken?'

Tallis made a gesture and a forensics officer went to huddle over the body. After a moment or two, he glanced back at us. 'The teeth haven't been touched but there is something caught at the back of his throat. Give me a second.' He went to work with a pair of tweezers before finally dislodging some foreign object. 'Got it.'

Although the scrawled biblical quotation from Exodus had not been attached to Thorn's doll, a different passage had been left inside the victim. On a scrap of moist paper, I read: *1 Timothy 6:10*. Tallis looked it up on his phone.

'"For the love of money is the root of all evil."'

I nodded. 'He mocked Genevieve's power by taking her hands. He mocked Tilda by claiming she was a fool. Now he's condemning the legacy of Sebastian Thorn, a man who made his fortune from the promotion of witches. I wonder what he'll be laughing at while his fourth victim burns.'

Chapter Thirty-Three

'Burns?' Tallis echoed.

'If the pattern holds, that's the fate of the last victim. The burned witch.'

Before leaving the hanged man, I took a final look around the entrance hall. In the shadow behind the doorway, I could see a scatter of white pills, left like a trail of breadcrumbs in a children's story. There were about a dozen in all, each the same size and shape.

'We're checking his medical records, but we assume they're Thorn's,' Tallis said, following my gaze. 'Maybe they dropped out of his pocket when he fell.'

I knew the DCI was too smart to believe this explanation. Was he already aware that Ben had been sent by Everwood to check in on Thorn? His constables in the car park would have made a note of the time the Bentley left the site. Perhaps someone had told Tallis about Ben's addiction. He might even be aware of our past association and was waiting for me to reveal it before he asked the question himself.

All I could think of when I saw the pills was a pair of pinprick pupils and trembling hands. Hands that in a panic would reach instinctively for the dulling reassurance of the pain meds, and fumbling, drop them. Of course, in his time, Ben had seen sights as bad as this, worse even, but he was trying to leave such horrors behind. Now, finding the battered corpse of Sebastian Thorn, had the blood and agony of other men returned to him? Men he'd broken under his fists? In my mind's eye, I pictured Ben fleeing both the scene of the crime and the dark memories that pursued him.

'But if they were Thorn's, why would he be carrying them loose?' Tallis said.

Our eyes met and I asked, 'Any CCTV installed?'

'Not that we can find.' He led the way back to the SOCO tent where we started to change out of our forensics gear. 'We'll check any local cameras for vehicles coming this way, but it's a pretty rural spot. I doubt there'll be much we can work with.'

He walked me to my car, where we shook hands again.

'Do you think they'll go ahead with the broadcast after this?' I asked.

'I haven't managed to speak with Everwood yet,' Tallis said. 'But I have touched base with the network people this morning. They tell me that postponing the event would be the last thing Sebastian Thorn would have wanted.'

I almost laughed. 'That, I do believe. Well, I suppose with millions watching, Darrel's as safe as he can be, although I imagine his paranoia will go into overdrive when he hears about what's happened here. If it *is* paranoia.'

The inspector gave me one last, long look. 'Let me know if anything else occurs to you, Mr Jericho. And thanks for the tip-off about Thorn.'

Cursing myself for not having taken Ben's number, I'd just got back into the car when my phone rang. No caller ID.

Praying that this was him, I started rehearsing a couple of reassuring lines that might settle his nerves and bring him out of hiding. I had no doubt he'd scurried away to some secret bolthole, terrified that the police would take one look at his record and implicate him in the murder. If I could convince Ben that Tallis would give him a fair hearing, then everything might still work out.

I answered the call.

'Hello, Scottster, long time no speaky, eh? If I didn't know better, I could swear you've been avoiding me.'

As soon as I heard that voice, I knew it was too late for Ben.

'What do you want, Mark?'

The mobster Mark Noonan cooed softly in my ear. 'Now, is that any way to speak to an old friend? Let's keep our manners nice and sociable, shall we? Cos if you do get snappish with me, Scottster, I might have to start snapping back, and that wouldn't be pretty.'

I took a breath. 'Have you heard from Ben Halliday?'

'Yes indeed, I might have to snap back very, very hard.' He laughed. 'You stabbed me right to the heart when you went off and joined the filth, but I didn't bear a grudge. Long as you kept shtum about my business, I was happy enough to let you run around with your new detective friends. Oh, I heard you got into a bit of trouble, though. Beat up some Nazi cunt, wasn't it? Landed yourself a nice little stretch. I also heard,' he said in a delicate whisper, 'that some big boys jumped you in the showers up at Hazelhurst. Hurt you pretty bad, so the story goes. Well, I want you to know, Scottster, that unpleasantness had nothing to do with me.'

I closed my eyes, fought back the vision of myself curled up on those blood-streaked tiles. I didn't have time for this.

'Say what you've got to say, Mark. I'm listening.'

'No, no,' he cooed again. 'This ain't no kind of reunion. If you want to know what Ben has just told me regarding a certain murder he might have witnessed last night, you come see me at Nana's. I got a little favour I need taking care of and, if you agree to scratch my back, I'll tell you what I know.'

'Fine,' I grunted. 'But first you let Ben go.'

'You're not in any position to be dictating terms,' the mobster snapped. 'No, I think I'll be keeping our Benny tucked safely under my wing for the foreseeable future. So you just hurry on over now, my boy. I'll have the kettle on ready.'

The line went dead.

'Fuck,' I muttered. 'Ben, what have you done?'

It was hardly a question worth asking. Frightened and confused, high on his illegal meds, Ben had sought the protection of the only man in his life who had ever offered it. Executing a quick three-point turn in the lane, I wondered why he hadn't come to me. The answer was equally obvious – he knew that I was just starting again and that I had someone I cared for. Conscious of his own now-shattered hopes for a new life, he wouldn't have wanted to bring trouble to my door. In the end, Ben had seen Noonan as his only option.

Now I ran through mine. I could inform Tallis that Ben was being held against his will and that he possessed information about Thorn's murder but required police protection. Even if the DCI was willing to action a raid on Noonan's base, however, that sort of operation would require time to organise and implement. Meanwhile, any delay in me reaching the house would arouse Noonan's suspicion. In any case, it was likely that Ben was being kept at a separate location.

Time wasn't the only factor. I could call my dad and have a crowd of local Travellers waiting for me outside the house when I arrived. Backup in case things turned nasty. But given the ingenious set-up of the place, that probably wasn't wise. If I wanted to learn what Ben had seen last night, then I had to play by Noonan's rules. And that apparently also meant doing him some 'little favour'. I batted away the anxiety those words aroused and checked the dashboard clock: 9.50 a.m. Plenty of time to swing by the house in Hounslow and get back to Purley for the broadcast at eight.

If I survived, of course.

An hour and twenty minutes later, I pulled into a charming crescent of semi-detached houses that backed onto the Hounslow Loop railway. At one end stood the overground station, at the other, a community allotment and the hump-backed railway bridge. The street was clean and litter-free, its pavements weeded, its hedges neatly trimmed. Pensioners in old-fashioned housecoats and peaked caps looked out from their gardens as I parked up. They all smiled and waved as if they knew me. Lending a hand in the gardens, washing cars, carrying shopping were a few good-looking young men with biceps for days and necks like tree trunks. I felt every eye on me as I pushed open Nana's gate and walked up the path to number 56 Sanford Crescent.

This wasn't only Noonan's base, it was his street. He owned every house and let them rent-free to a select club of pensioners – men and women of impeccable reputation who had never so much as received a parking ticket. Noonan's 'husbands' helped to maintain the properties and were always delighted to carry out any small chore that was asked of them. People strolling down Sanford Crescent might wonder at so many attentive grandsons and the fact there seemed to be no one here aged between forty and sixty, but the charm of the place would soon overwhelm their misgivings.

It was the perfect camouflage for organised crime. All that was asked of the residents was that they keep their eyes peeled and their mouths shut. That was why I knew I couldn't risk bringing in backup. A worried call from an old dear about strangers congregating in her street would only end in the Travellers' arrest. And so, under that keen surveillance, I turned and knocked at the smartly painted front door.

There was no nana at Nana's house. Noonan's grandmother, who had brought him up in this modest Edwardian terrace, had died some years ago. Still, the beloved matriarch was memorialised on every wall. As the door swung open, I saw her ruddy, puggish features grinning down at me from half a dozen different angles. I didn't recognise the kid in the doorway, but he was wearing one of those tacky diamonds on his ring finger, so it was safe to assume he was a husband.

'You're a new one,' I said, pushing my way inside. 'So where is he?'

'Mark's been called away on urgent business,' he squeaked. 'Says to offer you his apologies. He'll be back in an hour or two.'

Chemically inflated with steroids, the kid tried to front up to me. I cuffed the back of his head and pushed him towards the kitchen.

'I was promised tea. Milk, one sugar. If you spit in it, I'll know and I'll kick your arse up and down the railway tracks.'

Moving into the back sitting room, I picked up the local paper from the sideboard and collapsed into Noonan's favourite armchair.

'All right, Scott?' muttered a man-mountain sitting on the other side of the electric fire. 'Been keeping your nose clean?'

'Clean as a daisy,' I said, before turning my attention to the paper. 'Nice to see a face from the old days, Charlie. That busted elbow still giving you trouble?'

Time crept by. I drank my tea, read the *Herald*, ignored the occasional buzz from my phone, reminisced with Charlie – who, at the grand old age of thirty-six, was one of the more senior husbands. Charlie left on an errand at around midday, and by one thirty, I was ready to call it quits. Just over six hours until the broadcast and a three-hour drive ahead of me, if I didn't hit any substantial traffic on the M25. I wanted to know what Ben had seen, but every instinct told me that I needed to be back at Purley when the cameras started rolling. According to Everwood, the media event of the century was at hand.

I'd just started to rise when the door swung open and Noonan came bouncing into the room. He looked twenty years older than the last time I'd seen him, the toll of his fentanyl addiction showing in the loose grey flesh that hung from his face.

'Scottster! I'm so sorry to have kept you waiting. I hear young Timmo here has been supplying you with tea and biscuits. Isn't he a peach!' The fifty-year-old gangster play-wrestled the kid against the wall. Meanwhile, six other young men watched on, their faces gripped with the tightest of smiles. A little breathless, Mark turned back to me. 'Now, here's the thing, Scott, you've presented me with a bit of a dilemma today. I've been talking about you for years, you see? How you betrayed me by joining the other side and what I'd do if our paths ever crossed again. Course, I couldn't do anything to you while you were with the filth, and then they had you banged up for such a long time, my opportunity's only really just come round.'

I settled back into the armchair. There was no way I was getting through that door, not with seven hard bodies and Noonan's pudgy frame blocking it. I'd just have to see how things played out.

'Well,' the mobster went on, stroking a forefinger under Timmo's jaw. 'I can't let my boys think I'm a weak old man, now, can I? These youngsters smell blood in the water, they'll tear me to pieces. Won't you, gorgeous?'

Sweat starting on his brow, Timmo vehemently denied he would ever do such a thing. Noonan just chuckled, and reaching into the holster under his designer tracksuit jacket, pulled out a Beretta pistol and pointed it at my head.

'So I gotta make an example of you, Scottster,' he sighed. 'But I don't want you to worry about a thing. We'll box you up nice and pretty when it's done, and get you sent straight back to the fair.'

Chapter Thirty-Four

THE COLD MUZZLE OF THE semi-automatic grazed a path around my kneecap, its touch as tender as a lover's kiss. Bending a little to his task, Noonan then shot me a sly wink before smashing the butt of the magazine repeatedly against the bone. The sound, a hard, hollow clacking, mimicked the bright tick of Nana Noonan's cuckoo clock on the wall. I gripped the arms of the chair as my leg spasmed in response. Set my jaw, breathed through my nose, ignored the jackal laughter of the husbands. The gun mouth was back, moving on, zigzagging up the inner thigh of my jeans, pressing under the bulge of my balls before resting against my groin. Noonan licked his lips. He glanced over his shoulder, eager for the jittery support of his boys, as he thumbed back the Beretta's hammer.

'Better not chamber a full round, eh, loves? When this thing goes off it won't stop until the mag's empty. Don't want to cut the poor sod in half, do we?' He turned back to me, that saggy grey skin flopping from his jaws like elephant hide. 'Just a single shot to make my point. What do you say, Scott?'

I stayed perfectly still. Let him have his fun.

Beyond the patio doors behind me, I could hear the sound of kids kicking a ball in a neighbouring street, a couple's muffled argument, a lawnmower chuntering into life, the summery chimes of an ice cream van, incongruous in the autumn dank. Life rolling on, oblivious to the psychopath currently threatening to emasculate me in his late grandmother's armchair.

Noonan moved the gun up and down my groin before tutting at himself. 'I just can't bring myself to do it.' He sighed. 'I've heard such wonderful things, it would be like desecrating a work of art. But perhaps a bullet to the gut would satisfy me?' He jabbed the barrel into my navel and hissed between his teeth. 'Such a bad way to go. Takes a fucking age for them to die. I'm not sure I'd want him rolling around on the floor, squealing like a stuck pig for the rest of the afternoon. What about we just cut to the chase and finish this thing?'

He played the pistol around my jaw, over my left cheek, and into the tumble of curls that curtained my forehead. I felt the muzzle find that hot, throbbing wound Christopher Cloade had inflicted, and at its slightest touch, stars exploded before my eyes.

'Oh dear, but I can see you've been pissing off other people behind my back.' Noonan pouted. 'And I thought we were exclusive.'

'What can I say?' I grunted back at him. 'I'm too much of a pain in the arse for just one crazy motherfucker.'

'You know your problem, Scott?' he seethed.

'I'm acutely aware of about half a dozen. Look, Mark, if there's a choice between being psychoanalysed by a certified sociopath in a tracksuit that does nothing for him, and having my brains blown out, please hurry up and feed me the fucking bullet already.'

'Well, isn't she a sassy princess?' The mobster straightened up and raked the gun hard across my forehead, splitting the surgical glue, reopening the wound, and making me roar. 'Maybe her fairy godfather should make her wish come true.'

The pain burned under my skin, ran like liquid fire down my spine, made my fists clench and my toes curl. I felt the warm cascade of blood flow down my face. I wanted to wipe the spill from my chin, but it was important to let Noonan have his moment. He had to make enough of an example of me to save face and to keep the husbands in check. I might have made it easier for myself just now by not running my mouth off – but hey, nice to meet you, I'm Scott Jericho.

Finally, he pushed the weapon between my eyes and pulled the trigger.

A single, impotent click.

'Ha!' he cried ecstatically. 'Oh, poor Scottster. Didn't you know I was only fucking with you?'

He flicked the gun away, and returning it to his holster, spun on tiptoes to face his crew. The husbands all burst into competitive applause, as if Noonan had just pulled the crown jewels out of his arse. After a moment or two, he seemed satisfied and ordered Timmo to go to the bathroom and fetch clean towels and the first aid box. While I thumbed blood from my eyes, the middle-aged mobster came and sat on the arm of the chair, his diamond-encrusted sausage fingers massaging my shoulder.

'You know that was nothing personal, don't you?' he whispered. 'It's just the way things have always been done. And I think you'll agree that I let you off quite lightly. No hard feelings, eh?'

'Never where you're concerned, Mark,' I assured him. 'And I knew you wouldn't dishonour Nana's memory by killing me in her favourite chair. I remembered her rule – no severe beatings in the sitting room.'

We both looked up at the portrait of the long-dead gargoyle, leering down at us from her spot above the mantelpiece. In her final years, Nana Noonan had sported the kind of moustache a nineteenth-century strongman might have envied, but a loving eye is very forgiving. Mark patted my hand almost affectionately.

'Wasn't she a handsome old lady? Always had a soft spot for you, you know.'

I was saved from inventing any fond feelings for Nana by the arrival of Timmo and the towels. Mark asked for the room to be cleared while he personally cleaned and bandaged my wound. His personality had flipped again, switching from Old Testament tyrant – thou shalt not worship any gang boss but me – to forgiving mobster messiah. The husbands looked relieved to be dismissed and the door clicked shut behind them. While Noonan fussed, sterilised and bandaged, I tried to return us to the topic in hand.

'I knew you wouldn't blow my brains out,' I said. 'Not when you've apparently got some favour you want from me. Anyway, now you've had your fun, can we talk about Ben?'

'Stop squirming or you'll open this cut right back up again,' Noonan chided. 'And we'll get to Benjamin in a moment. First, you mentioned that favour. Yes indeed, this little production today doesn't even begin to rebalance the scales between us. But, like I said, it was important to show the boys that no one crosses me with impunity, no matter how handsome.'

'Mark,' I sighed. 'There's no way I'm coming back to work for you. Not even for a one-off job.'

'All right, you great virtuous saint,' he said lightly. 'It isn't anything that will compromise all these new-found morals of yours. I'll fill you in on the details once this business you're involved with up north is done and dusted.' For Noonan, anywhere beyond the end of the Piccadilly Line was classified as 'up north'. 'I just need you to look into a little family matter for me, that's all.'

'And if I say yes, you'll tell me about Ben?'

'If you say yes, I won't cut off your balls and feed them to Doris's cat over the road.'

I admitted defeat as he secured the last bandage and patted my curls back into place. 'Fine.' Standing up, I checked my reflection in the mirror next to Nana's portrait. I had to hand it to Noonan, thirty years of digging out bullets and patching up husbands had made him a pretty skilled first-aider. 'Just promise me this favour won't get me arrested.'

'Can anyone guarantee such a thing with Scott Jericho?'

I shrugged. He had a point. 'I've said I'll do it. Now, what has Ben told you about last night?'

Mark settled himself in the chair I'd just vacated while I went and leaned against the wall. He kicked his legs up onto the arm in a way he clearly imagined was coquettish, and which certainly would have earned him a slap from a certain dead moustachioed grandmother.

'He turned up here at about four in the morning,' Mark said, picking at a piece of fluff around his groin. 'I must admit, I wasn't fabulously excited to hear from him. You're aware that I offered Benny the chance to become one of my very special beloveds? He threw it back in my face. Never trust the young ones, Scottster, they always disappoint you in the end. But you know what a pushover I am. Last night, he begged me to come back. Literally got down on his knees and *begged*.'

'And I bet you didn't enjoy that one bit, did you, Mark?'

'Such a big brain,' Noonan purred. 'But you're not always on the money. Fact is, I wasn't even here. I was spending the night with some friends in Vauxhall. Timmo got me on the phone and told me this adorable redhead had shown up and was pleading for my protection. Our Benny was well and truly tripping off his tits by that stage. Timmo put him on the blower, and from what I could make out, Ben had stumbled into something he wasn't supposed to see.'

'The murder of Sebastian Thorn.'

'The telly producer?' Mark whistled. 'I didn't know that. All Benny boy said was that he'd seen someone rubbed out and would I help him to disappear for a while. Not being the purest lamb in the flock, he reckoned the filth would think he was involved.'

'But what exactly did he see?' I asked.

Noonan rolled his eyes. 'Christ Almighty. You know I could never understand half of what that gorgeous boy was saying, even when he wasn't off his head on pills and slurring his words. Why don't they teach these Northerners how to speak the Queen's proper English? It's like they're jabbering away in a foreign language half the time. Anyway, from what I could make out, Benny had been asked to check in on this old man who wasn't picking up his calls. He arrives at the house around two in the morning to find the front door open and the old fella's brains splashed across the staircase. He says he froze.

Couldn't move a muscle. Panic attack. Said he had flashbacks to some of the stuff he'd done for me in the past. I never asked him to murder anyone, so I don't know what he's on about there. Anyway, according to our boy, he just stands there like a statue while the killers run straight past him.'

I stared at the gangster. '*Killers?* He told you there was more than one?'

'Two, from the sound of it,' Noonan confirmed. 'After I said I'd take him back and look after him, he asked me to phone you. The fear was on him by then, and he thought if he contacted you himself, the cops would be able to track him from the call.'

I pushed off from the wall and went to stand in front of Noonan.

'Tell me exactly what he said.'

He sighed and examined his fingernails, as if the effort was beneath him.

'"Both, Mark,"' Noonan said. '"Tell Scott, I saw both of them."'

Chapter Thirty-Five

BOTH OF THEM.

A parade of conspirators ran through my mind, each striking me as either unlikely or absurd: Dr Gillespie and one of his worshipping disciples; Evangeline Bell and her dementia-afflicted mother; Darrel Everwood and Deepal Chandra; Christopher Cloade and a member of his homeless congregation; John and Anne Chambers; Miss Rowell acting in concert with someone as yet unsuspected. Like partnered cards in a tarot reading, I tried to deal them in as many combinations as possible, yet none seemed to fit.

I had pictured this killer throughout as a lone predator and that image wasn't easy to dislodge. But did the idea of two murderers answer at least one of the questions that had been puzzling me? A committed, ferocious, fixated monster, zealously working to his design of eradicating witches, and a confederate, perhaps less sure of their mission – a moderating voice that had begun to have an effect, toning down the extreme features of their macabre ritual. It was possible, and yet something about the theory didn't sit right.

I turned back to Noonan. 'You're absolutely sure that's what he said? "Both, Mark. Tell Scott, I saw both of them."'

'That's how he said it,' Noonan assured me.

I shook my head. 'Maybe if I could speak to him myself?'

'Oh, no, no, no.' He hauled himself out of the chair and fronted up to me. I had to virtually drop my chin to my chest to return his gaze. 'I know you two had something going on back in the day, but he didn't come to you for protection. He came to *me*. Ben Halliday is my husband now and no grey-eyed Romeo is going to sweep in and take him from me. I've given you his message and that's all you're getting, understood?'

I nodded. 'Thanks for the tea and biscuits.'

I turned away from the little man and headed back through the hall and out the door of number fifty-six. It killed me to think of Ben trapped in this world he had tried so hard to escape, but there was nothing I could do. Armed to the gills and surrounded by his husbands, I couldn't force Noonan to tell me where he was keeping Ben. Perhaps one day I could devise a plan to rescue him, but for now, I had to focus on the case and get back to Purley before the broadcast.

'You know why you worked for me all those years, don't you, Scottster?' Noonan called after me, as I pushed open the gate and stepped into the street. 'You had the brains to be whatever you wanted, but you were drawn to me, just like you were drawn to the filth.'

Timmo and a couple of the other husbands were standing around my ancient Merc, blocking access to the driver's-side door. I jerked my thumb sideways and they fell back readily enough. There was a smirk on Timmo's face, however, that I didn't quite like.

'You enjoy it,' Noonan laughed. 'That's why. The fear, the violence, the adrenalin. You can't get enough, can you?'

I looked back at him. In their neat, ordered gardens, his pensioner tenants stood watching, their comfortable suburban smiles chillingly robotic.

'Maybe you're right, Mark,' I said. 'And maybe that ought to worry you, just a little. I'll wait to hear from you about that favour.'

I dropped into the driver's seat and turned the ignition. Thank God the old Merc was an automatic so my left leg wasn't required all that much. I'd forced myself not to limp to the car, but now the freshly tenderised nerves in my kneecap started to scream. Leaning over to the cluttered glove compartment, I rooted around before eventually excavating the holy grail of half a box of paracetamol. I swallowed two tablets dry and then pulled out into the road.

According to the dashboard clock, it was 2.36 p.m. Still plenty of time to make it back. Leaving Hounslow via the Great West Road, I rolled down the window and took a breath of cold, gritty air. I could smell the promise of rain on the breeze, and within half an hour, a few spots had started to streak my windscreen. The traffic on the M25 was heavy but moving, no trundling lorries hogging the fast lane as I sped the Merc around that dreary London orbital. With the dull ache of my head and the sickening pain in my knee, it was difficult to focus on anything except the road. Each time my thoughts strayed to the case, some bright new agony would make itself felt.

In the end, I decided to give up trying and turned on the radio.

'... and so despite the news that has leaked this morning, the *Ghost Seekers* team is adamant that the broadcast will go ahead as planned?'

'That's right, Sinead. I've been in touch with the producers and they're saying that, while Darrel Everwood is naturally devastated by his manager's death, he knows that Sebastian Thorn would want the show to go on. In fact, Darrel claims that Thorn has already been in touch with him from the "other side" and has urged him not to cancel.'

'Might be helpful if he also happened to mention who murdered him,' I muttered to myself.

'We have to remember that Darrel Everwood has a lot riding on the success of this Halloween special,' the reporter continued. 'His celebrity stock has plummeted in recent weeks. The revelations about his personal life, and the challenge of Dr Joseph Gillespie, whose own pre-recorded documentary, *Ghost Scammers*, will air at the same time on a rival channel.'

'But you say Everwood is confident about the show?' the host asked.

'More than confident, Sinead. Here's a clip of what he had to say to us earlier ...'

The mockney accent was firmly back in place, but Darrel sounded more keyed up than ever. 'No one is going to believe the shocks we've got in store. This isn't just going to be a television event – it will stand as an epoch in world history. For centuries to come, our descendants will look back on this day and say, "That was the point when everything we thought we understood about life and death was changed forever." At eight o'clock this evening, I, Darrel Everwood, will shake the very fortress of mortality and allow the dead to return.'

Switching off the radio, I thought back to the phone call Everwood had received, the one after which his entire attitude towards the broadcast had changed. If the killer – or killers – were playing with him, then perhaps this time the plan was to mock their victim *before* he met his fate. Public humiliation preceding his ultimate punishment.

I was so caught up in this idea that I'd automatically slowed the car to a standstill before I realised what had happened. The motorway before me dipped gently downwards, and I could now make out half a mile of gridlocked traffic with the distant speck of a jackknifed lorry tipped onto its side. Hundreds of engines were suddenly silenced as we all settled in for the long wait.

An hour passed. Then another. By five o'clock, I was still eighty miles from Purley and we hadn't moved an inch. There were rumours among the other motorists that the crash had been a bad one with multiple fatalities. I threw another couple of paracetamols down my throat and called Tallis.

'Jericho?' he said. 'Where are you?'

I could hear the buzz of the fair in the background.

'Sorry, I had to call in on an old friend. Look, in case I don't make it back in time, there's something you should know.' I explained to him the possibility that we might be hunting two killers. When he started questioning me about my sources, I shut him down. 'Just bear it in mind. I'll be with you when I can.'

I ended the call just as the traffic started moving again. Still enough time if … The key turned uselessly in the ignition. Immediately, a barrage of horns blared behind me as my eyes snapped to the dashboard. The needle on the fuel gauge stood at empty. I had topped up the tank on my way over to Noonan's so how the hell—? That smirk of Timmo's came back to me. Siphoning off my fuel – a petty prank he imagined might win him kudos with the boss.

'Little bastard,' I muttered.

In the end, a kindly Samaritan helped me push the car onto the hard shoulder, where I waited for a breakdown service to come to the rescue. They promised to arrive in half an hour. At six o'clock, the rain started in earnest, great sheets lashing the motorway, throwing up a pale mist through which headlights glanced like passing phantoms. I knew I wasn't getting back to Purley by eight. Instead, once my tank had been replenished, I drove on for another thirty miles before pulling into a huge service station complex.

My phone buzzed as I limped across the car park and into the vast food court. Every taste catered for here, so long as that taste ran to bland, oversalted, and served with chips. I glanced at the caller ID: Haz. I was tempted to answer, to put myself out of my misery, but at that moment I was cold, wet, hungry, in pain, and trying to make sense of a clue that wouldn't fit. I didn't have the energy for a break-up too. I let it go to voicemail.

Grabbing a powdery coffee and a listless burger from one of the outlets, I shuffled my way around the eating area until I found a clean table. I ate mechanically, drank the coffee, and stretched out my injured knee. A bulge of swollen flesh bloomed at the joint. I knew that when I finally peeled off my jeans, it wasn't going to be a pretty sight.

'You're telling it wrong! It's "Why are there no aspirin in the jungle? Because the parrots-eat-'em-all." Not, "Why are there no paracetamol in the jungle?" If you start it that way, the joke doesn't make sense.'

'Well, that's how Mark told me it at school.'

Two kids arguing at the next table. The younger looked about Jodie's age, his brother perhaps twelve or thirteen.

'Well, you're probably not remembering *exactly* what he said.' Big Brother sighed in a teacherly tone. 'People never repeat what they've been told. Not word for word.'

'I s'pose,' the smaller kid agreed. 'Maybe they put things into their own words instead?'

The mother, a long-suffering parent with the look of someone who'd already endured many hours of backseat bickering, caught my eye. 'Sorry, are they disturbing you? Please, turn down the volume, boys.'

'"People never repeat what they've been told",' I echoed. '"Not word for word."'

Taking in my bandaged head and the dried bloodstains on my shirt, the mother seemed to decide that making small talk had probably been a mistake. The quarrelling brothers were quickly ushered to a table on the far side of the food court. Meanwhile, I sat and stared into space. *Both, Mark. Tell Scott, I saw both of them.* But as those little geniuses had just said, we very rarely repeat back precisely what we've been told. Instead, we interpret what we believe was the meaning behind the words and then rephrase them. And of course, there was the fact that Noonan had always had trouble interpreting Ben's broad Yorkshire inflections.

The breath caught in my throat.

That was the moment the truth hit me, in all its horrific inevitability.

'Jesus Christ,' I whispered. 'But that's impossible.'

Chapter Thirty-Six

I WAS REACHING FOR MY PHONE to call Tallis when the big screens mounted around the food court snagged my attention. The broadcast from Purley had begun.

As Everwood had promised, the intro to the *Ghost Seekers* Halloween special was spectacular – an aerial drone shot of the clearing, the blaze of the fair glowing in the dark bowl of the forest like embers in a witch's pyre. The shot swept on, zooming around the track of the roller coaster as punters screamed from their carriages, zipping to the heights of the Ferris wheel, and then down to take in the mannequin monsters stationed outside Tommy Radlett's ghost train. As the show's misty logo materialised on-screen, so Purley Rectory came into view. I had to admit, with the low-angled spotlights enhancing its aloof and chaotic façade, the house looked suitably spectral.

There was a small stir in the food court around me. At a table nearby, a young woman with dyed purple hair and an impish face grabbed her friend's hand.

'Oh my God, it's that Darrel Everwood thing!' she cried, pointing up at the screen. 'I totally forgot this was on. My mum loves him, but I reckon he's a complete nutcase. Aw, I'd like to have watched it, though. Steph at work said he's going to actually summon a real ghost or something. I wonder if we can get them to put the sound on?'

Every screen was currently muted.

'Billy's got his tablet,' her friend said, looking over at the third occupant of their table. 'Be a love and put it on for us, Bill.'

Clearly not the biggest *Ghost Seekers* fan, Billy groaned and started rifling through the backpack on the seat next to him. Meanwhile, I staggered to my feet and hobbled over to their table.

'Excuse me, I happened to overhear your conversation and I wondered if I could join you for a moment?' All three looked up at me with expressions of concern similar to that of the long-suffering mother. 'I'm supposed to be there tonight, you see?' I said, gesturing towards the screens where Everwood had just appeared. 'My name's Scott Jericho and I—'

'Oh. My. Freaking. God!' the impish girl squealed. 'That was the name of the fair! My mum told me, and it stuck in my head because it sounded so pretty and unusual. So you're, like, the owner?'

'Son of.' I smiled.

Billy glanced up from his tablet. 'Then why aren't you there?'

'I had a car accident,' I said, eliciting sympathetic pouts from the girls. 'My family's been working on this with Everwood for months, so I'm really gutted I won't be able to make it back. I would try watching it on my phone, but for some reason the volume doesn't work on my media player.' This, at least, was true. 'Do you think—?'

'Of course!' the impish girl said, grabbing Billy's bag and dumping it on the floor so that I could sit. 'This is *so* exciting. You'll have to tell us what he's really like. I mean, is it true what his ex has been saying? That he can't really speak to dead people? That he makes it all up?'

'I guess we're going to find out,' I said.

Billy perched the tablet at the end of the table so that we could all see. Behind it, a silent big screen played along in time. From multiple tables nearby, I could hear excited chatter as other diners followed our lead and crowded around their own phones and devices. The buzz was palpable, and I wondered if Gillespie's sceptical documentary would be generating the same kind of reaction. For all the doctor's showmanship, I doubted it. The unromantic reality of the real world could never compete with the promise of ghosts. Perhaps, in the end, that was the only sane explanation for these killings.

I looked down at the phone in my hand. When the show was over, I would have to decide how the case played out. Sam Urnshaw had wanted Tilda's murderer delivered up to private justice – an instinct that I'd once thought jibed with my own rage and desire to see the guilty punished. But Sal had urged me not to lose myself in the hunt. My dad hadn't made his view known but had seemed to trust my judgement. I already knew what Harry would say. As for myself, I was undecided. Would I end up calling Tallis or the killer?

The sound kicked in on Billy's tablet and my gaze returned to the screen.

Everwood was standing in the Victorian sitting room where, not many hours ago, Miss Rowell had confided her secret. Much of the clutter had been cleared away so that the only furniture remaining was a single high-backed armchair. The lighting was subdued, the glow of a fire in the grate providing an atmospheric flicker. The medium was dressed in a red silk smoking jacket with a mustard-coloured cravat tied around his throat. A bold choice of costume that provoked sniggers from Billy.

'The time has come,' Darrel said, his intense, mascara-rimmed gaze focused down the camera. 'As many of you know, the entire *Ghost Seekers* team and I are grieving the loss of one of our own. Just today, our friend and colleague Sebastian Thorn was ripped from this world in the most violent and despicable way imaginable. Our dear Seb, who for decades has been an advocate and champion of powerful and gifted psychics. But I am here tonight to tell you ... He is *not* lost to us.'

I could hear hysteria in Everwood's voice, keen as razor wire. It even seemed to be infecting his limbs, small shudders animating his hands and shoulders.

'He's doing it,' the girl beside me squealed. 'The possession thing!'

I thought back to the clip they'd played on breakfast television. Everwood in the darkened passage of a Scottish castle, shuddering and whining as the spirit of some long-dead laird spoke through him. In the ghostless environment of Purley Rectory, I wondered which fictional personality he would claim had taken control of his body. Perhaps one suggested by a killer, whose very existence, I now realised, accounted for Darrel Everwood's new-found enthusiasm for the event. In his manic and paranoid state, he must have not only accepted that existence but embraced it as a vindication of his life's work.

'Some of you watching will also be m-mourning the pr-premature deaths of loved ones,' he said, his words suddenly stilted. Halting. Spasmodic. 'Muh-others, fathers, s-sons, daughters, ch-children, all taken from you before their time.

Well, take heart. I have *suh-een* the dead returned! Not just in spirit. But b-body.'

'Oh, this is priceless!' The impish girl and her friend both had their phones out and were busy scrolling. 'He's trending already. Hashtag: Darrel is losing it. Hashtag: Everwood is the real deal.'

'I will pr-prove to everyone that death is not the end,' Everwood went on. 'Here in the most h-haunted house in Britain, I call upon the veil to be t-torn aside and for the dead to appear. Let the wuh-world see you as I have seen you. The doubters. The scoffers. The sc-sceptics. Their time is over and ours has begun.'

Suddenly, he dropped into the high-backed armchair, and the spasms which, until that point had been no more than tiny jerks and twitches, intensified. He raised his hands to his face, his fingers closing into frozen claws. His lower jaw jutted outwards, the bottom shelf of teeth projecting in front of his top lip and then roving side to side in a strange rhythmic motion. Eyes horribly wide, he appeared to be fascinated with the hands that remained bunched up in front of his face. Then a huge convulsion shot through his body like an electric current. His legs appeared to stiffen until his heels rested on the floorboards and his shoulders arched into the chairback.

'I don't like it,' a child whispered behind us. 'Daddy, turn it off. It's too scary.'

The girls at our table exchanged glances and even Billy looked a little unnerved.

Our attention returned to the screen. A long, low whine was projecting from the throat of Darrel Everwood. His head began to thrash up and down as if he was violently agreeing with some imperceptible spectre standing before him. Then his eyes rolled white in their sockets and that jutting jaw fell open, yawning wider and wider, stretching to an almost impossible degree. With his chin resting against his chest, those straining lips appeared grey and bloodless.

'He's trending number one in the UK,' the girl murmured. 'But that little kid's right. I don't like it either.'

Neither did I.

Because suddenly I realised what was happening here. I'd seen it once before in a case Garris and I had investigated a few years ago. Not a common method of murder these days, but the odd instance cropped up from time to time. In that case, a wife had been forced to ingest a lethal quantity of rat poison. We'd received a tip-off and arrived at the house an hour after she'd swallowed the stuff. Everything was done to save her but there was no known antidote for this particular toxin.

I pulled out my phone and fired off a text to Tallis:

STOP IT RIGHT NOW. NOT AN ACT. EVERWOOD POISONED WITH STRYCHNINE.

On-screen, the medium was now balanced on his heels and shoulders, the centre of his body arching outwards. It was as if his arms and legs had been weighted down while an invisible rope had been tied around his middle. Slowly, this unseen tether appeared to be winched in, concaving Darrel Everwood's spine to the breaking point. Then all at once, he collapsed into the chair, gasping, choking, only to be jerked back into that same exaggerated posture. This happened five or six times, the heels of his boots rapping out a hollow tattoo on the floorboards.

'Make it stop,' the child wailed at its father. 'Someone help him.'

But no one could help Darrel Everwood. Not now.

It was as clever as it was cruel. The ultimate act of mockery, not enacted prior to death, as I'd originally thought, but at the very same moment. No one was rushing to Everwood's aid. They had seen his possession routine before. They believed his death throes were all part of the show.

We watched on as the killer's final victim jerked and thrashed, foaming at the mouth, clenching his jaw, bending his spine until surely it had to snap. Watched the inexpressible agony in his every hideous contortion. Watched the unspoken pleading glisten in his eyes. Watched until at last the life went out of him and he slumped back into the chair.

As a nation, we watched a man murdered live on-air.

Watched and did nothing. Darrel Everwood had been right all along.

This would be remembered forever as the media event of the century.

Chapter Thirty-Seven

I HAD THOUGHT THAT THE KILLER might have entirely abandoned their ritual in the public execution of Darrel Everwood. But replaying those final moments in my head, I wondered if that was true – the flame-red smoking jacket, the mustard-yellow cravat, the glow of the firelight flickering across his agonised body, and then there was the choice of strychnine as the poison. Perhaps not only to mimic the medium's possession routine, but in those flailing, tortured movements, to suggest the agony of a burning witch.

That was what I thought as I limped out of the motorway services towards my car. In fact, this insight turned out to be yet another that didn't quite hit the mark.

I had left the people at the table in a state of confusion and horror. A reaction that was probably being shared in households up and down the country. Many might think that what they'd just witnessed was a joke – a gruesome Halloween stunt designed to shock the nation. I imagined furious parents jamming the phone lines of the TV station, demanding to know why Darrel Everwood had just traumatised their little tykes. From what the girls had told me, I knew social media was in meltdown. As well as the public, reporters, politicians, influencers and celebrities all appeared to be gripped by a collective hysteria, everyone posing theories and demanding answers.

I dropped into the driver's seat. The rain was still falling, a drenching blast that came in gusty waves across the windscreen. I wiped my face on my sleeve and spent a few minutes staring through the downpour. I knew I couldn't have saved Everwood. My realisation of what had really been happening in this case had come too late. But still, the clues had been there right from the beginning, their true significance just waiting to be appreciated. If I hadn't been so distracted at the prospect of losing Haz, would I have seen it earlier? I only knew that the fury I had expected to experience at this moment was not there. Instead, all I felt was a weary sort of sorrow that made me dread the confrontation to come.

My phone pulsed into life. A call from Tallis. I turned off the handset and went back to staring at the rain.

I left it until just after one in the morning before starting the car and continuing my journey to Purley. In those long, dark hours, I had checked and rechecked my theory against the facts. One clue central to the murders had suddenly illuminated a separate puzzle. A human drama that had been running alongside the main event and which had also distracted me. If the players in that little production were still up and about, then it might be worth having a word with them too.

I moved on from A-roads into country lanes, confident that, by the time I arrived, the main police presence would have left the site. In fact, a couple of constables were still on duty when I pulled into the car park. I grabbed my beanie from the back seat, pulling it low so that it obscured my freshly bandaged forehead.

'Mr Jericho,' an officer said as he checked my ID. 'I was told to keep a lookout for you, sir. DCI Tallis says you must contact him as a matter of urgency. Guvnor said for you not to do anything without his say-so. Said you'd understand.'

I flourished my mobile. 'I intend to call him in the next few minutes, Constable. I just need to check in on someone first.'

'Long as you steer clear of the house, that should be OK. I suppose you know what happened here tonight?'

'Yes,' I said. 'I believe I do.'

Stalking through the last of the drizzle, I headed straight for the production trailers. Just a few hours ago, this entire area must have been a hive of activity, the *Ghost Seekers* crew dashing around in preparation for their big broadcast. Now, like the fair, Purley Rectory lay cloaked in silence and darkness. I guessed most of the team would have been interviewed and released back to their hotel hours ago. I imagined them now, crowded into each other's rooms, passing around drinks, all trying to process what they'd seen.

All except one.

A light was on in the small trailer next to the late Darrel Everwood's. I mounted the step and knocked.

'Mr Jericho? I ... I'm so sorry, I can't see you now. I can't see anyone.'

Deepal Chandra tried to close the door on me. I wedged my foot in the gap.

'Is your partner with you?' I asked. 'I'd like to speak to him too.'

She swallowed hard. If she'd looked stressed yesterday, she now appeared utterly at the end of her tether, her eyes bloodshot from crying, the smell of whisky on her breath.

'I don't know what you're talking about. There's no one else here.'

I nodded. 'Then I'd better call DCI Tallis and pass on my suspicion that you and your partner have been involved in a plot to undermine Darrel Everwood. That this may have led to his increasing sense of persecution and paranoia. That you might have falsified your credentials in order to gain the position as his personal assistant. That, given the ongoing murder investigation that began to centre around Darrel, your continuing failure to divulge this little conspiracy could be regarded as highly suspicious. Of course, the police would use all endeavours to keep any non-relevant facts from the press, but as *you* know very well, such things have a way of leaking out.' I called through the gap. 'Dr Gillespie, don't you think it's time we spoke?'

A hollow voice, quite unlike that of the smooth public speaker, answered, 'Let him in, Deepal. For Christ's sake.'

The door swung open and I limped up the final step. Much more modest than Everwood's extravagant model, his PA's trailer was still at the luxurious end of the market. I watched as Deepal went to sit on the leather sofa beside Gillespie, folding his hands into hers.

'It isn't us,' she said, as I eased myself into the seat opposite. 'You have to believe me. We only wanted—'

'I'm a humanitarian,' Gillespie insisted. 'I would never harm a fellow creature. Never.'

His oddly lineless face suddenly appeared very old and tired.

'But your humanitarianism only seems to extend to those who agree with you,' I said. 'The others, like Darrel Everwood and Genevieve Bell? They're fair game, aren't they? For ridicule and humiliation. That was the purpose of this undercover mission of yours, wasn't it? To dig up some solid dirt on Britain's most famous psychic and then to expose him to the world?'

The doctor shifted uncomfortably in his seat.

'I think you began to realise that, as clever as you are, it was impossible to compete with the allure of these people. What Darrel and his kind offer might well be fool's gold, but it glitters nonetheless. The cold, hard reality you tried to sell the public was a truth they didn't want to buy into. But if you could plant a spy in his camp and she could bring you irrefutable evidence of fraud, then it wouldn't just be Everwood's reputation destroyed. As the most celebrated of them, he would stand and fall as a totem for all psychics.'

'How did you know?' Deepal asked.

'I've been thinking a lot about names tonight,' I said. 'How they're used, how we interpret them. Doctor, in your TV interview before you came to Purley, you insisted that the interviewer call you Joseph, saying only your mother and your partner called you Joe. You did the same with me when we met. Yet when Deepal interrupted your rally in circumstances where you might easily have rebuked her, she called you Joe and you never said a word.' I turned to the PA. 'You were his PhD student? The one he had a relationship with?' She nodded. 'Your disgust for the doctor also felt overplayed at times. Describing him as a vulture picking over the bones of the dead. For an abused employee who didn't even seem to like her employer all that much, your contempt for Everwood's enemy struck me as insincere. Like someone trying to ensure that no one would suspect her loyalties.'

'Stupid.' She shot Gillespie an apologetic glance and he wrapped his arm around her.

'Do you remember what you said to me when I suggested Darrel might do anything to get out of the Halloween event, even murder? You said, "He's a complete egomaniac but not even *we* think he'd go that far." Because Ben was with you, he assumed that "we" included him. In fact, you were talking about a view of Darrel you shared with your partner. You both thought he was a ruthless fraud but didn't believe he was dangerous to that degree.'

Gillespie inclined his head in acknowledgement.

'But I think the most suggestive thing was how you provided each other with an alibi on the night of the murder,' I continued. 'Without me even asking, Deepal, you volunteered the idea that you'd been contacted by a mysterious journalist who wanted to get Everwood's take on Dr Gillespie's press stunt. You went to meet this person, but he didn't show up. However, this apparently put you in a position to witness the doctor leave the area at exactly eight twenty, a time that conveniently coincided with an alarm on your phone to check in on Darrel's social media platforms.

'I'd suggest that even the most committed PA doesn't vet her employer's online presence every twenty minutes. But guess what? When I questioned Dr Gillespie about his movements, he confirmed your story. When I then asked him why he'd hung around after the press conference, he couldn't give me an answer. Because I think it was to meet with you for a debrief. Later, when you discovered the time window for the murder from your bribed police contact, you agreed on a story that would give the doctor his alibi. Why? Because the ritualistic slaughter of a medium might just implicate an obsessive academic who had, on more than one occasion, said he would stop at nothing to eradicate belief in the supernatural.'

'It was just talk.' Gillespie sighed. 'A bit of hyperbole to get some press attention.'

'And then there was your detailed knowledge of the murder,' I went on. 'Information that must have been fed to you by Deepal after she learned it from her police contact.'

'I got the job easily enough,' Deepal said. 'You're right, we faked my CV and references. I don't even think Darrel's manager checked them. He ran through personal assistants at the rate of one a month. Thorn was just glad to find one who'd put up with him.'

'Do you know what Everwood intended to do tonight?' I asked. 'The nature of his big reveal?'

She shook her head. 'He went completely off-script. With Seb gone, there was no one to rein him in. He even asked for a change of outfit at the very last minute and then got them to restage the sitting room. Said he wanted it cleared of furniture and the fire lit.'

'You told me earlier that he also wanted some time alone before the broadcast, to "attune with the spirits". How long before?'

'A couple of hours. Does it matter?'

'It's crucial,' I said, getting to my feet. 'After being administered, strychnine takes roughly two hours before taking full effect.'

The pair of them rose as I moved towards the door.

'The backlash against me will be devastating,' Gillespie said. 'When the public find out what we did, they won't believe we weren't involved in the murder. My reputation will never recover.'

Every shred of the man's pride and pomposity appeared to have abandoned him. He leaned heavily against the young woman who stood at his side.

'Did you find any solid evidence that Darrel was a fraud?' I asked.

'No. I actually think...' Deepal glanced at the man she loved. 'I think he believed it himself, in the end. That he really had spoken to the dead.'

'I know he believed it,' I confirmed. 'And don't worry about your reputation, Doctor. I don't think there's any need for me to report this to the police. Only, perhaps you might extend the same kindness to the next believer you encounter. There are gentler ways to convince someone of your arguments than to tear their beliefs to shreds.'

Gillespie's whispered thanks accompanied me out of the trailer.

I limped slowly back to the perimeter of the fairground. The main strip was empty, everything shut down and boarded up. Jericho Fairs had played its final night in the grounds of Purley Rectory. I stumbled on, feeling the pain twist around my knee like a hot wire, sensing the despair of these murders seep into my bones. Away to my right, I caught a glimpse of Tilda's darkened tent, a hill of dying flowers stacked outside the door.

It was time.

I took out my phone and called the killer.

Chapter Thirty-Eight

'HELLO GENEVIEVE,' I SAID.

The woman I had known as Evangeline Bell came slowly through the mist. The grey-white vapour that had begun rolling out from the forest an hour ago now swam around her. It left its damp touch on her hair and clothes, streaking her long coat and reforming into droplets that trailed down her face like tears. The self-possessed, forthright woman I had met at Cedar Gables was gone. In her place stood a dreamier, somehow less substantial presence.

'It's over,' she said, even her voice sounding airier than the one she'd used for Evangeline. 'Thank God. You're a clever man, Mr Jericho. I wonder, did you always suspect you were speaking to the wrong Bell sister?'

'Not until tonight,' I said. 'The man who saw you at Sebastian Thorn's gave me the clue.'

She continued walking along the empty avenue of the fair, cutting through a mist that seemed almost as ethereal as herself. Despite the pain in my knee, I kept pace, my hand closed around the phone in my pocket.

'That poor young man,' she sighed. 'He stood in the doorway while I finished arranging Sebastian's doll. At first, he startled me and I thought of running, but then I realised that he'd become frozen by what he saw. Almost catatonic. In the end, I simply walked straight past him. I wasn't even sure he'd seen my face.'

'He hadn't,' I said. 'He'd seen something else.'

People never repeat what they've been told. Not word for word – the wisdom I'd learned from the two quarrelling brothers in the food court. Mark Noonan had been remembering a conversation he'd had with a confused and frightened Ben Halliday at four in the morning. Ben, fuzzy-headed from his pain meds, mumbling away in an accent the London mobster had always struggled to understand, led to Noonan misinterpreting the message and then rephrasing it to reflect what he believed was its meaning – 'Both, Mark. Tell Scott, I saw both of them.' What Ben had most likely said was something like, *Birthmark. Tell Scott I saw her birthmark.*

I gestured towards the port-wine stain on Genevieve's hand.

'I've always hated this thing,' she said, rubbing the side of her thumb. 'Right from when I was a little girl. It felt like some kind of ill omen that had been branded on my flesh.'

I nodded. 'And that was the real reason Tilda gave you the gloves, wasn't it? For the most part, I believe the story you told me back at Cedar Gables. Of how your sister Evangeline started the game, of how your cousin, Miss Grice, then invited Tilda to come to the house to confirm your psychic abilities. How Tilda felt sorry for you and taught you the fake dukkerin techniques so that Miss Grice might treat you better. How in the months and years afterwards, you slowly became convinced of the reality of your powers. But the gloves were a separate matter.

'The talent you described as psychometry, the ability to receive psychic messages through touch? Tilda never suggested that you mimic that particular ability. It isn't mentioned in *Hearing the Dead* as being part of your repertoire, and when Darrel Everwood was praising your incredible gifts to me, he didn't list it among your accomplishments. Tilda gave you the gloves because she felt sorry for a shy little girl who was self-conscious about her hand. Which was ultimately why your first victim had to be so savagely mutilated.'

The woman walking beside me didn't so much as flinch as I went on.

'To make the world believe that Genevieve Bell had been murdered, you were forced to remove your sister's hands in case anyone ever mentioned that the real Genevieve had possessed an identifying birthmark. For the same reason, although you didn't look dissimilar to Evangeline, you had to disfigure her face and remove her teeth in case of dental comparison. That was why the ritualism of the murders became necessary. If it hadn't been for the arcane set dressing of the dolls and the Bible quotes, then the natural question might have been asked: what was the purpose of those original mutilations? And the obvious answer: to mislead the police about who was really lying dead in the sitting room of Cedar Gables.

'But some kind of identification would have to be made. So you cleaned the house thoroughly, scrubbing away your own fingerprints and removing hairs from your pillows and brushes. These you replaced with hair from your dead sister so that a DNA match could be made and the police would believe that it was the occupant of the house who'd been murdered.'

'Please go on.' Genevieve nodded. 'You're doing very well.'

We had now reached the steps of my father's Waltzer and Genevieve began to climb up to the ride's undulating wooden walkway. I followed a pace or two behind, keen not to startle her. Something wasn't right here. I could feel it in my gut.

'My guess is that you invited Evangeline down from Scotland on some pretext,' I said. 'Perhaps to discuss your mother's deteriorating health. Evangeline was in the house long enough to leave some of her own fingerprints on the freshly dusted surfaces, but not quite enough to account for any normal inhabitant. But of course, you had a ready-made explanation for that. In your guise as Evangeline, you would claim that Genevieve had become fixated on always wearing her gloves. Not because she wished to disguise any blemish, of course, but because she absolutely believed in her power of psychometry.'

The slick shining boards groaned under our feet as we made a slow circuit of the ride. I gripped the phone hard in my pocket while my heart hammered in my chest. Why had she brought us here? Was she simply walking as if in a dream or did she have some purpose in mind?

'The red herring of the ritual had been crucial for the first murder,' I continued. 'You wanted your sister dead, and by taking on her identity, you were also given the freedom to continue your campaign without any suspicion settling on you. I briefly considered Evangeline as a suspect but dismissed the idea because of a total lack of motive. However, the extreme violence that had been so necessary for the first killing soon began to sicken you.

'In Tilda's case, you managed the mutilation of her face but couldn't go through with the removal of her hands. The same happened in the killing of Seb Thorn. Most serial killers become ever more intricate and obsessive in their rituals whereas here the reverse was true. From the beginning, I thought the ritualistic aspects were both overdone and yet somehow half-hearted. A jumble of ideas and symbolism that soon started to fall apart in the execution. It was Tilda herself who suggested the true motive when she said the poppet doll felt *personal*.

'This was never a case of some religious fanatic determined to wipe out witches. That was just an elaborate smokescreen to disguise the most intimate of motives.'

Genevieve nodded, absently trailing her fingers along the Waltzer's dripping handrail. 'Did I make any other slips?'

'Your mother was a weak link,' I said. 'You allowed her to discover your sister's body – a fitting punishment perhaps for her emotional neglect and exploitation of you as a child. But despite her dementia, you couldn't disguise your identity from the woman you'd lived with all those years. And so a small sleight of hand was required. To anyone asking questions, it became crucial to establish from the outset that your family had called you "Gennie". Because of your mother's wandering mind, everything hung on the idea of this particular diminutive. When your mother then used the name "Eve" we'd assume she was referring to her living daughter, Evangeline. In reality, your family had always used "Eve" for Genevieve and "Eva" for Evangeline. I think you'd tried to explain this in some way to Patricia, and in those times when it came back to her, she would put emphasis, almost apologetically, on Ev*ah* to show that she understood and remembered. By the way, the idea that Eve was a reference to yourself was reinforced by Darrel Everwood. He seemed puzzled when I spoke of "Gennie" because, of course, he would have heard Sebastian Thorn refer to you using "Eve". But going back to Patricia – her drifting attention was a risk.'

'A risk indeed,' Genevieve said with a smile, and stepping onto the ride's revolve, she began to cross the Waltzer plates. When I tried to follow, she turned and waved me back. 'I'm not going anywhere, Mr Jericho. Please, continue.'

I shook my head, uncertain if I should follow. In the end, I obeyed her wish and remained on the walkway. This situation, whatever it really was, felt delicate, as if one clumsy move on my part might tip us into disaster.

'At one point, your mother almost gave away the fact that her favourite daughter was still alive,' I said. 'When she told me that Genevieve remained at Cedar Gables, that she spoke to her, and that her youngest child would never leave, she wasn't referring to a restless spirit. She was speaking about the *living* daughter that stood beside her. And then there was the night of Sebastian Thorn's murder. When I called you to discuss your former publicist, Patricia cried out, "Eve, where have you been? You said you wouldn't leave again." She wasn't confused. She was referring to the fact that you *had* left the house once already that night. She must have woken while you were away murdering Thorn and panicked. Later, while you were speaking to me, that anxiety of waking in an empty house returned to her.

'I really ought to have listened to Patricia more closely,' I said. 'If I had, then who knows how things might have worked out? That morning I met her stumbling out of the conifers, for example. The assortment of possessions she imagined had been taken from her – her hat, her scarf, her underthings – had included one real item. Her bedsheets. I'd already guessed that the killer must have been wearing some kind of Halloween costume in order to pass through the fair, bloodstained but unnoticed. My father had only announced the costume concession that morning.

'Seeing the opportunity this afforded you, I think that was the day you fixed on for Tilda to die. But sourcing a costume quickly might prove difficult, especially as you lived in the middle of nowhere. Then again, there's an item in every house that can be quickly adapted into a rudimentary Halloween costume. A white-sheet ghost, this one a little more gruesome than is traditional, with its bloody smatters, but still unremarkable in a crowd of monsters. Unfortunately, while crossing the drive to Purley you dropped a couple of the masonry nails from your bag and was then spotted lurking in the trees.'

Genevieve had come to one of the far gondolas when, quite suddenly, she reached out and spun the thing on its squealing casters. The back of the carriage rotated slowly around to reveal a single occupant, a wild-haired old woman sitting with her hands locked firmly around the safety bar. There was no understanding in Patricia's eyes, no comprehension of where she was, only a glazed emptiness.

'Poor dear,' Genevieve sighed, pulling back the bar and dragging her loose-limbed mother out of the ride. 'It might have been easier to kill her, too. But as selfish and manipulative as she was, she did love me.' The killer ran a lazy finger down that slack, almost immobile face. 'I think even in her addled state, she remembered how she'd exploited me as a child. Trying her best to go along with my plan might have been her way of making amends.'

Genevieve then slipped a hand into her coat and, positioning herself behind Patricia, pulled out a long-bladed knife. In the next instant, the keen edge was laid against her mother's throat. I took a step forward but the flexing of her fingers around the handle made me think better of it.

'Please, put down the knife,' I said, my voice a little louder as I gripped the phone in my pocket. 'You don't have to do this.'

'Don't I?' She smiled. 'We'll see. But do go on, Mr Jericho, this is all most interesting.'

I took a breath and complied. 'You weren't only seen in the trees. I was speaking to Christopher Cloade at the fair when he glimpsed you over my shoulder.'

I thought back to that look of stark terror that had washed over the preacher's face. Then his words, almost a whisper, *So it's true. What they say about Purley*... A woman he knew by sight, who he believed had been brutally murdered, now stood looking back at him. A phantom returned.

'I could tell straightaway what he thought.' Génevieve laughed. 'It was the same ridiculous thing Darrel Everwood would come to believe. You know, Mr Jericho, there is no fool on earth like a man desperate to wallow in his own fantasies.'

'And of course his belief became useful to you.' I nodded. 'You already had the perfect alibi for these murders. After all, who in their right mind would suspect the first victim? But why not take this chance to muddy the waters even further? You began turning up outside Cloade's home at night, showing yourself to him in the street, slipping in among his homeless congregation. Haunting him. Then, seeing me waiting outside the schoolhouse to interview him, you took the opportunity of leaving your bloodied gloves on the altar.'

She gave me an oddly bashful look and the knife slipped a little from her mother's throat. 'He came to me after the podcast with Dr Gillespie had been aired. Caught me at my moment of crisis, waving his pamphlets, evangelising, saying he could save my wayward soul. He even got some money out of me before he left. Afterwards, when I came to my senses, I wondered if I should add him to my list: Evangeline, Tilda, Sebastian, Darrel, and Christopher Cloade. But that pitiful man wasn't part of the legacy I needed to eradicate. Still, I thought he deserved a good scare for his impudence, and he made a rather enticing suspect, didn't he?'

'The legacy you needed to eradicate,' I echoed.

She blinked at me and, in that moment, tightened her grip again on the knife. 'Of course. Why else do you think they all had to die?'

Chapter Thirty-Nine

'As soon as you discount the ritualism of the murders, you not only see that the identity of the first victim becomes the crucial question, but that the motive must be linked to that question as well,' I said. 'Who was the most likely person to bear a grudge against Evangeline Bell?'

'Grudge?' She stared at me. 'You think it was only that? Some pathetic resentment I harboured against my sister?'

'Why don't you tell me?'

She took a moment, closed her eyes, appeared to gather herself. Meanwhile that unmoving presence at her side gazed back at me through the twisting tendrils of mist. This wasn't merely a catatonic state induced by Patricia's dementia, the old woman must have been drugged. Some kind of sedative to keep her calm and compliant, but to what purpose? Was Genevieve really going to cut her mother's throat in front of me? The image felt wrong somehow.

'Remember me saying that I had always been a consummate little actress?' Genevieve asked. 'Well, that was true. In the plays we'd sometimes invent for our father before his death, Eva was the narrator while I played all the parts. Even as a child of eight, I had a flair for it, pulling on a mask and inhabiting other lives. It was how Eva knew that I could pull off that original trick and make Miss Grice believe that I was communicating with the dead. I was a quick study, as I told you, picking up the dramatic flourishes used by the clairvoyants who visited the house, learning how they threw their voices and contorted their features while apparently possessed. Of course, I didn't realise then that I'd be playing the role of a medium for the rest of my life.

'What I gave you in my performance of Eva, Mr Jericho, was an idealised version of my older sister. The one I wished and longed for. A failed protector who'd tried her best to save me. A remorseful soul tormented by what she'd done. In reality, Evangeline regretted nothing. In fact, after she had come up with the "joke" of fooling our cousin, she realised that the trick had to be sustained. Our lives had been transformed overnight, remember. No more endless domestic chores, no more drudgery, no more earning our keep. We had become honoured guests at Cedar Gables. But I was just an eight-year-old kid who might give the game away at any minute. To maintain our new lifestyle, it therefore became crucial that I start to *believe* in my powers.'

She looked down at her hand for a moment, perhaps picturing those black lace gloves that had been so much a part of her life.

'You have to understand, a young mind is pliable,' she said. 'Its understanding of reality is a day-to-day exploration of ideas, constantly evolving and shifting. There are no set laws, no boundaries, no absolutes. We'd been visited by Tilda Urnshaw, who showed us how to create the illusion of psychic powers but who also claimed that I *did* possess some latent paranormal ability. Eva seized on this. She began to suggest that perhaps we hadn't played a prank on Miss Grice after all. That although that had been our intention we had, in fact, unlocked gifts already there. We should continue to use the tricks Tilda had taught us, just as a convenience, but there was no doubt, she said, that I was a *very* special young lady.

'Those were the kindest words my sister ever said to me. Over the coming months, she began to reconfigure my reality, changing the very idea I had of myself, adapting my personality so that, slowly, gradually, I came to accept my new identity. I wasn't playing a part anymore. I *was* the child who spoke to ghosts. She'd whisper to me at night, going over the ordinary incidents of the day, infusing them with a sense of wonder, always ensuring that I was at the centre of each rewritten event. For a lonely child, shunned at school due to her increasingly odd reputation, it was an irresistible fantasy. I was special. That's why I was bullied, called names, set apart.'

'Genevieve,' I murmured. 'I'm so sorry.'

Despite what she had done, the horrors she'd perpetrated, I did feel for her then. Or at least, for the isolated, manipulated child she had once been.

'I'm not entirely sure whether Mother knew what Eva was doing. Did you, my dear?' she asked the unresponsive old woman. Receiving no answer, Genevieve drew the knife higher until it rested tight under her mother's jaw. 'Did you, you malevolent old bitch?'

'Geneveive, don't,' I shouted, stepping up onto the Waltzer plates.

'One more step and I'll cut her wide open, I swear to God ... That's it, back you go, Mr Jericho.' Genevieve smiled and nodded at my compliance. 'On some level, I suppose she must have known. In any case, after months of my sister's manipulation, the reality of my world had been set for the next thirty years. And, of course, Evangeline happily accepted all the benefits. First, the little luxuries showered on us by Miss Grice, then the generous annual allowance I gave her out of the estate I'd inherited from our cousin. I even handed over a percentage of my earnings from the private readings I performed after I'd withdrawn from the public spotlight. Eva never had to work a day in her life.

'And what a life! She left us at twenty, travelled abroad, had adventures, love affairs, saw the world. Meanwhile, I remained at home with this grasping husk of a woman.' Genevieve spat the words into her mother's ear. 'Oh, I might get the odd phone call when Eva needed money, but otherwise, she became a stranger. She never regretted what she'd done. Never tried to dissuade me from the fantasy she had invented. Eva created a person who was never supposed to exist and then abandoned her creation to live out its make-believe life. A life in which I was utterly invested, convinced I was helping grieving people. That I was making a difference.'

'And then you were invited onto the podcast with Dr Gillespie,' I said.

'The offer came through Seb Thorn.' She nodded. 'Another lie, I'm afraid, Mr Jericho. We did remain in contact after I stepped away from the limelight. I didn't need the money, but I was intrigued by the idea of proving my abilities to such a renowned sceptic as Dr Gillespie. You know the result.'

She glanced again at that blemished hand, currently fixed around the glinting knife.

'What I told you about the effect it had on me was true. Imagine if for thirty years – pretty much your entire life – you'd believed in an identity that was suddenly torn away from you. Systemically, ruthlessly, brilliantly stripped away within ten minutes. Decades of self-deception crashing down until you're forced to peer through the wreckage of your personality, only to find a stranger staring back at you. It was like waking from a beautiful dream to a howling, indifferent wasteland.

'And so, *no*, Mr Jericho, I didn't just bear a grudge against my sister. I wanted her dead. Erased from existence. Unmade, like I had been unmade.'

'And unwittingly, Dr Gillespie provided inspiration for how you might do it,' I said. 'He told you that what you'd suffered had been a form of abuse. That if there really was a God of the Old Testament, then this was deserving of all His fury and vengeance.'

'It made me think of that line from the Bible,' she confirmed. '"Thou shalt not suffer a witch to live." That was the beginning of the smokescreen, as you call it. I did a little research into the old witchfinders, the poppet dolls, all the paraphernalia that might mislead the police. Christopher Cloade played his part, too. After his visit, I saw that such a fanatic could easily make a viable suspect. I had to give myself time, you see? To keep everyone guessing long enough so that I could finish the thing.'

'To eradicate your legacy.'

'I thought I'd been helping people,' she said. 'Instead, I'd been lying to them. There are no ghosts. Nothing beyond death except the empty scream of the universe. When I looked back at my life, all I could hear was that scream and all I could see were the people responsible.

'I invited my sister down for a visit, as you said. Not an easy thing to arrange, Eva had barely set foot in the house for years. She planned to stay just a single night to discuss our mother's failing health.' At that word – mother – I thought I noticed the first flinch of cognisance from Patricia Bell. A flicker of the eye, no more. 'Eva's solution? Put the old bitch in a home and forget about her. I knew that would be her response and I made sure Mother overheard it. Despite her confusion, the old self-interest was still there, and, later, it made her more amenable to my plans – discovering the body, playing along as best she could with the names.

'Eva's is the one death where I feel no remorse.' Genevieve grinned. 'I even enjoyed it. The obliteration of the person who started it all, the taking away of *her* identity. By the way, we had both turned grey in our late thirties, but after the murder, I dyed my hair to resemble her old copper tint so that I could further distinguish myself from "Genevieve". As I told you, Eva was divorced and estranged from her daughter, so she could easily disappear for a couple of weeks without being missed. And I never intended this thing to go on forever.'

'Just until your four victims were accounted for?' I said, my gaze moving between mother and daughter. Yes, just a flicker in those dull, almost lifeless eyes. 'The first three, you knew. That was why they were comfortable turning their back to you. Thorn must have been shocked to see his old client had returned from the dead, but at that moment there would have been nothing to alert him to any danger. Like with Eva and Tilda, you caved in his skull with a hammer before attending to the ritual elements of the scene.'

'I turned up at the house in the early hours, saying I could explain everything.' Genevieve nodded. 'He was shocked, as you say, but he'd only taken a few steps across the hall when I struck him.'

'And Tilda?'

She hesitated, her focus moving away from me to follow the dreamy undulations of the mist. Could I cross the Waltzer plates before she swept that blade across her mother's throat? Was there time? Was this even the end Genevieve truly envisaged? Again, something about the whole notion of the knife, Genevieve and Patricia felt wrong.

'Tilda. She didn't seem surprised at all. She said, "I knew you weren't dead, little Eve." She even . . .' Genevieve lifted her free hand to the side of her face. 'She saw the hammer in my fist and she just turned her back, as if she'd accepted what was coming.'

Even hearing this part of her confession, I didn't feel angry. At least, I didn't feel that old unreasoning fury that had so often coursed through me in the past. Dr Gillespie had been right, Genevieve had suffered a form of abuse – the warping of her identity to the extent that, when the trick played on her had finally been revealed, her mind had utterly shattered.

'I didn't blame Tilda,' she said. 'Not in the same way I blamed Evangeline for starting it all. But still, she'd played her part.'

'And you mocked her,' I said. 'Just like you mocked Thorn and Everwood.'

'The tarot card?' She raised an eyebrow. 'That wasn't a comment on Tilda alone. All believers are fools. Deep down, some of them even know it. That's what they're terrified of – that one day someone like Gillespie will come along and show them just how ridiculous their hopes and dreams really are.'

It was a suggestion I might once have privately agreed with. Now I baulked at it. 'What was done to you was terrible, Eve, but that doesn't mean belief itself should be despised as foolish.'

She shrugged. 'Everwood was certainly a fool.'

'Evangeline started the deception,' I said. 'Tilda played her part in establishing it. Thorn then came along and reinforced it, spreading your fame.'

'My lies.'

'And Everwood was your legacy.'

'When I heard about how he'd been inspired by my story? I felt this suffocating sense of responsibility. It had to end. Had to be torn up, root and branch.'

'Before killing Eva, you got Darrel's personal number off Thorn,' I said. 'Despite what you told me, you'd always stayed in touch with your old manager. I should have known. You were so precise over details, yet you misnamed the man who'd made you a star. Rose instead of Thorn. Just to keep him out of the limelight long enough for you to get to him.'

'I said that I'd been flattered by Darrel's comments and wanted to speak to him personally,' she said. 'But for Thorn not to say anything. I wanted it to be a surprise.'

'And it was. When you finally placed the call, he thought it was a prank.'

I remembered what Ben had said about Darrel's reaction, *That's some sick shit you're talking. How dare you even pretend to be . . .*

'Thorn had told me weeks ago that Darrel was becoming increasingly unstable,' Genevieve said. 'Losing his grip on reality. It wasn't hard to play on that sense of paranoia and persecution. He wanted to feel vindicated, justified in his self-belief, armoured against his enemies. In his delusions, I saw an echo of my own. He'd passed beyond the conscious trickster and into a state of wilful self-deception.

'I convinced him that I was physically returning to the world. That the guiding light of his psychic gift had reached me on the other side. At the same time, I fed his fears that shadowy figures were working to undermine not just his own career but the truth of all psychic phenomena. He ate it up. I told Darrel I'd visit him two hours before the broadcast, and if he summoned me, I would make an appearance on live television.'

'The media event of the century,' I said.

'He dismissed his security staff and waited for me inside his trailer.' She laughed. 'He sat there, amazed as I walked through the door. A corporeal manifestation! I understand that it might sound ridiculous, but there is a rich history of mediums apparently summoning solid spirits. He even had to leave the room for a moment to gather himself.'

'And that was when you administered the strychnine into the water tank of his coffee machine?'

Patricia suddenly shifted a little, her hands twitching at her sides. I licked my lips, checked Genevieve to see if she had noticed anything, but the killer was too caught up in her story.

'Thorn had told me he was a caffeine addict,' she said. 'Drinking cup after cup in quick succession. The strong flavour would disguise the bitter taste of the poison to perfection.'

'You intended him to die live on-air.' I took a small step up onto the ride's revolve. 'To show the world how human and fallible these so-called psychics are. Because if he was the real deal, surely Darrel would have foreseen his murder.'

'As you've probably guessed, I also suggested a costume change and for the fire in the sitting room to be lit.' She nodded. 'He would be my last victim. There was no more need for the red herring of the ritual, but I knew you'd be watching, Mr Jericho. I thought the neatness of the idea might appeal to you.'

'The burned witch.'

'Perhaps ... Or perhaps I'm spinning you yet another tale. Was Darrel Everwood really my last victim?' She smiled down at her mother. 'Or is there another pyre to come?'

My heart lurched into my throat. I had underestimated her. As I took my next step forward, Genevieve retreated, moving backwards off the revolve and onto the walkway, dragging her suddenly shrieking mother with her. If not full comprehension, then a kind of understanding had begun to animate Patricia Bell. She struggled and the knife fell from Genevieve's hand. Relief surged through me, but in the next instant, I saw the awful smirk on the killer's face and, taking in that long wet coat that she had draped around herself, I realised with a cold horror that she'd never had any intention of using the knife on her mother. That had been a mere delaying tactic to keep me at bay. Her real plan was something far more dreadful. Pulling the almost limp body with her, Genevieve rested her back against one of the posts that held up the ride's canopy.

'Don't,' I cried out. 'For God's sake, don't. Please, just listen to me. I once thought that the only real justice is the kind we make for ourselves. Private justice, personal revenge. I was wrong. *This* is wrong. I don't hate you, Genevieve. What you did to Tilda was cruel beyond imagining. What was done to you was almost equally inhuman. Not just in your childhood, but how you were forced to confront that truth. Everything that followed grew out of that trauma. I need you to know that I forgive you.'

I plunged my hand into my pocket and pulled out the phone, planting it against my ear. 'Tallis? Are you there? Did you hear everything? Where the fuck are you?'

As if I'd conjured him, a solid form suddenly emerged out of the mist and raced towards the Waltzer. I'd called the inspector after making contact with Genevieve, hoping that a live confession would provide him with the evidence he needed to prosecute her. Now all that seemed irrelevant.

Genevieve Bell pressed her back hard against the wooden post. She smiled a beautiful, almost ecstatic smile, and reaching inside her coat, brought out a small silver object. She played it between her fingers, thumbing the wheel. I had already realised too late that it wasn't only the touch of the mist that had dampened her hair and clothes. Powered by engines and generators, the air of fairgrounds is always laced with diesel and so I had missed the smell.

'Eve,' I murmured. '*Please.*'

That awful smile broadened. 'You're a good man, Scott Jericho. But I reject your justice.'

Hair slick, coat saturated, face wet, she locked her arm around her squealing mother's chest.

And then, quite calmly, Genevieve pressed the lighter to her body and struck the wheel.

Chapter Forty

THE GLARE OF THE INFERNO accompanied me into the darkness. I remembered lunging across the Waltzer's revolve, grasping at a piece of tarpaulin that covered one of the gondolas, wrenching it free of its fastening. Already, Genevieve Bell and her mother were aflame. A vortex of fire engulfed their bodies, catching at the post that rose behind them like the stake in a witch's pyre. It could only have been seconds before I reached them, but the accelerant was working fast. Genevieve's features could barely be glimpsed inside that raging cowl.

I had a vague idea of someone shouting my name before I hugged the tarpaulin around them. That was when I felt their bodies collapse and the fire catch at my own clothes. My injured knee twisted as we fell together, a jolt of internal pain vying for my attention against the searing kiss of the flames. My head must have struck something, perhaps the lip of the revolve, and almost at once my vision tunnelled. I thought I could make out a hand lying against my chest. Crabbed, unmoving, blemished from birth, wreathed in fire, the flesh sloughing from it like the wax of a melted candle.

Then, darkness.

Except not quite. Nothing came to haunt my dreams – not the faces of unavenged victims, no poppet dolls or slaughtered fortune tellers, no bloodied tarot cards or burning witches, not even the shattered corpse of Lenny Kerrigan clawing its way from beneath the marigolds planted in Pete Garris's back garden. Instead, a simple white candle fluttered in the void.

It faded only as the light of the hospital ward broke in upon me.

'Take it easy, Scott. Here, have a sip of water.'

I blinked up at Thomas Tallis as he held the plastic cup to my lips. He looked as youthful and unruffled as ever, just a black smudge marking his chin. I wondered if it might be some atomised remnant of Genevieve or Patricia Bell. The water was warm and yet to my parched throat it felt like heaven. Adjusting to the glare, my gaze played around the curtained-off cubicle, taking in my bandaged left leg that poked from under the bedsheet, a bulge the size of a tangerine at my kneecap.

'You've been having adventures before last night,' Tallis said, replacing the cup on the bedside cabinet and folding his arms. 'Care to tell me about them ... ? No? Well, never mind. The doctors say that, with a little physio, that knee should heal up just fine. Your hand and neck, however?'

My eyes drifted to my bandaged right hand. I didn't feel any pain, but then I imagined there was a drip somewhere feeding the good stuff into my veins.

'Some scarring, I'm afraid,' Tallis murmured.

I shrugged, then pushed with my right leg, raising myself up the bed while the inspector rearranged my pillows.

'Genevieve?' I croaked. 'Patricia?'

He stood back and refolded his arms. 'They didn't make it.'

I swallowed hard. 'She'd had her entire existence torn away from her. The person she'd been was a lie and the one she became afterwards had only one purpose, to destroy every trace of that old life. When that was accomplished?' I locked eyes with Tallis. 'She never thought she'd get away with it.'

'I don't think she wanted to. She had no idea how to build a new life for herself.' He gripped the back of the plastic chair that stood beside the bed. 'Thank you for the call, Scott. You made the right choice in the end. Course, I would have preferred you to contact me with the full details of your theory so that we could've brought her in for an interview, but I suppose I should be grateful for small mercies. When you're up to it, I'll need you down at the station to make a statement. Maybe we should talk beforehand, just to get our stories straight? As I remember it, a disturbed Genevieve Bell sought you out to make a personal confession because she was overwhelmed by the guilt of killing your aunt? Sound about right?'

'Thank you, Tom.' I nodded.

He was about to pull aside the curtain when he looked back. 'I met your boyfriend, by the way. Harry? He's been here ever since you were brought in last night. We got to chatting in the waiting room. I understand you've been going through a bit of a bumpy patch. Just so you know, I didn't say anything about that drink. I'm not sure you really meant it, and anyway, the fact is, I don't swing your way. I actually don't swing any way, if you catch my drift. Relationships, romance, dating?' He made a face. 'Not really my thing. Ah, and here he is.'

Tallis pulled the curtain aside and Haz stepped into the cubicle.

'I'll leave you to it,' the inspector said. 'Goodbye, for now, Scott Jericho.'

Haz stood there for a moment, those big jade eyes looking everywhere except at me. His long, nervous fingers twined together as a single tear tracked down the side of his face. He rubbed at it with the back of his hand, smiled a little, then came and sat on the edge of the bed.

'Haz,' I whispered. 'Look at me.'

At last, he did, and laughing and crying, brushed back my curls. 'You bloody idiot. Will you stop trying to get yourself killed?'

I took his hand and kissed the bowl of his palm. 'I'm ready to talk now, if you are?'

'Do you know what's been happening with me?' he asked.

I glanced at the sleeve of his canary-coloured coat, finding the ghostly mark of spilled wax on the sleeve. 'You've been lighting candles?' I said softly, remembering something Miss Rowell had said about the white prayer candles she'd found in the cellar of the rectory. 'In memory of your dad?'

His fingertips brushed the pale traces. 'I'd kept the memory of what I did at bay. Pushed it away for ten long years. If I didn't acknowledge it then it wasn't real. But then this person comes back into my life.' He leaned forward and kissed my brow. 'This clever, infuriating, moody, messed-up, big-hearted idiot, and with him comes all these memories. The good and the bad. And suddenly I'm facing the thing that ripped us apart all those years ago, and it feels fresh and raw and terrible.'

'Harry, you saved him so much pain.'

'I did. But I killed him, too. I took a life, and that is a huge, huge thing, Scott. I needed to find a way to deal with that. To come to terms with it. Then one day, I found myself outside the cathedral in Aumbry and before I knew it, I was at the altar, lighting a candle, writing a prayer card. Just the simplest thing, but it brought me peace.'

A splash of wax, the stub of a pencil dropped absently into his music bag after filling in the prayer card. I squeezed Haz's hand.

'I didn't think you'd understand,' he said. 'I know all that stuff is just mumbo-jumbo and wishful thinking as far as you're concerned. But it started to mean something to me. Just those visits every Tuesday and Thursday evening, to light my candle, to write my prayer, to sit in the church and be with my thoughts. To think that maybe part of him had survived and that he could forgive me.'

'Haz ...'

'And I couldn't have you picking at that belief,' he said. 'Probing me and questioning me about it the way you do. Maybe even taking it away from me. So I lied about where I was going, what I was doing. Do you understand, Scott?'

I nodded. Something Genevieve had said echoed in my mind, *It can be a dangerous thing, you know, to systematically strip away a person's certainties. It can leave them with nothing to hold onto.*

'And I need to tell you,' Haz sighed. 'I've met someone who understands.'

I closed my eyes. I would rather the meds be turned off and feel every scrap of pain from my tortured leg and burned skin than experience this agony. I'd only just found him again, and in my arrogance and stupidity, I'd lost him already.

'I know,' I said softly. 'I know, my love. I saw you together. Haz, I'm really happy that you've found someone who—'

'Oh, but you are the biggest idiot!' he said, framing my face with his hands. 'Scott, look at me. Look at *me*. The man you saw me with? That's David Yarrow. I met him at the cathedral while I was lighting my candle. He was doing the same and we started laughing because we're both so clumsy and always spill the wax. David lost his wife last year to ovarian cancer. Anyway, we got chatting and it helped, you know? To talk about stuff. He's a lovely, lovely man, and quite possibly, the straightest person I've ever met.' Haz's expression twisted. 'Scott, why would you ever think I'd cheat on you?'

I took a breath. 'Because why wouldn't you? Harry, I'm a mess. Fucked up.'

'Yes, you are.' He prodded my nose with his finger. 'Welcome to the club.'

We sat in silence for a moment, Haz stroking my hair. When at last I thought I could speak without breaking down, I said, 'I don't believe in the things you believe in, my love. At least, I don't think I do. But I want to support you. I want to try. I'm so sorry.'

He gave a determined nod. 'And I want to support you too. You've been coping alone with what happened back in Bradbury End. So tell me. Tell me all of it.'

'You're sure?'

'No. But maybe we can be brave, together.'

'Then I will. But not today. Bradbury End is history and I want to talk about what comes next.' I laughed and threaded my fingers between his. 'Do you know the last thing Aunt Tilda ever said to me? She'd read our cards – the Star and the Lovers combined. Faith, hope, rejuvenation.' I pressed my lips to his. 'All will be well.'

'She saw a lot, that old lady.' Haz smiled, pulling out his phone and holding it up so that we could both see the screen. 'Maybe even further than you think. This started hitting the headlines about an hour before you came round.'

He thumbed the screen and a news clip started to play. A couple was standing outside the entrance to a hospital, tired but euphoric, caught in a blaze of flashbulbs. John and Anne Chambers clutching at each other as if desperate to confirm that this wasn't a dream.

'It's a miracle,' Anne said in a strong, measured voice. 'A miracle that was promised to us. Debbie, our little girl, has found her way home. She's being treated here at St Giles', but it seems that the person who abducted her has treated her well. A woman who couldn't have children of her own. A poor, lost soul who didn't know what she was doing. But she kept Debbie safe and hasn't harmed her.' A babble of questions from the journalists was met by Anne's raised hand. 'We won't be making any further comments today. We just want to get back to our little girl – there are lots of cuddles we need to catch up on. But I want to say one last thing. Thank you to the late Tilda Urnshaw. You told us Debbie would come back to us on All Hallows' Day and she has.'

The screen switched to a reporter standing at a rural roadside, behind him, the glowing sign of a small petrol station.

'It was here, at six o'clock this morning that little Debbie stumbled into the kiosk of this family-owned business. She was tired, soaking wet from the rain, and scratched from her dazed walk through the surrounding woodland. The owners immediately called the police, ending what had been a six-month nightmare for the Chambers family. People in the area are—'

'Pause it, please,' I said.

Haz touched the screen. Behind the reporter, the red neon sign had started to flicker: PARKER'S SERVICES. Every letter but one had phased out. I suddenly remembered what Anne had said about Tilda's prediction – that Debbie would *find her way back to us, through water and wood, until the red eye guided her home*. Now I stared at that static scarlet letter 'I'.

'How did she know?' I wondered.

Haz smiled. 'There are more things in heaven and earth than are dreamed of in your philosophy, Scott Jericho.'

Epilogue

BEFORE HE LEFT, HAZ RETRIEVED my phone from the bedside cabinet and laid it beside me.

'It's been ringing pretty non-stop,' he said. 'You must have a million voicemails. I didn't realise you were so popular.'

If it hadn't been for the dulling effect of the analgesics pumping through my veins, I might have guessed who had been trying so desperately to contact me. As it was, I could already feel my eyelids beginning to droop. I caught clumsily at Haz's sleeve as he turned away from the bed.

'Still going to love me when they take off these bandages and my neck looks like a boiled chicken?' I asked.

He bent down and brushed his lips against mine. 'We'll see.'

I lay there for a while, drifting in and out of sleep, listening to the muffled conversation of visitors in the next bay, wondering about an old woman and her prophecies. Like me, my mother had possessed a dual soul, caught up in the romance of her stories but infused with a practical hard-headedness. Although sceptical about many things, she'd still believed in her friend Tilda Urnshaw. I remembered a scene not long before she died in which my mother had overheard her cocky seventeen-year-old son scoffing at something Tilda had said.

'Don't ever let me catch you laughing at your auntie that way again,' she had seethed. 'That woman has more wisdom in her little finger than you'll possess in a lifetime. You might very well need her advice and comfort one day.'

And I had needed it. Tilda was the first person I went to when, a month later, my mother was found dead.

Only half conscious of what I was doing, I picked up the phone and called my voicemail. 'You have seventeen new messages. First message received at 8.30 a.m. on 1 November . . .'

The somewhat breathless voice of the private detective I'd employed to watch Garris panted down the line, 'Jericho? It's Gary Treadaway. Look, we've had a bit of a balls-up on our end. The boss said not to worry about the last few days' pay that you owe us. Call it evens, eh? Anyway, this is just to say, we've lost him. Not exactly sure when it happened, but the old bastard's fucked off somewhere all right. I've had one of the boys pose as a window cleaner to take a look through the upstairs windows. The house is empty. We're thinking he might have bunked over the neighbour's fence, but that's just guesswork. I knew you must have a good reason for wanting us to keep an eye on him, so I'll try you again later. I only hope he's not going to cause you any trouble. I mean . . .' The detective chuckled uncertainly. 'What trouble could he cause?'

I'd been so focused on the call that I hadn't even acknowledged the doctor who'd stepped inside the curtain to take my blood pressure. Now, as the cuff around my arm deflated, a hand reached out and took the phone from me.

'One hundred and sixty over eighty. I think you need to calm down a little, Scott.'

I looked up into the vacant face of Peter Garris.

'Now, now,' he said, as I made a grab for the front of his shirt. 'No drama. If you kick up a fuss, I'll be forced to use this on the first nurse that pokes their head through the curtain.'

A surgeon's scalpel flashed in his hand and I settled back onto the bed. Meanwhile, Garris moved around the cubicle, finally taking the plastic seat beside me. He laid the blade flat against his thigh and treated me to a paternal smile.

'Been getting yourself into trouble again? Perhaps next time it can be a less bruising adventure?'

A flicker of the old rage ignited in my chest. 'What do you want?'

He looked at me for a long time, something new in his gaze. A hint of indecision. 'To make amends,' he said at last. And reaching into his jacket pocket, he brought out a scuffed and battered digital recorder. 'It contains the audio file in which you revealed Harry's act of mercy. It's the original. I didn't make any copies. I'm sorry ...' He frowned, as if he couldn't quite believe what he was saying. 'I don't want to hold it over you anymore. What I did to save you in Bradbury End, I did to save *you*. Not some twisted version of yourself. Back in my garden a few days ago, I realised that you were beginning to frighten me. That the position I had put you in was changing you in some fundamental way. You shouldn't frighten people, Scott. That's what men like me do best. I'm the villain of this story – you're the hero. Always remember that.'

He stood, smiling at the scalpel like an old friend before sliding it into his pocket.

'You won't be seeing me for a while. Being who I am, I've always had plans in place if ever I needed to run. So take a breath, Scott Jericho. Try to be happy. And maybe we'll see each other again someday.'

He had pulled back the curtain and was about to step through when he clicked his fingers.

'Of course, I almost forgot. I'm such a muddle-head when I've got a long journey before me, but I meant to say: I know the murders I committed for your sake have weighed heavily on you. Well, you can stop torturing your conscience about one thing, at least.'

'Oh, yes?' I almost laughed. 'And what's that?'

In the harsh hospital glare, the dead marble of his eyes appeared to glitter.

'Lenny Kerrigan is alive and well and sends his compliments.'

I stared at Garris. My old mentor shrugged.

'Well, you never actually saw him die, now, did you?'

Glossary of Traveller Slang:

Chap:	a worker on the fairground who is not himself a showperson.
Chavvy:	a Traveller child.
Chor:	to steal.
Dinlo:	an idiot; a moron.
Dukker/dukkerin:	fortune telling.
Gavvers:	the police.
Ground:	abbreviation for 'fairground'.
Jel:	to go/to leave.
Joskin:	a non-traveller (see also gorger).
Juk:	a fairground dog; usually a watchdog.
Juvenile:	a child's ride.
Mooie:	face.
Mulardi:	haunted/creepy.
Muller:	to die or murder.
Mush:	a man.
Posh:	earnings, wages, profit.
Rokker:	to speak.
Ruk:	a fight.
Scran:	food

Acknowledgements

A huge thank you, as ever, to my wonderful agent Veronique Baxter, my TV/film rights agent Clare Israel, Sara Langham, Deidre Power, Emmanuel Omodeinde and everyone at David Higham Associates for their continuing support. The best agency in the biz!

Undying gratitude to Ben Willis, my fabulous editor whose eagle eye spots all my mistakes and whose insightful suggestions make me (and Scott!) look much cleverer than we really are. Thanks also to the brilliant team at Zaffre – Isabella Boyne, Isabel Smith, Sarah Benton, Chelsea Graham, Jenny Richards, Ellie Pilcher, Katie Sadler, Sophie Raoufi and Arzu Tahsin.

For some of the technical aspects of the book, my thanks go to DC David Bettison and the wonderful author and advisor on all things police procedural, Graham Bartlett (check out Graham's spellbinding books and his advice for crime novelists, established and aspiring, at www.policeadvisor.co.uk). Thanks also to Dr Carl Gibson for his advice on matters relating to academia. Naturally, all mistakes are my own! Thanks are also owed to Hanna Elizabeth, Dawn Andrew, Jacqueline Beard, Stephanie King, and Debbie Scarrow for their early insights and advice on the manuscript.

I have been truly overwhelmed by the generosity of the crime writing community, welcoming a newbie into their midst. I've worked for many years as an author of Young Adult novels, and so I entered this new arena with some trepidation. But from my first Harrogate Crime Festival onwards, I've been blown away by a very warm welcome. With this in mind, thanks to the following authors whose work I've long admired and who have had some nice things to say about Scott Jericho: Val McDermid, SJ Watson, Sarah Pinborough, Chris Whitaker, John Connolly, Sarah Hilary, Janice Hallett, Graham Bartlett, TM Logan, Ian Moore, Ajay Chowdhury, Tina Baker and David Fennell. I'm sure I'm missing some lovely people, so apologies for that!

Thanks also to the following wonderful bloggers, reviewers, podcasters and booksellers for their support: Frankie and Sarah of the brilliant Read and Buried pod; Luke Deckard; Donna Mortfett; Caroline Maston; Samantha Brownley (and the whole community over at UK Crime Book Club on Facebook); Lisa Howells; Stu Cummins; Craig Sisterson; Matthew, Lukasz and Grey at the spectacular Queer Lit in Manchester; the amazing team at Lighthouse Bookshop in Edinburgh; the fab bunch at Goldsboro Books, London; Andreas Alambritis of Watersones Wimbledon; Edouard Gallais of Waterstones Bristol & Bath; Daniel Bassett of Waterstones Bristol; Danny of the gorgeous Quinns Bookshop in Market Harborough; Nick, Emma and Mel at the wonderful Rabbit Hole bookshop in Brigg; Sam Cains at Waterstones Glasgow; and far too many others to list here. Just know, all booksellers are my heroes and I appreciate the support you've shown for my big-hearted, flawed but well-intentioned Traveller detective!

Thank you, as always, to my family: Dad, Georgia and Jon, Carly and Jamie, Johnny, Lyla, Jackson and Charly. And to my extended fairground family for their positive response to the series and their insights into a still largely hidden world.

And finally, and most importantly, all my love to my biggest fan, my most loyal supporter, and my best friend. I love you, Christopher White. Thank you for everything you do for me (and Scott Jericho!).

A last word. If you have enjoyed JERICHO'S DEAD, I would really appreciate you taking a moment to leave a review on the site from which you purchased the book or the usual review places online. Just a few short words will do. It will help other readers like you find the book and encourages word-of-mouth support so that there can be more in series!

Until next time, farewell to Travellers and joskins alike! We hope to see you again at Jericho's Fair very, very soon ...

Keep reading for an exclusive extract from the next Detective Scott Jericho thriller...

BURYING JERICHO

Coming April 2025

Chapter One

HARRY TRIED TO PASS ME the walking stick and I wrenched it roughly from his grasp, throwing it onto the backseat of the Merc and slamming the door. Then my gaze swept that peaceful suburban crescent, hunting out potential threats behind lace-curtained windows, anxious as a condemned man who'd just been handed his death sentence.

'What the hell do you think you're doing, you rank joskin?' I hissed at him. 'Do you want to get us both killed?'

Swaddled in my long trench coat, a thick minder's scarf wound around my throat, still I shivered. And not just through the cold. The coat felt two sizes too big for me, like I was a little chavvy all dressed up in his father's duds. Harry stood at my side in his canary-yellow cagoule, those gentle jade eyes crinkled with concern. He looked seasonably elfish with his green beanie hat and the pink tip of his nose. Altogether too innocent for a job like this.

'I'm sorry, but we can't risk it,' I told him, moderating my tone. 'Not here. We show any sign of weakness to these people, it'll be like throwing chum to a school of sharks. Sharks with knuckledusters and beretta pistols.'

'But you can hardly walk without it,' Harry objected. 'You've only been in physio a couple of weeks, and admit it, Scott, you're crap at keeping up with your exercises. You're not strong enough for this. Not yet.'

I stole a glance at myself in the Merc's driver-side window. He's right. Who was this wiry-framed stranger, his strong-featured face thin and pinched; whose were those hollowed-out eyes staring from behind a curtain of dishevelled blue-black curls?

I've lived what some might call a hardscrabble existence, born in my parents' trailer on a travelling fair; moving from place to place, building up and pulling down rides and stalls, working ever since I could hold a spanner. The kind of life that tempers a boy into a man early on, forging him hard and flinty. It was also a life I'd longed to escape. And I had, for a time. My head full of romance and books, in my late teens I'd waved farewell to the fair and run away to university. The only good thing I'd found among those dreaming spires was the man standing next to me. Harry Moorhouse. My love, my conscience, my lodestar in the darkness.

When I had lost him for a decade, to his own guilt and despair following the death of his father, the physical strength I'd built in my travelling days had served me well. In the misery of those lonely years, when I'd wanted nothing more than to forget the man I'd loved, I had become a thug for hire, collecting the debts and repaying the grievances of gangsters. Actions that chipped away at my soul, until finally a man named Peter Garris entered my life. A mentor and a monster who had drawn me over that thin blue line. I had flourished working in CID, but again only for a time. My attack on a far-right lunatic and suspected child-murderer had been rewarded with imprisonment and disgrace, following which my fairground family had, without question, taken me back. All that was six months ago, and since then I had reforged something of a reputation as a detective, albeit now in a private capacity.

Cases had come my way, strange and harrowing mysteries which called to that darkness that seemed to move inside me like a shadow self. And so yes, a hard, eventful life. Until recently, however, it seemed to have taken little out of me. I had never once looked my thirty-one years.

Now I looked it, and more. The best part of six weeks in a coma will do that to you, I suppose.

'You're not strong enough for this,' Harry repeated, his gaze on one of those nondescript terraced houses across the street. Again, he pulled open the rear door and offered me the walking stick; again I ordered him to put it back.

'Then I'd better learn to fake it,' I said. 'And quickly. Or else neither of us might be getting out of here alive.'

'Scott, please—'

'Come on,' I said, leading the way. 'A favour is owed, and we've left Mark Noonan waiting long enough.'

A hard frost glinted across the roofs and bonnets of the cars lining that charming West London crescent, landscaping windscreens into miniature tundra and laying thick cataracts over mirrors and headlights. Above us, a nothing December sky capped the borough of Hounslow. It was freezing, the pavements death traps, the paths up to the houses a fractured hip waiting to happen. Still, at our approach to number 56 Sanford Crescent, doors were opened and neighbours gathered on those lethal steps, cardiganed arms folded, snorting steam and monitoring us with fixed smiles. These were the mobster's watchdogs. Mark Noonan owned all the houses on this street and let them rent-free to a select club of pensioners who kept their eyes open and their mouths shut. It was the perfect camouflage for the headquarters of that wily old cockney gangster, in whose service I had once forfeited my conscience.

The gate squeaked on its frosted hinge as we stepped into the front garden of number 56. The neatly ordered flowerbeds, tended in spring and summer by those old dears who stood sentinel on their doorsteps, now lay dead or dormant. We were halfway along the path when I grasped at the fence for support, the coma-wasted muscles of my left leg almost giving way. Harry made a grab for me, but a word was enough to usher him back. I glared at my gloved hand, planted on the fencepost. Under the leather, this was no longer a strong showman's hand, bunched with muscle. What lay beneath was now more like a withered claw.

'Compliments of the season, stranger,' an age-cracked voice called out. I turned my head and the pensioners waved in unison, like festive figures in some automated shopping centre tableau. *Stranger?* I'd been here before, many times, but perhaps I could forgive them not recognising me now.

'And to you,' I called back. 'Merry Christmas.'

A holly wreath hung from the letterbox of number 56. Plastic blood-red berries among sprigs of artificial ivy, as synthetic as the street behind me. I rang the doorbell and a burst of *Good King Wenceslas* trilled out.

'I must be mad, letting you come here,' I murmured to Harry.

'You didn't let me,' he said. 'It was my decision. We're a team now, remember?'

I shivered and he rubbed a little warmth into my arm. I never used to feel the cold. Travellers never do. We stand out in all seasons, face every element to earn our living. It inures us to the chill.

'Here, let me, it's slipped a bit.' Harry reached up, pulling aside the scarf and adjusting the collar of my polo neck, just at the point where my burns became visible. The puckered pathways of flame, a memento from my last case. 'There.' He smiled. 'Like I said, a team.'

'We are,' I agreed. 'God forgive me.'

I thumbed the bell again and this time we're treated to *O Little Town of Bethlehem.* Harry grimaced. I could tell the offkey jangle offended his musician's sensibilities. I stamped my feet, blew out a frustrated breath, rapped my knuckles on the door. It juddered in response, a little loose in its frame. I glanced over my shoulder to see the Stepford Geriatrics still watching from their perches. Fuck it. I pushed open the door. The short hallway beyond stood empty. My eyes followed a flight of ceramic ducks up the stairs to the vacant landing.

'Mark? You here ...?' Noonan, it's Scott Jericho. If you or your hubbies are about, don't fucking shoot us. We're coming in, all right?'

I opened the door to the dining room, kitchen, downstairs toilet, and finally the sitting room at the back of the house. A hideous gold and brown hexagonal-patterned carpet, two bow-seated armchairs and a violently green settee, the arms worn to the stuffing by generations of overflowing ashtrays and the tap of nervous fingers. I glanced up at the painting that hung over the electric fire, a strand of tinsel draped around the frame. Dear old Nana Noonan seemed to return my gaze. This pug-faced gorgon had raised her grandson faithfully in the family business, introduced him to a dozen pimps and drug-traffickers before the age of ten, then taken him along to the Mecca Bingo Hall every Friday night with her best friend Mabel Goodman. A beloved matriarch of the underworld who could turn children into psychopaths, make hardened criminals beg for mercy, and run a score of bingo cards simultaneously.

'Shit decorations,' Harry murmured.

'They were hers,' I said, nodding at the picture. 'Noonan is sentimental about stuff like that.'

I took a turn of the room, pulling aside stray sofa cushions as if they might conceal a rogue gangster. Where was he? And where were the husbands—those young men who courted the middle-aged mobster and played up to his vanities? The house breathed an unnatural kind of stillness.

It was as I drew the coffee-coloured curtains that covered the French window that I noticed movement at the far end of the garden, right where the fence ran up against the railway tracks. A large block of a boy, all steroid-enhanced biceps with the stick-thin legs that often goes along with such a physique, was holding something sharp and shiny under Mark Noonan's throat. Even from this distance and with the windows closed, I could hear the mobster's squeal.

I limped over to the artificial fireplace and plucked up a poker. Straight away I could tell it was hollow, ornamental, no weight to it at all. Noonan had money, not as much as he used to, admittedly, but he was still rolling in the posh. He could afford a real poker, but instead he insisted on keeping Nana's house pretty much as she had furnished it in the '50s, in memory of that moustachioed queen-pin. If only she'd known her beloved boy might one day be panting at the business end of a switchblade, she might have invested in the genuine article.

'Go back to the car and get my stick,' I whispered to Harry

'Oh, so you want it now?' he asked, his eyes wide as he followed my gaze.

'Just go.'

He didn't need telling twice.

I moved back into the hall, looked about again, called upstairs, hoping Charlie or one of the old timers might be on hand. The house continued to breathe that uncharacteristic emptiness. I studied the vintage Bakelite on the table by the door, wondering if I should put through an anonymous call to the gavvers. I wasn't sure Noonan would thank me for such an act, and anyway, by the time they arrived the godfather of Sanford Cresent might well be rolled up, snug as a bug in knock-off Persian rug, awaiting disposal.

The house was so still that I couldn't help flinching as Harry stepped back inside, my rubber-handled, height-adjustable, NHS-issued walking stick in hand. When I told him to return to the car and wait for me there, he shook his head. And so I reluctantly led the way to the kitchen and the side door.

'It will,' I said. 'If you keep them hopped up twenty-four-seven.'

A shout from the kitchen doorway as a host of husbands appeared, all loud voices and botoxed brows in search of an expression. They dropped their shopping bags and came running, clustering about their beloved boss like chemically-inflated hens around a middle-aged chick.

'Where the hell have you useless bastards been?' Noonan demanded. 'Out spending my money again while I'm stuck here with a blade riding my carotid. If it hadn't been for Scott and his handsome friend, I'd be a corpse right about now, ready to be dumped in the nearest landfill.'

For the first time, I glanced at Harry. In all the excitement I had forgotten him. A hard thing to admit, troubling yet true, nonetheless. He seemed a little shaken but I was proud to see he didn't show it. You'd have to know him like I did to pick up on the signs.

Looking back at the crowd of husbands, I scanned them for a familiar face but there was no sign of the man I most wanted to see among their number. Meanwhile Noonan continued to berate his men while laying in a final kick to the gasping Timmo. His voice had always been high and piping, but I'd never heard it crack before. I looked at that grey flesh dangling from his jaw, creased as rhino hide, the designer tracksuit grubby and unwashed, those sausage fingers sporting fewer diamond rings than before. His outrage sated, the mobster turned back to us.

'Let's get up to the house,' he said. 'I'll have one of these useless bitches stick the kettle on. Then we can talk about that favour you owe me.'

'Now listen, Timmo, I'll get you whatever you want, baby doll,' Noonan blubbered. 'Always been a good hubby to you, haven't I? Always looked after you like the precious boy you—' He blinked those piggy eyes in wonder as he caught sight of us over Timmo's shoulder, moving as noiselessly as we could down the garden path. *Yes, it's me, you psychotic fuck.* I made a rolling gesture with my hand: *keep him talking*.

'You want some ket? I'll get you some ket,' Noonan swallowed and the blade surfed the wave of his Adam's apple. 'All the ket my kitty can take. You don't even have to blow me for it. Just calm down and let's talk this through.'

'Talk it through, you ugly piece of shit?' Timmo shouted in his dear old hubby's face. 'You keep making promises but you never keep none of 'em. If I slit you open, right here and now, then I get to take what I want anyway. I know where you keep it, stored up like a fucking squirrel in the attic. And if I did saw through that fat throat of yours, I'd only be doing you a favour. Your time is done, old man.'

Focused on the need that burned through his veins, Timmo didn't hear the crack of my tread on the frozen ground behind him, didn't see my shadow fall at his victim's feet. I pulled the walking stick over my shoulder and took my swing. I'm a practised hand at such things and so calibrated the blow, enough to drop the kid without doing any permanent damage. Timmo went down like a swooning damsel in a Victorian novel anyway. In the next instant, Noonan was busy laying in the boot, a dozen vicious kicks to the groaning boy's midriff, red-faced and screaming, jowls jangling away like cheap earrings.

'Take it easy,' I said, pulling the mobster off the kid.

'Don't you dare interfere with my . . .' Noonan took a breath, then smiled and shook his head. 'Nah, you're right. I'll deal with him properly later. It happens from time to time with these young 'uns, you know?'